ENTANGLED

Amy Rose Capetta

HOUGHTON MIFFLIN HARCOURT
BOSTON NEW YORK

www.hmhbooks.com

The text of this book is set in ITC Slimbach.

Library of Congress Cataloging-in-Publication Data

Capetta, Amy Rose.

Entangled / by Amy Rose Capetta

p. cm.

Summary: Seventeen-year-old Cade, a fierce survivor, feels alone in the universe

until she learns that she was created in a lab in 3112 and entangled at a quantum

level with a boy named Xan, sending her on a galaxy-spanning journey toward a

real connection.

ISBN 978-0-544-08744-6

[1. Science fiction. 2. Adventure and adventurers—Fiction. 3. Life on other

planets—Fiction. 4. Friendship—Fiction. 5. Robots—Fiction. 6. Guitar—Fiction.

7. Musicians—Fiction.] I. Title.

PZ7.C173653Ent 2013

[Fic]—dc23

2013003937

Manufactured in The United States of America

DOC 10 9 8 7 6 5 4 3 2 1

4500431929

For Julia
QEF

And my family—
For being one of the best songs in the universe

CHAPTER 1

PURE STATE A quantum system that cannot be described as a mixture of any others

Saturday night, and Cade was headed to the one place on Andana that she didn't hate. The one place where she could be around other humans and almost stand it.

First she put on the right armor: black skirt, black gloves. Spiked her lashes with a bit of black-market mascara, checked the effect in a broken-tipped triangle of mirror. Added two matching oil slicks of eyeliner. Grabbed her guitar.

Slapped and echoed up the metal ladder, out of her glorified cement bunker, into the empty-stomach rattle of the desert.

Her footprints crumbled in the sand as soon as she shifted her weight. Each breath was dust and dust and air, in that order. Each breath made her lungs curl into fists, ready to fight their way back to some blinked-out mother planet — a place she would never see because it didn't exist.

Cade swung her guitar case over the line that meant the

end of the Andanan deserts and the beginning of Voidvil. It was a real line — dunes on one side, and, on the other, buildings that shot like dark fingers out of the sand.

Cade didn't love the deserts of Andana. But she wanted to peel off her own skin and give it a firm shake when she thought about living in Voidvil. It was a human town — really a human trap — a place where people piled on top of each other deep and high in apartment towers crusted with the black of fire escapes.

On the bubbled-tar sidewalks at the edge of town, men and women stared at Cade and her guitar case. Smiles crawled onto their faces. The closer she got to the center of town, the louder the voices grew, the closer skins got to each other, got to her, sweating to close the in-between inch. The lips here smiled too, but the eyes were empty, glassed-and-gone with spacesick.

Cade didn't have spacesick.

She had something worse than that.

Her destination sat deep in the ground, a blister under nine stories of pressing, smelling, never-stopping human. Cade dropped down a corkscrew of stairs into the wet-stone smell of Club V.

The room wasn't much when she looked at it. A small stage, set back and painted the shiny black of an insect shell. The space was good for a crowd, but half-crammed with a glass bar that Cade wasn't old enough to drink at. Four laws governed the humans on Andana and this, of course, was one of them. Not that she cared. She wasn't there to fuzz herself. Or fade out. Or meet people, even.

Or meet people, ever.

"You're late," said the owner, a nonhuman who liked to tell humans that his name was Mr. Smithjoneswhite. He held a drink, something amberish on the rocks, with one of his long arms. He had six of them, and two legs, spanning out from a central nervous system that was actually central. He could regrow a limb if he had to, in a process that was filled with pus and fascination. Handy in bar fights, too.

"You're late," he said again, and Cade wondered if he was trying to start a bar fight, right now, with her.

"I don't go on for two hours."

"Be on stage," he said. "On time." His accent was thick, like he was slurping the words off a plate. Cade could speak passable Andanan, but he insisted on English. Didn't want her mangling the mother tongue.

"It's the setup," he said, waving one limb at the stage. "Isn't it? It's taking you too long. Too much time staring at yourself in the mirror." It was a low and unoriginal punch. Humans were the only species that used mirrors. Other species knew what they looked like without a bit of glass-and-backing, or had gone past a looks-based understanding of each other.

"Too good to make a bit of talk with me, little girl?" Mr. Smithjoneswhite asked, rattling his slow-melt ice at her.

Cade put her tongue between her teeth, to keep herself from grinding them to white dust.

"Just make sure I get paid."

She shouldn't have come back without seeing the money from last week. Of the four laws that Cade and all the humans on Andana had to live with, the first one declared that they weren't cleared for work. Too weak. Not built for the climate here, and definitely not built for space. So they bartered and black-marketed. It was clear that Cade had a talent, so of course someone like Mr. Smithjoneswhite was willing to step in, fill out the official forms, shuffle a few coins into her hand at the end of the night. But last week had been two sets, three encores, shameless cheering, no coin. And she slithered back. It was a sour move, because it showed Mr. Smithjoneswhite how much she needed this place, needed it more than the money.

"I'll see you get paid," he said. "From the drink sales tonight."

Cade looked up into his face — a blur of features, like it had been stamped by someone with a shaky wrist. "Right," she said. "For *both* weeks."

He tipped the end of his two upper limbs, his version of a nod. Cade swept past, and kept up the stomping and scowling. But for the first time in seven days, she felt something other than pissed off.

Because Cade was at the club for the same reason as every other Saturday. She would wait out the amateur screechgasm of the opening acts, bits of foam tucked into her ears as insurance against awfulness. She would take the stage, set up her amps and pedals, and give a tender squeeze to the pegs on the neck of her impossible, unscratched, cherry red guitar. The color of a fruit no one had eaten in centuries, and still, it looked delicious.

Plug in.

Turn the volume up. up. up.

Drown the unbelievable noise that crashed through her head.

The Noise was the barrier, the thing that kept Cade from living with other humans. They made so much scurrying, screeching, nattering sound, and when that hit the Noise, pressure changed, and she was sure her brain would start leaking out through her nose.

Cade kicked the metal skeleton of a chair to an isolated spot backstage and sank her head between her hands.

She knew there must have been a time before the Noise, but it was roped off, along with a few glaring, all-white memories of her most primitive years. People in white. White rooms. White lights, clean and sharp as a seven-blade knife. Cade wanted to look at those memories but she didn't have clearance, even inside her own head. She was stuck with the years of less-than-life that had passed since she'd been dropped at the Parentless Center on Andana.

And she was stuck with the Noise. It wasn't a clear stream of words or music or even random screeches of sound. It was those things and more — unclear, unwashed, unbearable. There were different strands of it. Frequencies. Sometimes she could pick them out, sometimes she had to cave and crumble.

Cade was a smashed radio, all the stations of the universe pouring in.

The opening acts — Andanans on sand-skin drums, a band with four lead singers, a lone man on a battered trumpet — came and went. Cade set up the stage in record time, feeling the shift of muscles under skin. She never needed help with even the heaviest of her amps, and she never felt tired, and she never got sick. Two girls even younger than Cade, dressed in some kind of plastic strings and spacetrash, stood at the corner of the stage and whisper-shouted about it — a favorite snatch of gossip at Club V.

"She's not human, not all human."

"Some Hatchum in her bloodline, you think?"

"She doesn't have the double pupils. Or the orbital. Anyway, they don't snug humans."

"Something snugged something to make her."

"Yeah, but what?"

Cade made a note: Play an ear-obliterating chord in their faces.

She stood in the center of the stage and held Cherry-Red — just held her, the weight welcome and sinking. The different colors of the lights warmed into her. Blue on her right side, red on her left, a whole row of colors pressed up hot, breaking over her back. It was enough to convince her that all lights should have color. Not the dark nothing of space, or the bright nothing of the desert sun.

Cade fiddled with the strings until her fingertips were satisfied. If they fit just right, she could play harder and faster than anyone in Voidvil. And when she did that, the Noise retreated — if only a little bit. Last Saturday night, she'd been onstage and she was sure that for a moment she'd felt the Noise flicker. When she tried to play the same song at home, re-create the conditions, the static in her head had blasted on.

But another flicker? That was something to look forward to.

The crowd was bigger than last week, splitting the seams of the room. People spilled over the borders of each other — arms overlapping, backs pressed to chests. The crowd was a creature of its own, with a long tail stretched up the stairs. And when Cade raised her pick, not even in a brass way, the creature went quiet and held its breath.

Cade bit into the first chord.

The song chose itself. A wild, cat-scratch number that yowled when she added distortion. Within a few minutes, it gave way to something else — driving, drumming, a pop of knuckles against steel. Cade never planned sets. That made it easier for her to sneak up on the Noise, overwhelm it. But it gave her no ground tonight. When she dialed volumes up, the Noise dialed itself up. When she strung notes into melodies, the Noise melted into chaos.

Cade looked up from the snarl of her fingers on frets and distracted herself with the crowd.

The ones closest to the stage had spacesick. They loved to dance, a spastic dance that involved half snugging your neighbor in public. The spacesicks that touched each other the most, without even seeming to notice it, were the farthest gone. Cade wondered how long it had taken — how many months, years, of exposure to the dead black of space—to make them like that. She looked over their heads, into the safe middle.

But she snagged on someone in the second row, a man wearing a lab coat. Human, from the looks of him. Of course, humans weren't cleared for labwork on Andana. The man's eyes—clear, no glass—scanned her up and down.

Cade slammed into another song. Verse-chorus-verse. Comfort food. It was the kind of tune that raised its middle finger to the Noise, slapped order thick and sweet on top of chaos. But then she got to the bridge—and Cade was sour at getting over bridges. She couldn't see the other side, never reached the shore. When the bridge crumbled, the Noise was waiting.

Cade grabbed the audience and dragged it down with her.

She filled them with strange intervals, waves of feedback, tones that picked out other tones so high they could only be felt in the drone of the air, so low they foamed up through the floorboards. She gave people the Noise, thick as black market coffee. Unfiltered.

And she got loud. So loud that there was no room in her head, her body, the club, the planet, all of space.

She'd reached the part of the set when the crowd had the annoying tendency to fall in love with her. She could see it happening. Hands went loose, bodies fell into the troughs after notes, crashed into the new ones. Talk died out and cheers evolved, strange and throaty. Some of the glass went out of the spacesicks' eyes, but Cade didn't trust it to stay gone—the longer a person had the sickness, the thicker and more constant the film. The people in the front row glassed over one by one, then reached up weedy arms to touch her. Mr. Smithjoneswhite didn't care as long as no one rushed the stage.

Cade knew this had nothing to do with her. People didn't want her. They wanted the music, this string of notes that kept them beating in time with something other than themselves, in touch with something *more* than themselves. Cade wanted that, too. It was the only thing she and these slummers had in common.

The last chorus trickled out, weak. Cade wanted to play harder, faster, louder — but she would get one note away from hitting a stride and he would be there again, looking up at her, pale and patient. Lab coat.

Cade wondered if he was just another one of her looped-out admirers. But he didn't have the look. He was calm and at least halfway to old — with eyes that rarely seemed to blink. Like they had to be reminded to do it, for appearances.

He stared on and on, his eyes insisting on some kind of connection. But Cade was connected to no one, and the few people who had pretended to care about her were useless. At best. Cade sliced one of her meanest looks at lab coat, one of her very best *back offs*. Then she stared at the bar, at the stairs, at the walls, but the white of his coat was always there, catching the corner of her eye.

Cade stirred things up again, built a new and terrible song. The song to demolish all songs, to smash the Noise, to put an end to the horrible world in her head. She crested to the top of it, reached her fingers for the next note, felt the strings close around the trenches she dug, over and over, into her skin.

And then.

Dark. Quiet. *Hush.*

The Noise blinked off.

CHAPTER 2

QUANTUM UNCERTAINTY PRINCIPLE
States that the more carefully one property has
been measured, the less possible it becomes to
know any other property

Cade pummeled through song after song.

The Noise might have flickered last week, but this was full shutdown. Cade had trouble hearing notes over the wash of silence in her head. She needed to get clear and figure this out.

She made it to the end of her set, prodded by a splinter of hate for Mr. Smithjoneswhite. Then she ran off the stage and pinballed down a short black hall. The balance in her head was wrong, or gone. It felt like walking on a string over a deep ravine. With each step, she slipped, was deeper into the mist — or made of it. Cade was alone in her hollowed-out head.

She worked past the snake of the bathroom line to the room at the end of the hall where performers could trash whatever they needed to trash, fade out, snug fans. Cade went on last, which meant she had the place to herself. She plunked down in front of the mirror. A whole sheet of it, only cobwebbed at the corners with cracks.

I must have done it, she thought. *Actually done it. Played so loud that I scared off the Noise.*

She examined her head from twelve different angles. Tried to see past the sinkholes of knotted dark hair and the second skin of makeup, through her olive eyes, through their black pits, into the welcome new void.

I wonder how long it'll last.

And then.

At least I can still think in here. That's something.

Behind her, a voice slivered through the cracks around the door.

"Cade?"

No knock. Usually her fans knocked and when she opened the door — if she opened the door — they smiled up at her, little puddles of apology, like their hands just couldn't help themselves. She either flashed her nastiest smile or her seven-blade knife.

"Cade?"

She didn't have time to waste on this. She had a head to spread out in. Get comfortable.

"What?" she cried, toward the hall.

"Cade?"

She would stop this thing in utero. She put on her tough girl face, a third skin that clapped on tight over the makeup. Flung open the door.

The white outline of a man flashed against the dark hall. Lab coat. Of course.

He looked older than she'd thought, his hair a muddle of gray and black. His wrinkles seemed to — not fade, or shift as he moved his face, but — blink. Like wiggles of static.

"You felt it, didn't you," he said. "Just now. The shift."

Cade took a tiny step, like a caught breath, backwards. This old spacecadet must have been talking about some important event in the relationship he'd invented for them in his head. She thought of his showy, obvious spot in the second row. Best to be careful. Cade crossed her arms, pursed her mouth so tight the lipstick pebbled.

"Shift?"

"I need you to listen to me," the old man said. Urgent words, but his voice was even.

"Sure," Cade said. But her eyes said, *No. Get off. Step back.*

"I know things about you."

He reached out one wrinkle-spurting finger, and Cade crumpled away from it. But he didn't touch her. He didn't even try. Just hovered near her temple — a straight line from his cracked old fingernail into her brain.

"The shift," he said. "It's different now, Cadence. Can't you feel it?"

He waited for her to respond, but Cade was stunned to a full stop.

"What did you call me?" she asked.

"Cadence."

She let the old man in.

He stood in the armpit of shadow just behind the door, facing the sheet of mirror. Cade weighed her options—keep him, waste him, send him on his nerve-shattering way.

"Who are you?" she asked.

"I have both a name and a number," he said. "The number is for paperwork and formalities. You can call me Mr. Niven."

"How do you know what's happening to me?" she asked. "No, wait. First of all, how do you know—"

"Your name. Cadence. Born June third, 3112." He was using the Earth calendar. Definitely human. But the rote way he reported things—feeding them out like strings of facts—felt strange.

"I know your name because I know you," he said. "I know you because I was there on the night you were born, and for the first eight hundred and twenty-nine days of your life. This period and duration of acquaintance makes us old friends, Cadence."

"I don't have friends," she said. "New, old, or otherwise."

But she was still hung up on those three letters, tacked to the end of her name. The nudge from bare-bones Cade to the sweet, curving fleshiness of Cadence. There had been times—bottomless nights in the bunker—when she'd been sure she made the name up, just to prettify herself, or pretend she had a past that she didn't.

But she did. And here it was. Babbling at her.

"You weren't born on Andana," Mr. Niven said. "You were born on Firstbloom."

That was a mobile lab station. One of the few that had been set up — in space, of course, since no planet would host a troop of human scientists. Rotating crews so no one stayed long enough to turn spacesick.

Firstbloom. Cade had heard of it, sure, but it had just been a word. Not the place where she was born.

"No parents," Mr. Niven said. "You were bred and raised for Project QE." He kept slinging facts, and Cade took them like punches.

No parents. No parents? But she'd never had parents, so what did it matter if they were just globs of genetic material or flesh and blood? And this way she'd never have to waste one more thought on how they died, or if they had just left her, or if they had loved her. It was better this way. Cade had seen enough tubies to know that they turned out fine, and sometimes much better than their parented counterparts.

When she reached the other half of what Mr. Niven had said, though, it brought her brain up short.

"Project what?"

"Project QE. Shorthand, of course. For Quantum Entanglement."

Each new unknown was a serious blow to the side of the head. Cade sat down — slumped there, a heap of slit-up clothes and chipped nail polish and toughness melting off her in sheets.

"What is that?" Her words came out small. "What is quantum entanglement?"

"It will be easier if I show you." Mr. Niven reached for the top button of his shirt without so much as glancing down.

Cade's hand swerved three times. Once to fish out her knife, twice to unsnap it, three times to deal out the short, flat blade that worked best on humans. She slid the tip of the knife through the stale air of the dressing room toward Mr. Niven's chin — which didn't so much as bob. Cade never should have let him in that room. Her wrist itched to undo the mistake.

But Mr. Niven had a few buttons popped now, and what Cade saw against his pale, almost transparent skin stopped her. A hole in the gulch at the center of his collarbone. Or not a hole. It glinted. A dark circle of glass embedded in the skin. He closed his eyes and the hole flooded with light, and the light streamed together, focused itself on the grime-white wall, and burst into a picture.

Mr. Niven was a projector. Cade wondered if it was an upgrade that came standard with being a scientist.

The picture took a minute to set and harden. White walls. White light. A room full of babies.

Cade dropped the knife and didn't even know it until she heard the clatter.

"Am I one of those . . . ?"

"Shhh," Mr. Niven said, the sound full of crackle, like it was being heated on a burner. "We are about to begin."

"Hello," a voice boomed out of Mr. Niven's mouth. Not his voice. Hearty, cheerful. It even changed the shape of his lips, stretched them wide around the warm sounds. "Welcome to Project QE." A few shots of babies crawling at each other, blinking their damp eyes, crabbing their little hands. "You might wonder why you're looking at a room full of infants."

Here was the childhood Cade almost-remembered. She didn't know whether to touch the makeshift screen with soft fingertips or run as fast as she could back to her bunker.

"These children have been split into pairs based on careful breeding and selection," the voice boomed. "Final tests and preparations are being carried out, and soon this batch of standard human children will undergo the process of quantum entanglement."

"You've said that twice now," Cade muttered, "but what does it —"

A flash of white, so hot Cade had to throw a hand to her eyes. Something had been spliced out. The picture flicked back on two babies sharing the frame. Swaddled in spotless white diapers. Out of the two, it was simple enough to find herself. A swirl of black hair, light-brown skin, green-black eyes. The other was pale as a cloud and twice as fat, in a soft-folded, babyish way.

"Here we have Cadence and Xan."

Xan.

The name clinked, like Cade was a metal bank and the name Xan was the first coin she'd ever dropped into it.

Xan.

That name meant something. More than that. It was

worth something. But Cade would have to come back to it later to figure out what, because the great big mouthy voice boomed on.

"These two are optimally suited for entanglement. Our greatest hope lies with them."

Another white-hot flash. Another splice.

The two babies sprawled in a new room, whiter, if possible, than the last one. "Cadence and Xan took well to the process. After a brief period of confusion and rest, the two began to bond at an intense level long thought inaccessible to the human species."

Cade felt the prickle of something in her chest. Pride. Not that she had earned it. All she had done was be a baby, bred for a certain purpose. It was the same feeling she had to dismiss all the time, when she smashed through a new song or splayed her fingers into an unreachable chord. She wasn't a good musician. It was just a response to the Noise, a necessary knee jerk. And those babies were just bundles of instinct and genes.

"Cadence and Xan are a wonderful pair," the not-Niven said. "Perfectly entangled."

"Entangled?" Cade asked. Again.

"Shhh," Mr. Niven said, and he was just his old man self for a moment, thin-lipped and scolding.

Cade was one curled knuckle away from sending him to the floor. But Mr. Niven had answers, and Cade was only starting to slam together the questions. So she let him stay on his feet. For now.

The picture on the wall changed to a diagram of bouncing circles, chalk-white on black. "When we entangle two particles on a quantum level, they are no longer bound to the physics that restrict human action." Two circles flowed together, down a narrow stream, and parted, now picked out in blue to show they were different than the rest.

"Entangled particles react to each other, balance each other, and transmit impulses faster than the speed of light." One circle spun clockwise. Less than a blink later, the other circle spun, counter. "Entanglement is an ancient fact, known to humans for over a millennium, but applications have been limited. Certainly, prior to these trials, no one has attempted to entangle two humans on the quantum level."

Back to babies. They were older now — Cade could tell by the full heads of hair, the sprouting bottom teeth. It hurt to look at that little girl and see how different she was from the mostly grown version. How happy.

Baby Cadence smiled and Xan puckered his face into a frown. Baby Cadence laughed, and Xan shredded the air with a wail.

"Their moods are attuned when in proximity. But they can transmit even more fantastic streams of information. What's more, they exhibit none of the human tendencies toward spacesick. While the spacesick detach from themselves, the entangled remain grounded in the strength of their connection with each other. The state is permanent, unaffected by cell turnover, due to our unique method of bonding particle interactions with the Higgs Field prior to entanglement.

"We at Firstbloom can now say it is possible to keep the human mind safe from space. We can do more than struggle, more than survive. Our hope is that Cadence and Xan will show us how."

The picture faded to white, and soon there was only the wall.

Mr. Niven coughed, chasing off the other voice that had been making use of his throat. He didn't budge from his spot behind the door. It was Cade who made the move, closer, needing to know more.

"Xan," she said, and the name clinked inside her head again. "Why don't I know anything about him? I've never seen him. Never heard his name."

"Xan was not as strong as you were," Mr. Niven said. "The entanglement process is complicated, difficult. Xan has been asleep for fifteen years."

"You mean . . . in a coma?" A rare word on Andana. Most of those who lost consciousness were left to die.

"Yes."

Cade tried to dial the picture of baby Xan forward, and came up with a pale, soft-faced teenager with water-blue eyes and loops of brown hair. She thought of him waking up on Firstbloom. Into the white of it, the nonsmell of it, the blank but friendly rooms. Hearing the voices of the scientists who had dreamed him up — blurred, at first, but then gaining edges. Welcoming him to the world with noise.

And then Cade understood something.

The Noise. It had blinked off, but only because this boy,

somewhere else in the universe, had woken up. Xan had been in a coma — blank, static-filled, stuck between stations, for fifteen years.

Cade had been tuned into him.

There was only one thing she could understand now, only one thing that made sense. "So," she said, smoothing down the threads of her skirt, patting the nests in her hair, doing a spit-sour job of grooming herself. "When do I meet him?"

"Xan is gone."

The word made no sense. *"Gone?"*

"Firstbloom was raided two days after he first showed signs of consciousness."

The flicker.

The flicker while Cade was onstage last week. It *had* been real. Xan had woken up for just a second as she hammered out notes, and now he was up for good.

"He wakes up for the first time since he was a drooling baby," Cade said, "and you let the place get *raided?*"

"Xan was taken." Mr. Niven didn't seem too worked up about it. He recited the words with the same thin-soup non-thrill that he said everything else.

Cade curled that last knuckle.

"Humans will be much stronger if entanglement proves possible," Mr. Niven said. "Not every species in the universe would like to see that. Project QE has enemies, Cadence. You have enemies."

She got the distinct feeling that Mr. Niven wasn't going to help her fight those enemies. It made her want to get up in his wrinkle-scaped face. Tear his lab coat into a thousand white pieces.

"So I'm supposed to sit around waiting for some hostile nonhumans to swarm all over me? *Attack?*"

Mr. Niven reached into his pocket. "No," he said. "You are not supposed to fight. You are supposed to find Xan."

"What!"

She rushed him now, and his hand flew out of his pocket, arms high and sudden-white as solar flares.

"No contact," he said. "No contact. No contact."

He bleated it until she backed off.

"You weren't here to tell me what I should be doing for the last fifteen years," Cade said. "Isn't this in your job description? You bred us and raised us and entangled us — aren't you the ones who keep us safe?"

"The scientists of Firstbloom would like nothing more than to recover Xan and run Project QE to completion."

"You'd like nothing more than to make me do it *for* you. Why should I do that?" Cade kicked a fallen chair, and the echo of the metal shivered up her leg. "Here's another question, while we're at it. Why wasn't *I* recovered? I've been on this boiling excuse for a planet, and this whole time Xan was on Firstbloom . . ."

"It was never our intention to keep the entangled on First-bloom." Mr. Niven kept up the pace of the excuses, but his voice thinned out even more, like a tape at the end of its loop. "We needed to see how you would fare in a natural environment. We've kept a close watch all these years, Cadence. How do you think I located you?" He put his hand to the left of his undone buttons, over his heart. "You are our most treasured experiment. We would never let harm come to you."

The pride Cade had felt at being a good little entangled girl was gone, washed off on a stomach-sick tide.

"Your most treasured experiment?"

Cade pointed a harsh finger at Niven. "I don't owe you." Her voice trembled like a shadow on a hot day. "Find him yourself. And when you do, you can reunite us. No . . . better . . . you sweep me off this sand-nugget and get us both back to Firstbloom, or a planet where humans are cleared for work. You scientist types must have some intense clearance. I mean, look at what you're getting away with. Running experiments on babies."

Cade picked up Cherry-Red. It was time to drain out. "You let me know when you find him," she said. "When you do, bring him to me. I want to meet this Xan."

Mr. Niven stood firm in front of the door. It looked like he would take his encore, whether she applauded or not.

"That's impossible," he said with one of his too-rare blinks. "The scientists cannot find Xan. The scientists were killed in the raid."

"You're standing right in front of me. So at least one of you made it."

"No," Mr. Niven said. "I was not so fortunate."

The wrinkles on his face trembled and then — vanished. Mr. Niven was thin, then thinner, transparent. He flickered, same as the light from a distant star. Then he snuffed out.

CHAPTER 3

PRINCIPLE OF LOCALITY A once universal notion that an object can be influenced only by its immediate surroundings. An idea that is defied by quantum mechanics.

Cade stirred through the pile of Mr. Niven on the floor.

Her fingers crept and retreated—like practice. Playing scales. They would go so far, find nothing, come back. Go so far, find nothing, come back. Cade took all of the anger and confusion over what Mr. Niven had told her and crushed it down, kept herself to the repetition of these simple movements, to see if Mr. Niven's remains could tell her more of the story.

Cade wasn't afraid of dead bodies. But this was something else—a faceless, skinless, organless heap. A not-body. Mr. Niven was mostly lab coat and the clunk of brown shoes. A few white spokes that at first Cade avoided on the theory that she would be touching bone, but on second inspection turned out to be plastic struts.

Something had been filling out the struts and the clothes

and it had seemed so clearly, frustratingly human that Cade had convinced herself she was looking at a human. But now she thought about Mr. Niven's speech (stiff), his responses (limited), and his wrinkles (blinking).

He wasn't just a projector — he was a projection.

And he'd stopped the playback much too soon. Not that Cade longed for the company of the old spacecadet, but he'd barely dented her list of questions — and those were splitting into more questions, sub-questions, each one demanding an answer. Who had decided to dump her on Andana? Why hadn't she been kept safe, if Xan had? Who — or what — were these enemies of hers? And why should she face them to rescue a boy she hadn't seen since they were both test-subject babies?

Cade worked her way around the not-body, backed into her guitar case, and almost knocked it to the ground. She saved it with scrambling hands. Placed it down, smoothed the cheap locks flat. Cade had always thought it was her music and the Noise that marked her as different. But it turned out she'd been made that way by scientists who didn't care if she knew what she was — until they needed her help.

She thrust her fingers back into the wreckage of Mr. Niven. Another question rose. Why shouldn't she throw what was left of him out with the night's empty bottles, torn ticket stubs, smeared cocktail napkins, and forget the whole thing?

The heap of struts and old clothes declined to answer.

"Just so you know," she whispered to the pile, "I don't like you any better now."

In the thin fold of Mr. Niven's shirt pocket, Cade's hand caught on a new surface, with smooth facets and a dicey edge. The circle of dark glass. So that was real, at least. She pocketed it as her due and kept moving, hands sure and fast now. But she only found one more thing worth her precious pocket-space.

A scrap of paper swimming tight with letters that she couldn't quite make out. Cade could read, but it wasn't like she got a daily helping of the printed word. She stuffed it in her pocket with the circle-glass. She would sound it out later.

For now, she had a bathroom line to slink past and fans to disappoint.

She left the mess for Mr. Smithjoneswhite.

With the quiet in Cade's head, the desert sang a different tune, all sand-scratch and hollow-boned wind.

She pulled up the metal door to her bunker. Clinked down the metal steps and landed in her square of cement. The desert was scattered with squares like this one, meant for travelers caught in the sudden bite of a sandstorm. Cade's must have fallen off the maps. It had been empty — no visitors — for years.

But now Cade wasn't alone. Not quite. She had the pieces of Mr. Niven in her pocket. And, in her head, a picture of the boy. The cloud-skinned boy. The one she was entangled with.

She sat down on the piece of scavenged plastic foam she used as a bed. It squealed at her, but Cade bore down and squished it into silence. She needed silence so she could wander into the mists of her head and find the place where she'd dropped his name.

Xan.

She clinked in other words, one at a time.

Cadence.

Firstbloom.

Entangled.

These were tokens of a past that Cade had been cast out of. She didn't know if she wanted it back, but she did want these words. They belonged to her. There was another one she needed to add, waiting for her on that scrap of paper from Mr. Niven's pocket. She opened it, and the lines where it had been folded were scars — thick and white and raised.

The characters sprawled. The first one reminded her of an *s*, but backwards. The middle letter was a *b*, she was sure of it. The last was an *H*, tall and crossed in the middle, one of her ladder rungs. But it was a capital, and came at the end of a word. A capital at the end of a word couldn't be English — could it? Cade didn't think so. But her lessons in the Parentless Center hadn't been easy to sit through.

Cade was left with two letters, second and fourth. She spun through the alphabet, but she didn't know these shapes. She wondered if she was looking at the curves and angles of a lost Earth language. It had been half a millennium since the decision was made, by nonhumans, that English would be the one accepted form of speech and writing for all humans living in space. Not because it was the prettiest or the most practical or the easiest to understand. Because it was common, and nonhumans weren't interested in learning more than one stick-figured, thick-tongued set of words.

If this note really was written in something other than English, Cade was done. She could try to track down a translator, but she didn't know what she was translating from. Unless the note wasn't for her at all. Maybe it was for Xan.

Cade felt Mr. Niven's influence on her like fingerprints. She tossed the paper across the room. She wasn't Firstbloom's messenger girl. These scientists scrambling her particles didn't mean she owed them favors — in fact, it was the other way around.

Cade burrowed as deep as her plastic-foam bed let her. Tried to burrow even deeper, into sleep. She would think about Xan in the morning. About whether she wanted to think about him at all.

Cade woke up and wasn't even sure of it for five minutes. No more Noise meant there was no static-prickled difference between dreaming and awake.

The room she slept in didn't give her much to go on. In the dark, it could have been the slate of a standard nightmare. But one finger of light reached down from a crack in the cover of the bunker, and led Cade to a patch of shine on the other side of the room. The mirror-tip caught her eye and threw back a dim picture.

Which gave her an idea.

If Project QE had nonhuman enemies, writing something that could be read backwards, in a mirror, would keep it safe.

Cade thrashed onto her other side and faced the pocked cement wall. If she was right, it would mean her enemies were real. She tried to convince herself that everything Niven had said was a lie.

But he was from her white-painted past — her own faded memories and her gut confirmed it. He was real, Xan was real, and entanglement was real. If it wasn't, the inside of Cade's head would be just like everyone else's.

Maybe the danger was real, too. Maybe the boy who used to be the most important thing in her small universe had been taken.

Cade got up and scraped the tenderness of her feet on the cement. In the dark, she found the slip of paper and crawled up to the mirror. Refocused her eyes. Reversed the word. It was blocked out in perfect, plain English.

Hades.

There was a reason Cade didn't go to Voidvil on Sunday mornings.

A hundred reasons, really, and Cade could see them running thick and obvious in the streets.

Voidvil was at its worst after the riot of a Saturday night. Men and women with spacesick had been up for too long without sleep. The needing smiles of the night before were traded in for burst-vessel skin and slitted frowns. A few tents were propped in the crust of alleys or slung across empty lots, offering forgiveness for whatever-you-did-last-night, only a few coins. Nobody bought it.

Cade scanned the buildings. She'd seen the word *Hades* before, splashed in neon over a gape-mouthed door. It was the name of a club on the near side of town. She would find out what the word meant, and maybe that would tell her how much trouble Xan was in.

Not that she cared. She cared about being able to go right back to not-caring.

The staircase to Hades put the one at Club V to shame. It twisted down, a spiral with pegs and spikes set in at random. Cade climbed, listening to her steps as they tested, sounded, called the all-clear.

Club Hades was a circle of sand-brick, with a sand-brick stage set inside of it like a ripple. A single person worked around the rim of the stage, broom in hand.

She was nonhuman—and therefore the owner or the bartender. But she wasn't a native of Andana like Mr. Smithjoneswhite. She stood tall and slender and had a much more reasonable number of limbs. She was one of the Matalan—a species of women who had some of the qualities of plants. They could photosynthesize and wore clothes spun with threads of sunlight over birch-pale, paper skin. This one rustled as she swept the floor. She grew purple flowers in her hair.

"No drinks," she said. "Noon." Her English was clear and her voice bent with ease, like it was giving in to a wind Cade couldn't feel.

Cade walked up to the bar and set her guitar case on a stool. She was sure that the word on Mr. Niven's paper had something to do with the enemies of Project QE. She needed her cool, and she needed a cover.

"I play at Club V," she said. "Saturday nights. I go on last." That meant she was the best act the club had.

"Dregs," she said. "You're Cade?"

"No dregs. I am."

The Matalan dropped a few petals on the floor, bloomed new ones. It was like blushing.

"And you want to play here?"

"No," Cade said. "I want to look around. On the condition that none of this makes its way back to the too-many-fingers owner of a certain other club."

The Matalan's eyes were swirled dark, like wood knots, and she narrowed them at Cade. She knew that Cade was scoping the club — or at least, that's what Cade wanted her to think. The cover was working, but it didn't come without a risk. If the Matalan didn't trust Cade or didn't want to deal with the possible mess of Mr. Smithjoneswhite, she might kick Cade back up the stairs, or make a discreet call to the bouncer and — wait. Cade had heard of musicians whose hands had been mangled and guitars smashed to atoms for less. She tightened her clutch on Cherry-Red's case.

"Sure." The Matalan tipped her chin out at the club. "Take a look."

Cade walked away, but she couldn't keep herself from watching the Matalan. All the woman did was sweep — skitter and gather, dust and air. But she was so beautiful, it could have been a dance. Loveliness didn't shift through her and leave, like the passing of a season. It was part of her, sewed up in her skin. Even when she shed her coat and went winter-stark, she would be beautiful. This was how she could live in the void. Humans had nothing that touched the fringe of this grace.

Cade walked the stage, the back rooms, the bathrooms, the dusty-bottled strip behind the bar. Nothing made her think of Mr. Niven or Xan or Project QE. She circled back to the Matalan. Watched for a minute as she tipped at the waist, tapped dust into a bin.

"Nice place."

Cade tried to imagine for a second that the Matalan was one of her enemies. But the fight would have started bubbling under the skin of their conversation by now. Cade had a sense for these things. The Matalan kept one swirled-knot eye on her, but other than that she didn't seem to care.

"The name of this club," Cade said. "What does it mean?"

"Death," the woman said, with a smile.

Cade smiled back, but there was strain in the thread of her lips. "Brass."

"Stole the name from an Earth story," the Matalan said. "It means 'underworld,' and this club is an underworld. Took me years of seeing people come in and out to know how good a name it was."

Cade slapped the side of her guitar case. It was an unspoken agreement. Meant she could be counted on for a set. The Matalan widened her eyes — no, just the whites. Stretched them into white-pointed stars.

"Saturday?" Cade asked.

The Matalan nodded.

But Cade didn't leave, even though they both had their answers. She got the feeling, from the twist of the Matalan's mouth, that she had more to say. Cade pushed one foot at the edge of a pile of swept dust. Swirled it into a glittering cloud.

"You want to see the real Hades," the Matalan said, "take a trip out to my planet and keep spinning."

"It's an actual place?" The inside of Cade's skull rattled, empty, wanting to be filled with this.

"Sure."

A real place. Of course. Mr. Niven was telling Cade where to go.

She gritted her teeth and thought about Xan. Not Niven. Xan. He had been innocent like she was, used like she was. Two babies—one left to a coma-blanked life, the other spat down in the desert. It wasn't so different. Except now he was in a place named after death.

Alone.

"What's out there?" Cade asked.

"I've been there," the Matalan said. "Past the rock planets and the gas planets and the ice orbs. Where the systems go thin. A mean place. No life, just a few stray strands of light. All over, black holes. It is a place of negation. That's a name for it—Hades. One of its names."

Cade had to get off Andana.

It smacked into her over and over again, in waves, the

need to leave. It followed her down the noon-washed streets. It crossed the line into the desert with her. It made decent company on the walk.

This was a strong, pure feeling, one that comforted Cade when everything else was confused. It was enough to guide her feet, unruffle her nerves, and set the ragged rhythms of her heart at ease.

And then there was the other dimension of it, the one that shimmered in front of her, beautiful and strange.

Needing to leave wasn't Cade's idea.

Andana was the sort of planet that brought on an endless parade of escape fantasies. But Cade had given up on those a long time ago, for the same reason she'd stopped touching underneath her skirt after the first few times she'd tried. A girl could get lost in that sharp a wanting. So she shut down the fantasies, yanked down the hem. Screeched the production of desire to a halt.

Now here it was — the need to leave — whole and certain, set down in her head by somebody else.

When the Noise had turned off, Cade had been stunned by silence. And of course she had her thoughts, sometimes low and murmured — more often a rough, ragged mess. But this was different. It didn't come the way other thoughts or feelings came — rising up, trickling in. This arrived whole. Delivered, or dropped out of the sky. And it had the stamp of someone else on it. Impressions that didn't match Cade's — of another body, another mind. Senses that pulled the world in at a different slant than hers did.

This feeling, this need-to-leave, was laced with fear. But it wasn't Cade-fear. Cade-fear was deep and thumping, and it felt like bass, and it tasted like metal. This was someone else's fear. It screeched and clamored. It even had a smell. Antiseptic and old sheets and boy-sweat.

This was Xan-fear.

He needed Cade to come and find him. He was reaching out across millions of light-years and — asking her. Not demanding it. Just needing it.

Needing *her.*

She wouldn't go for the scientists on Firstbloom. She wouldn't even go for herself, firm in the stance that she didn't need anyone, and Xan was still one of anyone. But she would go for the boy. Maybe because he'd turned off the Noise, and this was the only way to thank him. Maybe because they'd drooled onto the same blankets once. Or because he was like her — lab-altered, experimental, with no one else to count on. It didn't matter.

She would find Hades. She would find Xan.

Cade felt something else, and this time she knew it was hers.

Happiness.

For the first time in years, a shock of happiness, knowing that she could help, and that it might even matter.

There was a new mechanism to her steps now, a coil in her heels that made them lighter. She could have filled the desert with music. She could almost hear it now, the spreading of warm-centered chords.

Once Cade had it all decided, she wanted to send a message to Xan. Some way of letting him know to hold tight.

I'll get there.

She used the words, but words alone wouldn't reach. What she needed was simpler than words. Raw thought. Not nuanced, but powerful. When her words reached Xan they would reach him as thought — a shape, an idea.

Hold on. I'll get there.

She sent two feelings with the words — inside the hollowed-out bodies of words — her new happiness, and a twist of courage, paid out like a rope.

But it didn't last.

She cut the rope, it went slack, mind to black, when she saw the smoke behind the dunes.

Her dunes. The ones that opened onto her bunker.

Cade flattened and fitted herself to the shadow side of the nearest rise. Crawled under a thin blanket of sand.

The smoke rose and spread, and with it came sounds. Piercing high, thrumming low, nothing in between.

Not death sounds. Death would have been a comfort compared to these. Death was a bed — warm, dark, waiting. These were the sounds of what waited *past* death. The sounds of undoing.

Cade pushed herself up on the heels of her hands, breathed in a mouthful of sand. She crawled to the line at the top of the dune — sharp, but at any second it could crumble or be carried off by wind, and show where she was hiding.

She raised her head and risked one look.

A circle of beasts. Not a species Cade knew — too broad, with ridged backs and bent legs. If they were common on Andana, she would have heard of them by now, or seen one in the club. But Cade had never caught wind of these creatures. Taller than the tallest man. Covered in rags of space-black. Moving in a slow, practiced shuffle. Each of them cast two shadows.

Cade's body was a chant.

Heart, muscle, blood.

No. No. No.

She couldn't go back to the bunker. She had the circle-glass and the paper that spelled out *Hades* in her pocket. She had money sewn into her clothes and stuffed into the toe-points of her boots. She had her guitar.

Cade knew she had to leave, but she sat there behind the crest of the dune, watching.

These were the enemies Mr. Niven had warned her about, the enemies of the entangled. Cade had only half believed in them but now she could see them, hear them, feel them much too close.

They had come to unmake her.

She wondered if, somewhere else in the universe, Xan could smell her fear, like smoke.

CHAPTER 4

ELEMENTARY PARTICLES The building
blocks of the universe

Getting off Andana seemed like a better idea with each sand-
filled step. Cade would have to start at the bottom, though, to
figure out how to get all the way up to space. She'd have to
visit the only people she knew who had ever been there.

The spacesick bay was one of the largest buildings in Voidvil, a converted hangar from the days when humans had been
cleared to pilot low-flying craft. It stood at the southern edge
of town, cramped by weeds, painted the color of bandages.

Cade shuddered at the thought of the spacesicks' glassed-
and-gone eyes, their sweat-pasted skins. Spacesick had notice-
able symptoms, and they marched in a predictable order—the
glassy look, the utterly detached and voided calm, the ab-
sentminded touching. For the ones who hadn't been in space
long, it came in fits and starts. Those who had been exposed
longest were completely adrift in their sickness, and didn't
know who they'd been before space claimed their minds—no

names, no histories. Cade had never known about her past, so maybe she should have felt a kinship with them.

But she didn't.

She knocked at a small door that had been cut into the larger, craft-sized door. A woman answered it, wearing a brown dress and unfortunate shoes. She couldn't have been more than five years older than Cade, but she looked as if she'd burrowed deep into each one of those years. She was a nurse, or had appointed herself as one. There was no money to be had in watching spacesicks; it was the work of people who were either pumped full of religion, or fuzzed on enough drugs to know what was worth stealing from the medical supplies. Cade decided not to trust her.

"Who are you here to see?" the woman asked in a voice like the best black-market nail polish — shiny and impossible to chip.

"Umm . . ." Cade didn't have a specific name. She didn't know the names of her fans, just that there were hordes of them in that bay. She could describe them by the way they looked, the way they danced. The white-haired teenage boy whose shrugging moves said I'm-Too-Good-For-This-Get-Me-Out-Of-Here. The clatch of girls with hips and hands that kneaded the air. The woman who hooted at the end of every number like a desert owl. The middle-aged men with rubber arms, roaming eyes. Cade knew them all. She couldn't ignore them, standing in the front row every Saturday night. But she didn't think that's what the pretend nurse wanted to hear.

"I need to see a friend."

"Your friend have a name?" the pretend nurse asked.

Cade edged in a shoulder and tried to see the inside of the hangar. "Yeah, well, that's the thing . . . ."

"Look, *miss*," she said, as if the word *miss* meant "slummer" in some other language. "This bay is filled with sick people. So unless you have business here—"

"Cade!" Her name rang out once, and then it came over and over in small dry whispers. A spacesick she knew from his tendency to give himself an endless hug through her sets rushed to the door.

"She's with me."

The pretend nurse looked at the man in his hug-stained shirt and then at Cade, and Cade could see her doing some quick math about whether it would be better to let this happen or to purse her lips and make a fuss. But just as she started to gather her mouth into cracks and lines, five more spacesicks rushed up and joined the first.

"She's with us."

"We know Cade."

"This is our old friend Cade. Right, Cade?"

She nodded and shrugged at the pretend nurse, like she just couldn't help what good old friends she was with all of these nuts.

Hug-stains led her through the hangar, which was lined on both sides with small beds spaced in even rows. Cade couldn't help thinking of teeth, white, a few of them worn or yellowed, and in some places shoved together. Keeping the spacesicks apart from each other was almost impossible.

What they wanted, more than warmth, more than chatter, even more than the rich, filling hum of Cade's music, was human contact. There were abundant stories of spacesicks who jumped into each other's beds and did universe-knows-what for universe-knows-how-long only to wake up and stare at each other for hours, not sure what to do with a human when they weren't touching it.

Maybe that's what Cade's issues with the spacesicks cooked down to: touching. Their hands were on her now, as she walked down the center aisle. They prodded at her from all directions, fluttered their palms on her shoulders. Cade had never liked hands unless they were fitted to the coolness of strings and frets. But she needed the spacesicks' help, so she let them have the warmth of her shoulder, the rough grain of her hair. She wondered if, to them, it would seem like a fair trade. But when they stopped whispering her name, it became clear that they wanted more.

"What are you going to play for us?" Hug-stains asked, gripping her arm.

"Yes, yes," the girls with the hips said.

"Play!"

Cade had forgotten that she had Cherry-Red. All of a sudden its weight announced itself at the end of her arm. It was a good thing, really. If Cade had left it in the bunker it would be one more left-behind part of her life on Andana.

"Playplayplay," the spacesicks said, some of them soft, some of them screaming. She hadn't played since the night in Club V, when her head had emptied out like the bar after the barking of last call. She wasn't sure what it would be like now, to piece together a song without the Noise that had driven her to do it in the first place.

And there was something sharp-edged and dangerous about playing at the spacesick bay, with no one to keep the fans back if they loved the music a little too much. As much as she hated Mr. Smithjoneswhite, all of his arms did have their uses.

"One question," Cade said. "Before I play."

"Of course," an old man said, like he was damp at the notion that she needed to ask about asking.

"Space," she said. The bodies around her sucked in breath and hissed it out. "If you wanted to get back there — for some reason, I'm not saying you would — but if you wanted to get back to space, what would you do about it?"

The room ripped apart into too many answers and the moans of the ones who didn't want to answer at all. At the end of the hangar, the pretend nurse raised her thin, old-before-their-time eyebrows.

"Why?" begged an old woman whose eyes had gone so glassy, they looked almost white. "Why would you ever want to go there?"

"Space is beautiful," Hug-stains said, "but it doesn't give a dreg."

"Stay here with us," the dark-haired girls cooed.

"Stay here."

"Yes, stay."

They put hands on her with abandon now — on her arms,

her back, her sides — holding her down like they could keep her planet-bound. Cade turned in a tight circle, but she couldn't brush them off without blasting through, hurting someone.

"I have to go," Cade said, but she wasn't sure if she meant up to space or rocketing out the door.

"Don't . . . you should stay . . ."

Cade wondered if the spacesicks were right. The scientists had seemed to think she couldn't come down with space-sick because she was entangled. But how could the scientists know that for sure? Cade had spent two years on Firstbloom, not a lifetime.

More spacesicks moved in close. Cade eyed the door through the cracks in the crowd, but the pretend nurse stood there, ticking her fingers against her crossed arms, looking at Cade like she had earned this.

Bodies blocked Cade's skin off from the air. Her heartbeat kicked out of time.

And that heartbeat was like a call that Xan answered without a second's pause. He was with her, in her mind, sending her the focus she needed to face the spacesicks and give them an answer.

"I'm going to save someone," Cade said, unsticking their hands one by one. "I'm going. So you might as well tell me what you know."

The spacesicks kept at her, repasted themselves. Xan pressed into her mind again. Cade liked the hesitation she felt, almost like he was asking if it was all right to help — instead of barging in. They'd both had enough of that from the scientists on Firstbloom. When Cade sent back a sort of mental nod, he responded with a crash of comfort. It felt cool, and the raw thought had a pulse to it, too, an underbelly of a beat, and it reminded her of —

— music.

"Look," she said, holding up the guitar case. "You can have what you want." Cade slapped the case onto the nearest bed and rushed to connect to the built-in amp, hoping the sand-crusted batteries still carried a charge.

She hurried her fingers into a sweet, simple chord. C. C. C. That sound was milk and cookies. It quieted the spacesicks. A few even sat at her feet.

"That's nice," one of the girls said. Cade noticed her for the first time, picked her apart from the knot of other girls who, until that moment, had looked just like her. Now Cade could see that this girl was the smallest, with the roundest face and a bit of softness in her eyes where most of the spacesicks just had glass.

"Thanks," Cade said, as if it had been an actual compliment.

"Lee," the girl said. Half of the heads around her nodded. "If I needed to get off-planet about now, I would go to the market and find Lee."

"Thanks," Cade said again.

The girl smiled and the smile shifted something in Cade, moved her fingers into formation. She started to play. A lullaby, to lure the spacesicks from their worries and into their teeth-white beds. But they took it the wrong way and started to dance. Their usual dances, with jolted arms and hard-grinding hips. Cade pushed her way through a verse and a chorus and then sped through one more chorus to end it.

"Dance with us, Cade."

"No, that's —"

"Dance, it feels good to dance."

Bodies shivered toward each other, filled in each other's spaces. But when they touched, nothing changed. It was like they were rubbing up against people-shaped walls. The soft-eyed girl stood apart and moved her feet up and down, just a gentle tapping. She was plugged into the beat. Cade would have played the whole song for her twice.

But there was Xan to think about. She got a hint of him at the edges of her mind. Anxious. Waiting. It was time for Cade to go to the market and find Lee.

She packed up Cherry-Red and walked away. The space-sicks were still dancing, and she knew they would dance for a long time after she left.

The market was busier than the spacesick bay, but it was better, too. At least the people there knew how many inches to leave between their skins and Cade's. They streamed in long lines through the basement of HumanScape, one of the larger apartment buildings, twelve floors. The market moved all the time. There were arrests made, one or two a month, but only when a merchant's trade got too big for its human roots and started to suck customers out of the big city markets.

The Voidvil black market didn't have much, but it made up for that with lots of brass and color. Cade passed booths that sold hand-dyed scarves, oversweetened candies, sand-blasted electronics, candles that smelled like places Cade would never see — Deep Forest, Ocean Wave. She wondered how many times those smells had been handed down, diluted, since someone here last filled their nostrils with the green smell of trees or salt-sweet brine. But that didn't stop people — including Cade — from sniffing the little stubs of wax.

Cade knew a lot of the merchants; besides candles, she bought bread from them, and fruit. She traded for guitar strings and new old clothes and tear-shaped bottles of nail-black. Cade was a steady customer, and the merchants didn't have to pretend to like her or care about her life. She browsed, she scowled, she bought, she moved on. Merchants loved it. But a strange thing happened when she stopped stirring her fingers through their wares, looked up with careful, half-bored eyes, and asked about someone named Lee.

"Lee? No."

"Not a name I remember, and I remember it all."

"I've never heard of her."

Cade felt sure none of the merchants were telling the truth — not the soap man, not the rat-gut seller. But the comment from the baker sealed it. *Never heard of her?* Lee was a boy's name, at least some of the time.

The stacks of round loaves at the baker's booth led into the labyrinth of a clothing stall. Cade spent a few coins on a pair of yellow leatherish gloves she didn't care about. She should have saved her money, but she had to make it look like she was just another girl in the market crowd. For the enemies of the entangled — the Unmakers, as Cade had started to think of them — the market would be too obvious a place to come looking. After her bunker and Club V, it was the clear choice.

Cade stuffed her guitar case behind a row of old coats and paid the owner a few more coins to make sure it wasn't sold or stolen. Cade knew he would do the right thing. He was a fan, and a good man besides.

What Cade needed now was a criminal.

Whatever this Lee was getting up to, it was big-time-brass illegal, because what happened in the market was illegal enough. If the merchants didn't want to be associated with her trouble, it was trouble of the sourest kind.

Cade cut a line across the market, toward the least reputable merchant she knew — an old woman with long strings of dark hair and a too-small set of false teeth. She dealt in the bodies and belongings of the dead. Her booth was lined with strings of teeth, bottled clumps of hair, and the little possessions that people tended to have on them at the end. Bowls of keys. Neat lines of shoes.

"You know someone named Lee?"

"No one by that name here," the old woman said, pointing to her wares and laughing.

"Lee's not dead, as far as I know. I was sent here to see her."

The old woman squinted, and the ancient skin around her eyes rearranged. "Sent to me?"

"No. To the market." Cade ran her fingers through a bowl of keys. They shifted like water. "I've been told Lee can help me get out of here. You know. Out of here and up?"

The old woman hissed, a thin kettle sound. "Better to live and die on the ground, even if it's barren. You buy some of my product and you'll see. This all comes from planetbound bodies, not a spacesick in the pile. Space rots a person, body and soul. Empties out, hardens the shell."

The dirt-and-metal smell of the keys stirred up, thick in the air. "You believe in souls?" Cade asked.

The old woman bent down under the surface of the booth, the curve of her back showing. She came up clattering a tray filled with tiny glass bottles. They were all different shapes, some faintly colored.

"Half off the first one, special for you, space-bound girl."

Cade felt a wash of sickness at the sight of those bottles, but she wasn't sure why. She'd never known people well enough to mourn them. Mr. Niven was the closest thing she had to someone from her childhood, and her feelings about him were mixed, at best. Besides, his collapse was less than a death. The echo of a death.

Cade hovered her hand over the bottles. "What if I told you that my soul was tangled up with someone else's?"

"I'd say you were cursed. I have something for that, too."

The old woman smiled, showing the gnarl and pucker of her gums. She stooped to find more of her specialties.

The idea of entanglement as a curse, a burden she'd never

asked for and that would — in the end — ruin her, worked at Cade, slid under her skin. She reached out for Xan.

Cursed. Do you believe that?

The raw thought trembled, overfilled with Cade's anger at being left on Andana, and her fears about crossing the universe to find him.

What she got back from Xan was complicated. Flashes of white — the first images that he'd ever sent. Their connection was getting stronger, and with that came more senses. The whiteness was paired with a sterile smell. Firstbloom. And then — a flood of dark feeling and fire, gasoline ignited and charging through Cade's veins. That was Xan's take on the scientists and what they'd done.

But then his thoughts turned to something new. Here was a flash even more familiar. The face of a baby girl with light-brown skin, dark green eyes. And with that came the strongest feeling yet, breaking over Cade shiny and hopeful, like the yearned-for chorus of a song.

Even if entanglement *was* a curse, this was the way Xan felt about her.

It made perfect sense to Cade.

The old woman bobbed up from under her table and started to unload more wares, but Cade put a hand out to stop her.

"Let's get right to it."

Cade slid a coin onto the table. A not-kidding-around coin. The old woman waved a hand at her soul tray, inviting Cade to pick one.

"I'll pass."

She didn't need any more souls to worry about. Not when she already had Xan's on the line.

The old woman picked up the coin, brought it to her lips, but seemed to remember the nature of her teeth at the last second and settled for sniffing it. After a deep nostrilful of copper, she nodded.

"Now," Cade said. "About Lee."

"That will take more than coin," she said. "It's not the sort of information a person passes out so easy."

"But I just . . ."

"Proved you were serious, is what you did. But this will require something more . . . personal."

Cade didn't have much on her, and what she had, she needed. She leaned over the table, shoulders first, and tried a bit of intimidation, but the old woman raised her knotted eyebrows and stood her ground.

"What do you want?" Cade asked.

"Part of you," the old woman said. "For the shop."

Cade leveled a glance at the woman, and stuffed in as much contempt as she could fit. "But I'm not dead."

"You go there," the old woman said, pointing up, "you're as good as." She leaned in and whispered, voice coated in age like layers of dust. "The customers, all they want is the tragedy. And that's thick on you, isn't it?"

Cade's stomach flashed cold.

"I might have asked for your hair on another day," the old woman said, with a glance that inspired Cade to gather it up and tuck it behind her shoulders. "Decent locks, nice shine to them, but I've got plenty at the moment. So . . ." The old woman rattled around with one hand, not taking her eyes off Cade, until she flourished a pair of pliers. She nodded at Cade's mouth. "I'll take one of those."

"You can't be . . ."

"Serious? But that's just what we are, you and I." She slapped the pliers down on the table.

Cade grabbed them. Made another frantic round of the market, but no one would slip her one word about Lee. So she stopped at the booth that sold splinter-thin vials of moonshine. Bartered for two of them and took her strange armload of items to the nearest bathroom. It had a mirror, which was good. Not because Cade wanted to see what she was about to do — but it would help her be precise. She uncapped the first bottle and poured the white-hot moonshine straight over the chosen tooth, second from the back on the bottom right-hand side. Then she opened the other bottle and rubbed the fire into her gums until she couldn't feel them. With each slide of her finger, her stomach clenched. The pliers went in cold, and her tongue fought back. But she reached in the prongs, clamped them down.

Cade called out to Xan and concentrated all of her efforts on sending him a picture of herself, staring into a film-blotched bathroom mirror with a pair of metal fingers deep in her mouth. She gave him a chance to tell her to turn back. Not to do it. Not to come for him. She felt the clench of his heart when he saw her, but he didn't tell her to stop.

She sent him one last flash of the plier-glint, the taste of rust.

You had better be worth this.

She pulled.

Xan couldn't keep her from feeling the pain, but he could feel it with her. He was there, and it felt like someone holding her hand tight enough to draw her away from the hurt. He couldn't stop her from slicking one hand with blood or throwing up twice, but he could distract her, shore her up, calm her down — do whatever it took to keep her upright as she stumbled across the market, her fist closed around the chip of bone.

"Back so soon?"

Cade slammed the tooth down.

"Didn't think you would do it," the old woman said, picking up the tooth as if it were some milk-white diamond, peering at it from all angles.

"Lee," Cade said through a mouthful of pain.

The old woman pulled the black felt of the curtains behind her booth and let Cade pass through. She smelled the pungence of shoes that, thankfully, masked the other smells of the old woman's trade, and felt the swish of the dark fabric against her screaming-tender cheek.

On the other side, Cade faced the emptiness created by the backs of the booths. A sort of enclosed square. A few merchants sat on crates and counted wares or coin. Cade was sure she'd have to ask at least one more person where she could find Lee, and didn't know how she'd manage with her puffing mouth. But then her eyes settled on a girl at the end of a short line, and Cade knew she could stop the search.

People waited patiently to see the girl, who couldn't have been more than eighteen, just a little older than Cade. She had wild sand-colored hair, pulled up into a complicated series of knots. She didn't have a booth set up, just the line, and from the looks of it, people would be waiting for a while.

She was in the middle of kissing a man, long and hard and studiously. She pulled away every once in a while to write something in a small black notebook.

Cade tacked herself onto the end of the line. The kissing went on and on. Cade wanted to stop watching, but it took her mind off the splintered ache in her mouth.

"All right," Lee called out. "Who's next?"

CHAPTER 5

CONSTRAINT VARIABLE The boundaries of a
system within which any process must work

Cade had to watch a few people come and go to figure it
out—what Lee was doing, and why the line to see her was
filled with feet-tapping, quick-breathing nervebags. It didn't
help that Cade had to think through the pain of her voided
tooth.

Lee finished with the first man, and a woman stepped forward—she could only be described as a mother, her clothes
wrinkled and her face ironed flat with worry. In the black
notebook, Lee took down the recipe for a certain kind of cake,
crammed with black-market sugar. Cade couldn't see the connection between the kiss and the cake—but more than that
she couldn't figure out how this girl was supposed to get her
up to space.

Then an old man with square-framed glasses taught Lee a
song. His voice shivered like skin at nightfall, but the pitch
was true. Cade basked in the distraction of it—at least, until

Lee started to sing. She repeated the old man's words, but the rhythm dissolved and the notes weren't right. Cade wanted to nudge them up, out of their flatness.

Lee tried again.

"Come unto these yellow sands, and then take hands: Curtsied when you have, and kiss'd the wild waves whist, Foot it featly here and there; And, sweet sprites, the burthen bear."

The words were strange and wild and not English. But the sounds made perfect sense to Cade.

Her Noise-free head was turning out to be just as musical as before, if not more so. Now Cade could hear one sound at the center of her skull and turn it around, examine it from different angles. Even with her butchered mouth, she could hum the notes better than Lee. The song had gone sour, and Cade knew it, and from the squint of the old man's eyes he knew it, too. But he put a hand on Lee's shoulder and thanked her anyway.

No two people offered Lee the same thing, but she greeted all of their offerings with the same wide smile. And then the man in front of Cade stepped up and she heard Lee ask, "What planet?" and it all made sense.

Lee was part of the Human Express.

Cade had thought it was just a story, a collection of mumbles to help humans feel less alone. The Human Express was a loose network of people who made it their business to deliver messages over tough and sometimes uncharted tracts of space. It was also, in every sense of the word, illegal. Nonhuman species weren't interested in humans keeping in contact with each other. It was one thing to send a few words on a passing work ship, or bribe a half-rotted pilot to carry a letter. But the Human Express did a lot more than that. They took whatever was most important to people as far as it needed to go. The only place the carriers were safe was in space, which was almost impossible to carve into patrollable territories.

The Express being real, and Lee being part of it, meant that Cade had a chance to make it out of the atmosphere. She rushed to send Xan the news — a flash of the scene at the market, a blast of her new hope.

Lee turned her smile on Cade, who had landed at the front of the line. Now she could see the girl in detail — her wide dark double-moon eyes, the freckles scrolled out on her pale skin. She was the negative image of a starry night.

The distance between them was only a few steps, but to Cade it seemed uncrossable.

"Hey," she called from where she stood in line.

"You." Lee took a giant step forward, did the real work for her. "Never seen you before."

"It's a high price of admission." Cade tapped a finger at her wound. The words came out puffed and soft.

Lee shook her head and swore under her breath. Her storm-iness was as full and complete as the smiling had been.

"I told that spacecadet, no more teeth."

She turned her back on Cade for a minute and rummaged around in a canvas pack. When she straightened up, she held a small bottle of antiseptic and a few swabs of cotton. She tossed them to Cade, who caught them in the hand that wasn't busy cradling her monstrous cheek.

"Keep those, courtesy of the Express," Lee said. "Now what can I do for you today?"

"I was told you could help me," Cade said. "By . . ." She didn't know how to describe the soft-eyed spacesick who had sent her. *Friend* wasn't the right word.

Lee didn't seem to care. "Don't need a reference." She flipped to a new page in the notebook. "What planet?"

"Not a planet at all," Cade said. "It's a place called Hades. I think."

"Hades, you think?" Lee widened her eyes and pushed a hand up into the wilds of her hair. "Yeah, I've heard of that one. There are humans out there? You sure? I mean, other than the ones that are stuck in hole-suck. I can't exactly get to them."

Xan was there, in Hades. Cade was sure of it. But she didn't want to leave Andana only to go hurtling in the wrong direction. There had to be some way of knowing where Xan was, of not wasting Lee's time. She got the feeling, just from looking at this girl, that she was someone you wanted on your side and not the other way around.

So Cade reached out to Xan and sent the thought of black holes. Dense and inescapable. Light-devouring. And she thought the words that the Matalan had given her.

A place of negation.

She waited for a response, and Xan sent something just like

it back to her — black holes, a string of them over and over. So many black holes that Cade's thoughts were sucked in a hundred different directions at once.

"Yeah," she said. "I'm sure."

Cade sighed as the pulling in her head let up. She was left alone with her own thoughts and Lee's face, which might as well have blinked a neon sign that said THEN AGAIN MAYBE I WON'T.

"Hades is going to cost." She consulted a list of prices in the back of her notebook. "It is going to cost big and terrible."

"I have money." Cade didn't spend much of what Mr. Smithjoneswhite paid her, when he remembered to do it.

"And what am I taking out there for you?" Lee asked, licking the end of her blue pen and spotting her tongue.

"Well. Me."

Lee shook her head so hard that one of her hair knots came undone. "Don't carry human cargo," she said. "It's part of the code. I'm twelfth generation. I know the rules. Human Express takes the intangible to the unreachable. And you . . ." She looked Cade up and down. "You're tangible as hell. I know you're a first-timer so I'm going to let this one drain. No humans. No exceptions."

"But someone told me —"

"Someone was wrong." Lee looked over Cade's shoulder at the next person in line. Crooked a finger. "Step up."

Cade was surprised by the sound of her own voice — sharp-edged and rising.

"But I need to get to him!"

She had Lee's attention now, and she couldn't waste it.

This was no time to stumble through an explanation of what it meant to be quantum entangled. Cade knew that those words wouldn't clink for Lee the way they did for her.

"I need to find my brother."

Lee's storminess gathered again. She stepped in close to Cade and lowered her voice to a rumble. "Look, everyone in this line has a brother, sister, husband, kids, somebody to miss. What do you think we're all here about?"

Xan wasn't another one of those much-misseds, those long-losts. Cade knew it sounded the same, but it wasn't the same. Like a note played in two different octaves. You could only tell the difference if you knew how to listen.

"He's in danger," Cade said. "He's going to be . . ." The word she wanted was *unmade,* but again, she had to scramble for a translation that Lee would understand. "He's going to be killed."

Cade expected some kind of gasp, but instead she got a lightning-sharp stare. Lee pushed Cade away from the line with two small but firm hands. She stopped at the back of one of the booths. "Wait here."

"But —"

"Wait. Here."

Lee went back to her brisk-but-friendly business. She didn't look at Cade once. Her dark-moon eyes didn't even flicker. Cade focused her energies on the little bottle of antiseptic and the cotton swabs, one of which she soaked and lodged in the pain-rimmed emptiness where her tooth had been.

It took the better part of an hour, and then the line was

gone. Cade heard a bell ring in the distance, muffled by the booths and the sounds of people scraping to make their last purchases. The market would close in ten minutes.

Lee shut the little black notebook.

"You have to understand," she said, strolling over to Cade, "if I had this conversation in front of all those people, I would have started a riot. Or had to find a bigger ship."

"Which conversation?" Cade asked.

Lee's face traded in its normal upbeat airs for something else. A seriously down-tempo cover song. "When you said your brother was going to be killed, you meant it, right? You're not some kind of space junkie using me for a ride?"

"I meant it."

Lee's dark eyes searched her again, and Cade couldn't help but feel like this girl was on the hunt for her soul. She scoured up and down, then moved in close. So close, Lee's nose almost stubbed hers.

"Fine."

Cade wondered what Lee found in her face that settled the matter.

"Here's the rest of it," Lee said. "You come with me, you carry."

Cade wasn't sure what that meant at first. Then she remembered. Human Express. She would have to work her way to Hades.

"What do you want me to take?" she asked, sick at the thought of people lining up to unload their secret messages and most heartfelt kisses on her.

"I'm done here," Lee said, as she tied up her pack. "But on the next planet. Start thinking how you can be a help to me. And don't keep me waiting. And don't make me late, ever, and don't make me sorry that I bent the biggest rule for you. Right?"

Lee smiled, big and toothy-white.

Cade decided it wasn't the best time to mention that her brother wasn't actually her brother, and that the creatures she was going to save him from were after her, too. That she was a danger, a drag, the worst kind of liability for a ship that needed to travel without attracting trouble. Cade wasn't used to being smiled at in a way that she liked. She didn't want to do anything to collapse that small, bright star.

"Right."

The nearest spaceport was in Dana City, a half day out. Cade and Lee stood on the Voidvil line, looking at the desert. It blared sun back at them. Midafternoon, and if they walked without stopping, they would get there in the dead center of the night. Not that spaceports slept. Just that the desert got meaner as it got cold. And now, without the Noise in her head, Cade could hear how empty this part of the world was.

"You sure you don't want to take a skimmer?" Cade asked.

She had handed all of her coin over to Lee for her fare to Hades, so she couldn't make the call on a skimmer herself. Taking one to Dana City would cost, especially because they were human. But when it came down to it, most palms on Andana were greaseable.

Lee shook her head and slung her pack over a shoulder. "I spend ninety percent of my time in a metal canister," she said. "We're walking." She turned and looked at Cade, sun caught in her sand-colored hair. "Besides. It can't be so bad with somebody to talk to."

It had honestly never occurred to Cade to talk to Lee the whole way to Dana. Or any of the way to Dana. Her mouth was still a swollen pit. Besides, Cade didn't tend to use her voice for much besides growling out songs. But this turned out to not be as difficult as she thought.

Lee would talk for a mile about the things she'd picked up on Andana.

Cade would nod.

Lee would talk for another three miles about where they were headed, and the people they might meet, and how Cade should talk to certain types of customers (overexcited, water-working), and what to do if their ship got boarded.

Cade would say, "Mmm-hmm."

At some point, night came on strong and the sun packed it in. Lee's words dribbled into quiet. Cade was left alone with her own head and the desert — sighs of sand on sand, a groan of wind every once in a while to liven things up. She wasn't sure how she'd lived in this place for so long without noticing it was unlivable. The Unmakers hadn't exactly done her a favor by torching her bunker, but she was glad to not be going back.

Hours slunk by, measured in the number of new sand-welts on Cade's ankles. She reached out for Xan, but instead of transmitting, she tuned in to the soft, patient beat of his waiting. A thrum that started in her mind, but reached out to find echoes in the line of her neck, her fingers. It felt good. Not that Cade had a real frame of reference. She had gotten so used to the club — hands grabbing at her, eyes unpeeling her clothes. But this was different. Good-different. Knowing that Xan waited for her made it easier for Cade to keep walking, over and over the dunes.

"Hey," Cade said. She was the first to see it.

The spaceport rose from the sand like a radioactive wart. It was the only lit-up building for miles. The rest of Dana City was just a winking suggestion in the background. The spaceport was the thing.

She sent a beaming flash of it to Xan.

"How do we get in?" Cade asked.

"You think I don't have a plan for this?" Lee said, dropping to a knee in the sweat-cold sand. She seemed to take most things as challenges. And so far, she'd risen to them all. But Cade still doubted that she could get them both off Andana without trouble.

"It's against the law to be human and in the spaceport at the same time," Cade said. "Unless you're getting dumped here."

"I know." Lee rummaged in her pack. "I'm Human Express. Twelfth generation."

With a winning smile and a flourish of the wrist, she shook out a uniform — the blue and white of a spaceport worker. It unwrinkled and Cade saw that it had a thin plastic film attached that would turn human skin a pale blue. There was also an extra rolling eye that could be fitted with a bit of adhesive to the back of the neck. It was an outfit designed to make a human look like a Saea, one of the closest known species. The stitching across the breast pocket read SAEANNA.

"This uniform is cargo class," Lee said. "Makes it easier to lump around a bunch of stuff and pretend I'm delivering it to someone else."

"Nice," Cade said. "But not really enough. I've never heard of a two-headed Saea, and the fit for both of us looks . . . snug." She dropped down and sifted her fingers through the pack. "Have another one of those lurking around in here?"

"I used to." Lee's voice fell out of its usual rapid firing and dropped to a rare, slower pace Cade had heard only once before. "Had to stop carrying it around. I've covered this route alone for three years now."

"Yeah, well, that's how I usually work, too," Cade said. "Alone."

She snatched up Lee's pack and started to walk toward the spaceport. The weight of it meant almost nothing to her arm muscles.

"What are you doing?" Lee asked, running after her and launching herself on Cade's back. "You rot-faced, sour-livered spacecadet, give it back!"

Cade shook Lee off with a twitch of the shoulder and turned to face her. She dropped the pack in the sand and backed off. Lee's storminess had returned full force. But this time Cade laughed.

"I'm just testing it," she said.

"For what?" Lee mumbled as she rubbed the sand off her pants and the side of her face.

"How much it carries."

Cade looked Lee over. Three full heads taller. But skinnier than she was, in every instance. A papery slip of a girl.

"Yeah," Cade said. "This should do."

Cade — dressed in a light blue skin and stuck with a bonus eye — entered the spaceport by the maintenance door. She marveled at the number of nonhumans streaming up the glass concourses, down the glass stairs. She couldn't have imagined the number of ships they packed into one dome.

Another Saea stopped her halfway up the stairs. Rolled both eyes at her — the two front ones, at least. It was a greeting. Cade rolled her eyes back.

"Do you know where you're going?" the Saea asked.

Cade didn't nod. She didn't shake her head. She just looked up at him with her best, wide, I'm-a-lost-little-girl eyes. She'd seen those work on almost every male in creation, regardless of species.

"What dock, sweet-arms?"

Cade flashed a four with her fingers, then a two. She could understand Saea well enough, but when it came to speaking it, she sounded like an ancient woman with a stutter and a head cold.

"Forty-two is up the main concourse, then down the left-hand side, all the way to the back."

She nodded and smiled her thanks at the Saea man, picked up her pack and her guitar case, and hurried onto the concourse. There were more Saea in that crowd, and lots of native Andanans whose slithering arms reminded her of Mr. Smithjoneswhite. She had hundreds of fingers to avoid. The concourse rose and Cade looked down to the crowds on the lower floor — the scuttling crablike Mems and the faintly colored clouds called Remembrists.

Cade couldn't help but wonder at the fantastic spread of nonhumans. She hoped she wouldn't run into a Lilin, who could taste other people's emotions. It would be able to tell how scared Cade was of going into space. A dark and bitter taste, no doubt, that lingered on the tongue.

Dock forty-two was one of the smallest in the spaceport, tucked away behind two workships, great and hulking, bottle-shaped and silver. The ship behind them was nothing so brass. It was a perfect sphere, but its beauty ended there. Fine, downy fur covered it — half gray, half brown.

"Great," Cade muttered. "A hairball that travels to space."

Standing on the scratchy pink walkway, a Hatchum stared out at the middle distance of the spaceport, eyes calm but quick. Cade couldn't help but snatch in a breath. She'd never seen a Hatchum before. They were rare on Andana. This one looked young — older than Lee and Cade, but still young — and almost human, but taller and thinner, with every angle a bit sharper, every curve more intense.

He looked up, and his gray-brown eyes skittered over Cade. He was waiting for something.

She went straight up to him and slung the pack forward so it dangled between them. The Hatchum looked down at her with a mild questioning in his mild-colored eyes. Cade wondered what he saw.

Lee must have thrown a wild kick, because the imprint of a shoe came through the canvas.

"I. Um. Have something for you," Cade said.

The Hatchum arched his eyebrows at her. That was it. No *hello* or *what-the-snug-are-you-talking-about*. Cade found herself reaching for more of a reaction.

"You'll want to see this."

She beckoned the Hatchum over to a spot behind the curve of the ship. He moved light on his feet, and kept a careful distance. Cade held the sack with one hand and tugged at the string with the other.

Lee was folded as close to in-half as a human can get, her chest doubled to her legs. Cade and Lee had tossed all of the nonessential items out of the pack, and the rest were stuffed into their clothes — so it was just Lee down there, smiling up at the Hatchum. She could have lit all of Dana City in a blackout.

"Rennik!" she cried. "I wasn't expecting you."

He didn't even double-blink. "And I was expecting you, an hour ago, not stuffed into a bag."

Lee's laughter shook the pack, and Cade felt it travel up into her shoulders.

"Fair enough."

Rennik shook his head, like maybe this was something that had happened before. Or happened all the time.

"Is there a place I can put this down?" Cade asked. She was somewhat more than human, but it didn't change certain realities. "My arms do get tired at some point."

"In the hold," Rennik said, pointing one of his long, four-knuckled fingers up the walkway. "All cargo in the hold."

"Who is he calling cargo?" Lee cried, muffled by the canvas.

Cade started walking, but Rennik grabbed her guitar case and set it on the ground. Cade picked it up. Rennik grabbed it again. Set it on the ground.

He was so tall that Cade had to arch to see more than his chin. She stared him full in the face, and there was nothing mild about it.

"I'm sorry," he said, with all the charm of an instructions manual, "but I can't let you take this onboard."

"But it's my guitar," Cade said. "I know there's not a lot of room but . . . it's the only thing I own."

"It's not an issue of room. It's the nature of the beast."

Cade clapped Cherry-Red to her stomach, held her close. "Don't call my guitar a —"

"I'm talking about the ship," he said. "My Renna." At the mention of its name, the ship gave a little jump. "She's sensitive to electricity. This is electric?" Rennik asked, touching the case with one of those odd, fine-carved fingers.

"Yes. What do you mean, sensitive? And what do you mean, *she?*"

"Renna is a girl-ship." Rennik's voice had been flat, but it took on peaks and valleys when he talked about Renna. "She's very much alive. And she gets sick. You know, she's, what's the word . . . *allergic* to electricity."

"She's . . . what?"

Rennik put a hand to the curve of the ship. "Renna is my orbital."

Every Hatchum had an orbital. They could sail through any atmosphere, cut through space to carry messages and small items for their Hatchum. But Cade had never heard of one growing to a size where it could take passengers or cargo. There was no arguing with it, though—this was a spaceship, and she was alive. Now that Cade really looked, she could see the blink of little black eyes all over the surface. And the scratchy pink walkway had definite tonguelike qualities.

"What if I keep the guitar unplugged?" Cade asked.

"It's much too dangerous." Rennik ran his hand in a soothing manner over a fine-haired patch of ship. "I would tell you what happened the time we made an exception for a battery-operated flashlight, but you wouldn't sleep soundly for a week."

There was another kick from inside the canvas pack. Cade knew that Lee was telling her to hurry it up.

Cade looked down at Cherry-Red. "When is blastoff?"

"Renna doesn't blast," the Hatchum said. "She lifts with delight and ease."

"All right," Cade said. "When do things get delightful?"

"Two minutes."

Rennik's calm inched Cade to anger. "I have *two minutes*

to decide what to do with the one thing in the universe I care about?"

Rennik looked her over — and Cade looked him over right back. He should have been easy to interpret. Dramatic, handsome, almost-human. But it all fell apart when she reached his face. It was one thing to take note of his sharp-ridged cheekbones, how they sucked in underneath like craters. But Cade wasn't a dreg-brained club girl. She needed a hint of how this Hatchum felt about taking her onboard.

And she couldn't find one.

"If Lee said you were coming, I'll carry you," Rennik said. "I owe her several hundred favors. But we're leaving in two minutes, so both of you have to go. Strap in."

Cade should have been grateful, but the Hatchum wasn't making it easy. Still, this was her ride. She stowed the guitar case behind the walkway to buy some time, and hurried onto the ship.

She found the cargo hold off the central chamber and put the pack down, doing her best not to thump Lee against the floor. With two minutes draining fast, she ran back down the walkway, grabbed her case, and snapped it open.

Cade ran her fingers across the frets and over the strings. Tightened a peg. Touched the hollow body.

Parting with Cherry-Red would be the worst thing Cade had to do since she decided to leave Andana. It would be harder than making nice with the spacesicks. It would hurt more than pulling her own teeth. That guitar was the one thing that had kept her from losing herself in the wilds of the Noise. If she wanted to find Xan, she had to leave it behind.

Far above her head, a chip of the spaceport's glass dome opened up into the dark. The ship — Renna — blinked all of her little black eyes open.

Cade snapped the case shut. Opened it again. Took in that deep red like a drink. No. Like a blood transfusion.

A scream reached across the spaceport and found Cade. The sort of wild scream that went straight past the higher functions of her brain and buried itself in the ancient parts.

Had the Unmakers caught up? Would they attack her? Here? Cade's body was a chant.

Heart, muscle, blood.

No, no, no.

And she started transmitting to Xan without meaning to. It was the second time that had happened. When her emotions ramped up and her heart ran fast and tight, the connection snapped on — like a built-in failsafe. Cade sent everything she was feeling, thinking, seeing, straight to him.

She ran up the walkway. The scream died down and she was a step from the door, thinking the sound had been some mistake, thinking she had made it.

A hand clamped tight over her mouth, and another slid around her waist. Three more arms on her, in different places. Over a shoulder, around a thigh. Then she heard the voice, thick and slurping.

"You can't leave, girlie. You'd miss me too much."

CHAPTER 6

ENTANGLED QUANTUM SYSTEMS Cannot
be fully described without considering both
systems

Cade put an elbow to Mr. Smithjoneswhite's soft middle. A few of his hands trickled off like dirty water, but he stuffed a set of fingers into her mouth just as she was about to call for Lee. Pain shot from the root of Cade's gone-tooth and came out as the crudest form of sound. Mr. Smithjoneswhite's hand soaked up the screams.

"This is a nice skin," he said, breathing warm down the neck of her Saea outfit. "You look almost like a woman. Doesn't matter to me what flavor so long as it's not human." More fingers on her. More breath. "Too bad I know the truth. One scream from you and everyone in the spaceport will know it, too."

Cade bit his hand and when he snatched it back, her teeth went into her own lip—puffed it up with the bright taste of blood.

"You won't do that," Cade said. "Get me arrested. You want

me to come back to the club." She'd figured it out by this point. He must have put a tracer on her, or had one of the bouncers do it, or the bartender.

"It's cute, girlie, watching you try to figure me out. Maybe I just want to see you pinned for breach of contract."

Cade scrabbled back against Mr. Smithjoneswhite, pressed her heels down, but got no purchase. "It's not Saturday. I never missed a show."

"But I have you booked," he said. "Every Saturday for the rest of your life."

Cade's voice rose against the spaceport's din. "You wrote that contract and signed it for me."

"Yes." Mr. Smithjoneswhite let out a low, blurry chuckle. "And if I remember right, you thanked me."

Renna started to shiver, then shake. She rose an inch above the ground and blinked one eye, right in front of Cade. The ship was waiting to take off. The gap in the glass dome wouldn't be open for long.

Now that Cade knew Xan needed her, she couldn't get stuck on Andana. Mattering to someone was like having a favorite song. If you'd never heard it, you wouldn't be able to miss it. But once you knew it was out there, there was no distance you wouldn't travel to hear it again.

"Let me go," she whispered.

Fingers tightened on her neck, ridged her arms, pressed their prints white and all over.

"You don't want me to."

Cade felt a rush coming from the edges of her mind to the

center; from the warm underside of her skin, flooding in. She'd always been strong, but now she had another person's strength, too, underlining her arms, crashing down her legs, pumping through her heart and double-beating.

She stomped back on Mr. Smithjoneswhite's feet, and spun around to crack a fist into his face. As he staggered, Cade grabbed the guitar case and clamped her other hand, one nail-blacked finger at a time, around his neck.

Xan sent more strength, enough to wring and knock out Mr. Smithjoneswhite. Cade sent a flash of her view — the Andanan at the end of her arm, his skin hurtling past deep red to purple — to let Xan know she had the situation under control.

"You think I care about the club? You think I need you? Cute," Cade said. "Watching you try to figure me out."

She raised the case over her head and tossed it. The fake brass latch clattered open in the air and the guitar did Einstein proud, stretching its two-second dive into forever.

Mr. Smithjoneswhite looked back at Cherry-Red and its sickly snapped neck, long enough for Cade to pound the walk-way as it curled and tucked itself, pink and scratchy, into the mouth of the ship.

And then Cade was up. Gone. The guitar and Mr. Smithjoneswhite and the spaceport smeared into one bright memory.

The world shook and then Cade remembered it wasn't the world, it was Renna. Gaining speed.

Cade ran for the cargo hold, the upward pull confusing her forward-moving feet.

I'm coming, Xan. I'm coming, Xan. I'm coming . . .

Cade chanted it soft, under her breath and in her head, over and over. She told herself that Xan needed to know, but she also had to remind herself why she was onboard an enormous floating burr, headed for the unknown of space.

I'm coming, Xan. I'm coming, Xan. I'm coming . . .

Cade made it to the cargo hold just in time for Lee to toss her a thick cloth strap to latch on to — otherwise, she might have smacked into the floor and spent the rest of liftoff unpasting herself.

Cade didn't want to spend too much time nursing the quease in her stomach, so instead she watched Lee. She had her hand wrapped expertly around a strap and she modulated her breath to match the thinning-out of the atmosphere. Nothing to indicate that she was worried about bursting off Andana. But her freckles leached pale.

"You all right?" Lee asked.

Cade knew that however bad Lee looked, she must have looked ten times worse.

"Sure."

She remembered the facts from the filmstrip. She was entangled. She was supposed to prance around in space like it was her job. A sloppy minute or two at liftoff was one thing. She would snap into the beat of it soon.

Cade pitched forward and almost cracked foreheads with Lee as the ship lurched out of the atmosphere.

"So this is what delight and ease feels like . . ." Cade muttered. She tilted her face so she was looking at Lee's forehead instead of the ground. "I've never heard of a cargo-ready orbital."

"Well, you've never met Rennik," Lee said. "He's not the average Hatchum."

"What does that have to do with Renna being a spaceship?"

Lee's voice drummed tight — defensive.

"Everything."

Cade hung there, motionless at the end of the strap, her nose at a sharp angle to the floor, as they hit the smooth emptiness of space. The change of pressure in the tender inner shell of Cade's ear reminded her of her old friend the Noise.

"Hey," she said, laboring to stand. "You think I can get another guitar on . . . what's the planet that comes after this?"

"Highlea."

"Right. Highlea. Do they have guitars there?"

"Guitars?" Lee said, perking up noticeably. "There are planets that don't even have *music*. On Mann, the nonhumans are deaf and communicate using this intricate form of sonar. They think music is a form of chaos and use it as an actual weapon. On Wex 9, it's a snugging *crime* to create music. Sound waves are a class of being, and each death is mourned. Back before music was outlawed, the Wexians didn't get much done, they were too busy sobbing over dead melodies."

Cade thought all of that was interesting. "But . . ."

"Your guitar," Lee said. "Right. Your mind just runs on one track and explodes when it meets something coming from another direction, doesn't it?" Cade didn't answer. She was too busy thinking about guitars.

"You might find something on Highlea. Not an exact replica of that model you had, but the Highleans do make music. Then again, if it runs electric, you won't be able to stash it onboard. And you did give me most of your money. And exchange rates are terrible right now."

"Perfect," Cade muttered.

The smile snuck back onto Lee's face. "You'll figure something out. Humans get first-class creative when they have to."

Cade nodded. The film of the Saea costume shifted against the back of her neck. She tested to make sure that she could stand and then detached from the takeoff strap, shook off the costume, and grabbed her old clothes from the pack. She was just pulling down her shirt when Rennik swung into the cargo hold. He swept the room once with his gray-brown eyes, taking in the crates, the packages, Lee and Cade.

"I didn't think you'd make it," he said.

His voice was flatter than a day-old sandcake. He didn't seem the least bit surprised to find out she was human.

"Since you're new, how about a tour?" Rennik asked. It sounded like some kind of welcome, until he added, "Renna doesn't like passengers who aren't . . . familiar."

Cade nodded. The last thing she needed was a hostile, furry ship that didn't want her onboard.

As she unwound her hand from the cloth strap, she saw that she'd mangled a hatch of raw lines into her skin. It would make a nice set with the bruises that had sprouted in all the places Mr. Smithjoneswhite had grabbed her. Cade rubbed her arms and tried to look tough. When that failed, she tried to look entangled.

Strong. Stable. At home in her enhanced skin.

"Cade, if your stomach needs to do the gravity ballet, there's a bucket I can show you," Lee said.

Rennik held out his hand, not that it could have reached Cade where she was. Not that she would have taken it if she could. His offer of a tour seemed halfhearted — and Cade was being generous with her fractions.

She picked her way around the crates, Lee close behind.

"Not you," Rennik said to Lee with a smile curved so deep and cool, it made Cade think of water. Maybe he was never going to smile at her, but it was nice to know he could manage it.

He waved Lee back. "You're not new."

"Hey, I'm as new as she is! I just got here! I'm as mint as a new coin!"

Rennik led Cade into the main cabin. Lee was still shouting at them from the cargo hold.

"There's the mess," he said, pointing at one of the rooms that spoked out from the round space, "and a common area. I have a small cabin down here, too."

Cade was well past curious about the Hatchum's cabin — all she could imagine for him were neat-cornered sheets and bare walls. She lingered outside the door, but he kept moving.

At the center of the main cabin a chute twisted up to another floor. It slanted at just the right angle so that Rennik and Cade could walk without slipping. But every step reminded

Cade that she was planting her feet on someone else's innards. It was a slippery sort of feeling.

"Renna has a knack for false gravity," Rennik said. He lowered his voice and leaned in. "Some people tell me it's like taking a long walk in deep pudding. But don't repeat that. It will make her sad and we'll drift for days."

As they climbed the chute, he pointed to the stubby, white-sheeted beds bunked along its sides.

"She's not much of a passenger ship, but I do like to keep these here in case we have guests."

"Like Lee?" Cade asked.

He laughed — such a rich sound that Cade could imagine it being something you drank, in mugs. "Lee is like family." His trademark flatness swapped out for something much more alive, the way it did when he talked about Renna. "Hatchums have big families, you know. I think the closest word for her is . . . *cousin*."

"Don't have those," Cade said. All she had was Xan, and there was no word for what he meant to her.

"She's the one who turns up twice a year or so, tells you her stories, eats all the rations, and leaves with a smile."

It sounded like an accurate picture of Lee. "She's started in on the stories," Cade said. "Guess that means I should watch my plate."

Rennik stopped in front of a panel just behind a stretch of the chute. He stretched out his four-knuckled fingers, and the white chip of wall slid to one side and revealed an empty space. A short, square tunnel opened up into a little room with four more bunks.

"I have to ask the human passengers to sleep in here," Rennik said.

Cade's heartbeat scratched, like bad feedback. She had known it was too good to be true — a Hatchum who respected humans.

"What," she said, "in case we go spacesick on you?"

He turned his wide-open-skies look on Cade. "No," he said. "In case we're boarded."

She slogged the last steps up the chute behind Rennik, wondering how bad she should feel about the misunderstanding. And then the second floor sprang into view, and she was too crammed full of wonder to feel anything else.

"This is the control room."

Cade had never been in a control room, but Rennik didn't have to tell her what it was. There were dials and knobs and levers on almost every surface. Every surface that wasn't the glass.

Straight ahead and looming in front of Cade, a stretch of glass that at first she thought was a window. But as she stepped closer, she could see that it was more — a full picture of space outside the ship. Renna's little black eyes, all of those compound bits of blinking, drinking-in, fed into this one glass.

When Cade was close enough that she could reach out and touch it, the black stretched and circled around, swallowing her. She could turn and see planets on all sides — the colored swirls of gas planets and the mean fists of ice planets and past those, stars, and the milk of galaxies.

"How does it work?" Cade asked, turning and turning.

"Organic hologram," Rennik said, looking like he could burst his own skin with pride.

Cade thought of Mr. Niven for the first time since she left Andana. He had been a hologram, too — a different kind. She clutched the circle-glass where it sat lodged in her pocket.

She turned again, searching for something out there in space. The snatch-and-hoard of black holes. Hades. Cade wanted to send Xan a picture so he could know, once and for certain, that she would be there soon.

But Rennik bounded to her side, crashing into her thoughts.

"You like her?"

His nonchalance drained, and in the slip of a heartbeat he was in the glass with her, star-freckled, all eagerness and nerves. Cade couldn't answer his question. The word *yes* wouldn't do it — wouldn't stretch far enough to fit how much she liked Renna.

Rennik must have been able to see that in Cade's face, because he broke into a smile — the first one he'd cracked for her.

"Does she like me, too?" Cade asked.

Rennik's smile kept cracking, until it was in pieces.

"She'll let us know soon enough."

Cade backed up a few steps, out of the panoramic hold of the glass. Rennik bent over a panel of glass-slicked dials with thin, wobbling copper needles. These were nothing like the electronics Cade was used to — the faceless black, the mystery buttons, the harsh lights. But Rennik didn't look up and tell her about the controls. He didn't look up at all.

The tour was over.

Cade hung around for a few minutes, watching Rennik's hands work out patterns. Cade tried to come up with a note for each dial, a chord for each movement of his fingers. She tried to turn the ship into a song. One to flood the emptiness in her head, calm the storm in her stomach.

But Rennik's fingers were too fast and the dials were too complicated and when Cade looked at the glass again, space was just too big. The wonder she had felt when she first saw the room came rushing back, but this time it pounded her small, flattened her.

She had to get out.

Cade headed down the chute, but down turned out to be more difficult than up. Or maybe that was Renna, sending her a little message. Maybe that was how you said *drain out* in Spaceship. Cade's eyes were stuck so hard-and-fast on her feet that she smashed into someone sitting at the bottom of the chute.

The seven-blade knife flew out.

Cade didn't meant to unsnap it — this was instinct, carved into her by too many years of Voidvil, too many nights backstage at Club V. She held out the thick, mean, all-purpose blade.

Cade waited for the creature to stiffen.

Say something.

But no.

Cade walked in a careful, creeping circle around the creature. It was inflated in a way Cade had never seen before, puffed with a gas dense enough that it didn't float. Its body took up a seriously large part of the main cabin. Cade couldn't tell if it was male or female, both or neither. It was clothed in simple white and its skin was dishwater gray, which seemed dingy and unimpressive until she caught a look at its face. Boulder-featured, solemn, still. She could have been holding a mountain at knifepoint.

"Hello?" Cade whispered.

The creature dragged in a breath. Held it.

Never seemed to let it out.

"Hello?" Cade asked again.

Her politeness didn't match the knife. Then again, this creature didn't match the description of any species she knew.

"I'm not going to hurt you," Cade said. "I just want to know who you are. What you're doing here. If you're one of the people who wants to kill me. You know. The basics."

The mountain dragged in another breath.

Cade ran to the door of the cargo hold, where Lee was stacking and labeling crates with an old-fashioned stamp.

"What is that in the cabin?" Cade asked.

Lee stacked and labeled, labeled and stacked. "I guess Rennik didn't give you the full tour, did he?"

"Guess not."

Lee glanced up, ink plastered up her arms and dabbed on one side of her face.

"Work to do."

Cade could take a hint. Lee was still mad that Rennik hadn't taken her around the ship. Cade was on her own. She backed out of the hold and into the main cabin. This time, at least she didn't stumble into the blank-faced heap of creature.

She headed up the chute again. Less than an hour and she had no guitar, three people who couldn't be bothered to talk to her, and a ship that might cough her up at the first chance.

It made sense to Cade. She was alone — had been since the Parentless Center. She only made it official when she ran off into the desert. No one had bothered to come after her — there were too many parentless and not enough adults to watch them, let alone form search parties. But even before Cade's bunker, in the shabby classrooms and the dorm bedrooms, she had kept to herself.

Alone was the note Cade knew best. It was the root of all her chords.

But when she pressed the panel aside and crawled through the square tunnel into the little room where humans slept, she felt a new sensation. It clawed a space out inside of her, one that needed filling. Cade was alone, but she was something more than that.

Lonely.

The white beds were all the same. She picked the one on the bottom left so she could see people coming in.

Cade climbed into the tight grip of the sheets and closed her eyes. With no real day or night, she'd have to bully herself into sleeping whenever it made sense. It was a long trip to

Hades, and she would need to be as strong as possible when she got there.

Cade tried to wrangle her breathing. Her mind softened at the edges. In the last slow-drip second before sleep, her mind wrenched open.

Xan was in trouble.

Cade sat up and skinned her head against the top bunk. This was the automatic part of her connection to Xan—the one that dictated they would be there for each other at the first rebel heartbeat. Cade hadn't been on the receiving end of the call before, but she knew it for what it was.

At the same time, this transmission was something new.

Cade's connection to Xan—from the first wisps of feeling to the flash of a few sensations— had built to this. A whole picture, a three-dimensional place, the full range of senses. A moment as he lived it.

Another room. Smaller, darker.

The smell of metal, boiled sheets—sterile things.

The door blew open and a double shadow fell long on the floor. Cade caught a glimpse of space-black robes and the flickers of the shadows as they passed. She couldn't see more than that, but she didn't have to.

She knew it was an Unmaker.

Cade sent her strength to Xan. She hummed it to him like a bass line. Drummed it in a steadfast beat.

And he wasn't afraid.

Xan got up to close the door. There was no lock. The small rectangle could just barely be called a room, but Xan found a way to pace it. Nothing in that small space but a mirror and a pile of plain dark clothes in one corner of the floor and a bed. Xan hadn't been tied up or tortured or thrown in a pit.

Whatever they meant to do to him, it hadn't started yet.

Xan's emotions bum-rushed Cade's system like a drug. Like an itch in her blood.

She braced for hatred and fear. But what Xan sent was stronger than that, and it hit Cade twice as hard. He let her feel how much he needed her. A deep-shuddering, full-frame need. It slipped the borders of Cade's mind and searched out homes all through her body. Sliced up and down her nerves and sank into her softest parts.

Some small fraction of Cade didn't want to feel it. She and Xan had been entangled such a long time ago — there were moments when he felt like one more decision that had been made for her.

What she had was the chance to choose him now, and keep choosing him. To wash away the last of her resistance, and really feel him. It helped that she understood the emotions he sent. Xan was impatient, hopeful, waiting. Cade was those things, too.

He needed her to come. And she needed to get to him, no matter the distance, no matter the danger. They both felt the same, even with so much space stretched dark and impossible between them.

Which meant neither one could be lonely.

CHAPTER 7

SPEED OF LIGHT   186,282 miles per second.
Exceeded by the connections of the entangled.

Cade woke up feeling fine. If there'd been sunshine, she would have let it warm her for a minute. If there'd been music, she would have hummed along. But there was just the little white room and Lee.

"Hey," Cade said.

She wasn't used to radiating cheer. On short notice, *hey* was the best she could do.

Lee popped up on the top right bunk, her smile back to fighting strength.

"These beds are the snugging best, aren't they? When I'm on other ships, I dream about these beds. Renna knows how to treat a girl right. I thought she was on a run to the Outer Esterlies and I wouldn't see her for another six months at least. But this . . . well . . . this is the best I could have hoped for, and a little bit more."

Lee had a lot more words for a good morning than Cade

did. And she whistled—tuneless, drifting notes—as she made the bed.

Cade wondered what kind of morning it was for Xan. He had paced in that small room for hours until he exhausted himself. Cade reached out now and sent him a feeling left over from last night, a loose strand of worry—a drifting bit of minor-key concern.

Xan sent her a jolt of reassurance. It was hard to believe his fears of the night before had changed so completely. Cade didn't think he would be able to lie to her, but it was the first time she wondered if he could send her less than the whole truth.

Lee tossed a set of clothes down to Cade. They flapped in the air for a second and landed next to the bed. It was the plainest set of rags she'd ever seen—a prehistoric pair of jeans and a wrinkled tan shirt, instead of the layers of skirts she was used to wearing.

"For Highlea."

"Right," Cade said.

This was her first day as part of the Human Express.

She slapped on the clothes and followed Lee out of the tunnel, down the chute, into the clatter of the mess. The air filled with smells that meant breakfast, no matter what planet. Rennik bent over the small gas stove, scrambling eggs into an indecipherable dish.

"Did you sleep well, ladies?"

Cade liked the old-fashioned way that Rennik talked. It made her feel like English wasn't a blotch on the brightness of the universe. It also made her wonder where he'd learned it.

"Would have been outstanding sleep," Lee said, cutting a glance at Rennik, "if someone's flightstyle wasn't so scrappy."

Rennik cracked an egg extra hard, but gave no other sign of being riled.

Cade looked at the thick walls of the mess. She still wanted Renna to like her — so it was a good thing she didn't have to lie about how she'd slept. "Best night I've snatched since last winter's sandstorms."

Rennik and Lee stared at her like she'd grown back the Saean third eye.

"When you're underground, safe, a sandstorm makes the best kind of lullaby." What Cade didn't mention was that, in the case of last night, she had been too busy keeping Xan company to fall asleep for hours.

She took a seat at the long table and bit into her eggs to find that the centers were soft and ran down her chin. She looked around for a napkin to swipe at her face. It was only then that she noticed the other passenger sitting at the far end of the table.

Gray-skinned, rock-faced, swaddled in white. A male, most like. He could have been the shrunken twin of the creature Cade had seen the day before. Or he could have been the same one, deflated.

"Cade," she said, holding out a hand, wanting to make a good impression. She needed to smash all memories he might have of her at the end of a seven-blade knife.

He nodded his head deep into the folds of his neck, but

said nothing. At least his dark, lashless eyes took her in this time.

"That's Gori," Lee said from her spot next to the stove, where she was dictating how her eggs should be cooked. "Saying his actual name takes about a week, so just call him Gori."

Gori stared.

Rennik slid a glass of juice down the table to Cade.

Gori stared.

"I think we . . . uh . . . met?" Cade said.

When Gori spoke, his voice made her think of space: deep and wide, with something like a wind that moved through it.

"I would have noticed," he said.

"Noticing didn't look like it was on top of your list at the time."

"Ohhhhhh." He drew the word out halfway to the next planet. "I was in a rapture state."

Lee plunked herself down, took a slurping bite of egg-dish off Cade's plate, and talked through it. "Gori is a Darkrider."

Cade almost hacked up her juice.

"A Darkrider?"

Gori nodded again, so deep she worried his neck would snap.

She had never seen a Darkrider before. Most people hadn't. They were a rare, planetless breed. Everything she'd heard about them was probably a rumor, but one thing was for sure —they were the only creatures in the universe that could see dark energy. Cade wanted to reach out and ask Xan if he knew anything about them, but Lee was pulling at her hand.

"Come on."

Cade grabbed whatever on the table would carry — two lump-hard biscuits, an unidentified purple fruit — and stuffed it in the stiff pockets of her jeans.

"Work," Lee said to Rennik. "Take us down."

Rennik flipped a last egg and turned off the gas. He touched Cade's arm as she hurried past.

She looked down at the place where his fingers met her skin. She still wasn't used to letting people touch her. Cade could see the absence of logic — there was someone prodding at her *mind* a lot of the time — but skin on skin was a different kind of connection. One that made her insides twist.

"Your first mission?" Rennik asked.

Cade reached down the table and nabbed another biscuit. "I've worked my whole life."

"But you're new to the Express?"

Gori still watched from the end of the table, those dark orbs trained on her.

"It shows all big and obvious, doesn't it?"

Rennik laughed. It made Cade hungry.

"Lee's a good person — the best — but she'll stomp on your feet if you don't keep them moving. And be careful."

Cade felt the stick of juice in her throat.

"Yeah," she said. "I'll do that."

She'd been so busy with worries about Xan and the Un-makers that it had slid right out the back door of her brain. Human Express was dangerous in its own right.

Cade and Lee waited in the main cabin as Rennik set the ship down. There was no way to see the planet as Renna dropped through layers of atmosphere. Cade got her first good glimpse when they settled on something firm, and the walkway uncurled.

Highlea could have been Andana's bigger, older, uglier sister.

Renna sat in an outdoor port. Past a few rows of ships in different stages of falling apart, a strip of dirt and crabgrass gave onto Highlea City. It was ten times as big as Voidvil, at least. Cade couldn't see the end of it.

Like an ocean.

A great big seething sea of human.

Lee slung a canvas pack over one shoulder and handed another to Cade.

"All right," she said. "Let's collect."

Highlea City was like an ocean in more ways than one. It looked calm, but once Cade tossed herself into it there were waves, and tides, and scuttling creatures that lurked in its dark.

Lee tried to shout directions back to Cade, but her words got lost in a constant smashing surf of voices.

It was almost as loud as the Noise.

But Cade had a clear head now, and it helped her work her way through this blaring new world. Every street she turned down seemed to open into a public square, and every square was busier than Club V on a Saturday night. The force of the crowd tore Cade away from Lee more than once. She had to use her extra strength to push through, brush off, catch up.

Lee led her down a narrow side street lined in tan brick. The smells of clay and bread and spice crowded her even as the people drained out. It was just the two of them, Cade and Lee, standing in front of a door with a hand-lettered sign.

DO NOT ENTER.

In fourteen different languages.

Lee smiled and tightened one of her stray hair knots.

"Universe, but I do love that sign."

She opened the door and plunged them both into the dark.

A narrow set of stone stairs dropped down story after story until it hit a platform. This was longer than it was wide, and the drop on the far side bottomed out in a damp, shallow curve that ran in both directions into carved-stone circles.

"Old tunnels," Lee said. "Used to vent natural gases up into the city, but they came up with better piping a couple of decades ago. Now these are filled with spacesicks."

Cade thought of the glass-eyed men and women she'd known on Andana skittering around in underground gloom.

"They come down here?"

"More like they're dropped down here."

"That's . . ." Cade couldn't find the word. *Awful* wasn't enough.

It was a good thing Lee had curses to spare. "It's snugging sour, right? The spacesicks get so used to the black out there, people think it doesn't matter if they can see the sun."

"People can snug themselves."

Lee grinned at Cade's choice of phrase. But then she cast her eyes down the tunnels and got serious. "I think that was the official reason they gave, you know? Really just wanted the sick out of sight. Reminds people what could happen to them, with one nudge out into space."

"But you've been in space your whole life." Cade studied Lee. Clear eyes, a solid set of muscles, hands that kept to themselves. Not one whiff of spacesick about her.

"I spent a lot of time with planetbound relations when I was little," she said. "Been in space full-time for six years. It takes some longer to catch it than others. I know all the signs, check myself right and regular. And I plan to retire at the ripe old age of twenty."

Lee turned to one end of the platform. Cade's eyes adjusted down through shades of dark until she could see a little crowd of people. Their edges were unclear, parts of them shaded into the murk.

"All right, all right, step up," Lee said. The group shuffled like a horde of unsure fans. Cade almost thought one would take out a shiny-barreled marker and ask for an autograph. "We're going to try something new today. If you have an item you're waiting on, come see me. Need to send something off-planet? Meet Cade."

Lee flourished one of her long, sharp-elbowed arms at Cade.

She did her best to smile.

When that failed miserably, she found a dry patch on the platform and got to work.

First up was a little girl with planet-sized eyes. All she wanted was to hug a mangy cloth rabbit and send it halfway across the known universe. Simple enough. Cade stuffed it in the canvas sack, took down the name, planet, and dropoff point.

Then came an old woman, drowning in her own wrinkles. Cade had a rougher time with this one.

"You want me to *what?*"

"Cry. Tears?"

"I know what they are," Cade said, but that didn't change the fact that she hadn't produced them, ever. She hadn't cried in the Parentless Center on Andana, when she was told to drum up some misery for the inspectors so the center would get more coin. She hadn't cried when her parents were uncreated in one sentence from Mr. Niven. And she definitely hadn't cried when a song she made up on the spot turned a room of men, women, and spacesicks into watery chaos.

"My son, he died in a cobalt mine collapse. I can't be there at the funeral. But I need them to have my tears."

Cade shivered away from the old woman's arms. "Look, I'm sorry . . ."

Lee shot her a *don't-snug-this-up* look. Cade remembered, just in time, how much she needed the job.

It was going to get her to Xan.

She had it easy, compared to him. She was surrounded by humans, and he fell asleep to the sounds of Unmakers.

Cade looked down the line of waiting faces, and startled to think that she had it better than they did, too. She doubted most of them were being hunted by double-shadowed beasts—but in one sense she had it good, and she knew it. Entanglement gave her a direct connection to the one person she cared about. If that was broken, how hard would she work, what wouldn't she do, to get a message to him?

Cade couldn't be sure about the trustiness of her tear ducts, but she knew that wasn't what the old woman cared about. "I can't promise sobs," Cade said. "I can't promise buckets. But I'll do my best."

The old woman folded her candle-wax hands over Cade's and leaned in close.

"Universe keep you."

The man at the top of the line jumped forward. He was average height, average weight, average everything. He bounced on the balls of his feet.

"I need to send this to my wife."

He leapt in, lips trembling an inch from Cade's, so close she could see the thin cracks, the white-chapped corners.

Cade smacked him so far, he tumbled the rest of the line to the ground.

"Hey, hey." Lee jumped into the mess. She sent wild eye-stabs at Cade as she hauled people to their feet. "Sorry, she's new. You understand."

Lee left the line behind her with a smile, and pushed Cade into the stairwell. Cade's instinct was to push back, but there was no use starting a fight with her boss.

"Look, I know what you're thinking," Lee said. "Kissing is the most we do. And it's about sending a message—not snugging. Anyone gets sloppy or handsy or too brass with you, send them to me."

Lee cracked a knuckle. Cade almost laughed. Lee had some real storminess in her, and Cade didn't doubt she could put up a decent scrap. But Cade had seen lips before, and knew where to send people who shoved them into her face. That wasn't the problem. It wasn't even the problem she expected — the not-wanting-to-be-touched.

It was this: Cade had never kissed someone. And with those cracked lips so close, all of a sudden, it mattered.

"I won't do it," Cade said.

"Then drain out."

"What?" Her yelp hit the walls, bounced into the tunnels.

The storm gathered in Lee's face and could break any second. Her words trembled, weighted and electric. "The stairs are right behind you," she said. "You know how to climb them."

"But —"

"You can't take tears, you can't take a simple kiss, what else won't you take, Cade? You told me you would work to get to Hades. Right now, all you're doing is dragging me under."

"Look," Cade said. "Let me try again —"

"No!" Lee's words lashed at Cade. "There's not one person here you can help that I can't help faster, not one thing you can carry that I can't carry better."

Cade tried to keep calm. If she let fear override her systems, Xan would be there in a blink. She didn't want him to know how close she was to ruining the whole thing, setting herself back so far that she might not make it before the beasts came to his small room and did something unspeakable.

"But my brother —"

"Is in danger. I know," Lee said. "That's why I gave you a chance. Not my fault if you squandered it."

Cade got the feeling that with each word, Xan was another light-year away.

"Please."

"Look." Lee burst out a breath. "I'll take you back to Andana. I won't strand you here."

Andana. Back to Mr. Smithjoneswhite and his tracker. Back to the ruins of Cherry-Red and the bunker. Back to the world she'd never wanted in the first place — and the Unmakers who waited there.

"There's no life for me on Andana."

Lee cut through the air with her hands. "I can't leave you here. The Highlea force is too active. They find you and trace you back to me, I'm done. That's not a risk I can take. *This* wasn't a risk I could take."

Lee turned to her waiting line, waved over the stragglers from Cade's. She beckoned the first woman.

Cade went and stood on the edge of the tunnel, breathing in the dark. She wanted a minute alone with her thoughts, but within four seconds she was captured by something more interesting — sounds. Small ones. If the Noise had been with her, she wouldn't have noticed them. The pretty plink of water down the right-hand tunnel. The scrape of shoes on stone.

People lived in this deep, forgotten place. Cade thought of stepping into it and never being seen again. She could outrun Lee, Mr. Cracked Lips, the whole crowd. She could disappear into a new world.

But she couldn't find Xan alone.

Then it burst into her perfectly clear head.

"Come unto these yellow sands, and then take hands: Curtsied when you have, and kiss'd the wild waves whist, Foot it featly here and there; And, sweet sprites, the burthen bear."

Cade's voice was high and sweeter than black-market sugar. The tunnel grabbed the strange words, and they traveled into the circles of dark, to live down there. To echo, maybe forever.

Lee half turned from the line to look at Cade. Her words still sharp, electric at the edges. "What was that?"

"What," Cade said with her best innocent-girl eyes. "Don't remember it?"

Lee's eyebrows crumpled.

"That's the song the old man taught you on Andana. You couldn't sing it to keep the sun from blinking out."

Cade spun away from the edge of the platform, crossed to Lee.

"So there is something I can carry better than you," Cade muttered. "A tune." She turned to the line. "Does anyone here have a song? Music?"

A woman in a long red robe stepped forward.

"I want to send this to my girls . . ."

"Perfect."

The woman dipped her head low, hair shifting pale under her hood. She hummed through notes that worked over and under each other like woven cloth. When a thread felt rich and full, another would enter and surprise Cade with its color, its fluttering movement, the way it fit so neatly with the others.

Cade picked up a thread and started to sing.

The notes were beautiful. And then the notes themselves weren't enough. Cade scratched the soles of her shoes against the platform, slapped her palms on her thighs, the floor. They came up gritted and pink as raw meat, but the ringing was just what she needed. It filled her head, fizzed in the half-healed space where her tooth had been.

Things would never be the same without Cherry-Red, but Cade could still make music. She could get people to listen. The little crowd stood around her now, in a half-circle, clapping to the beat when they could find it. And further, in the tunnels, other people clanged and rattled, throwing in their voices and their bodies. Wanting to be part of it. The space-sicks. Always her truest fans.

Lee watched the whole thing from her spot on the platform, and one twitch at a time, the smile came back to her face.

The song swelled and broke and swelled again, until it flooded the platform and spread deep into the tunnels and all the way up the long, steep stairs.

The door cracked open.

A thin point of light shone down and landed inches in front of Lee.

"Who's down there?"

The silence was thick, like a blanket, and it fooled Cade into feeling safe. Whoever was up there would close the door. Forget what they thought they heard. Keep moving.

Then the blanket ripped off.

Footsteps slammed down the stairs — so many sets that, even with her first-class hearing, Cade couldn't count them. People on the platform started to babble or moan. Lee brushed them to the edge and set them off down the right-hand tunnel. She grabbed the canvas sacks and Cade's hand in one sweep. Cade jumped into the left-hand tunnel just as the first pair of boots hit the bottom of the stairs.

Lee sped down one branch of the tunnel and then another, catching them up in puddles and slamming into circles of dead-end stone. Their shoes stuttered as they rounded back. Within three turns it was clear. Lee had no idea where she was going.

With Cade's heartbeat running triple-time, the connection to Xan kicked in. She could feel his worry — the worry that she would never reach him. Cade didn't need this. Not now. She didn't need a flood of someone else's feelings. She didn't even need his strength or steadiness.

She just needed a way out.

The thin beam of light nipped at her heels. Feet slammed behind them, close.

Cade hit a long stretch of tunnel with at least ten branches, and her ears picked out something new.

The beat she had been slapping into the floor, stinging into her palms. Now she heard it banged into the walls and splashed out in the water. At first she thought she was mad, a regular spacecadet.

But the beat drew her on, and then she knew.

The spacesicks were telling her the way.

As soon as she tugged on Lee's hand and started running in the right direction, other beats sprang up, other sounds. Someone who didn't know better would follow them. The Highlea force branched into two groups, then four. Their footsteps thinned and threaded in all the wrong directions.

Cade could have looked every one of those spacesicks in the glassy eye and planted kisses on their hungry lips.

She followed the right beat, let the rest fall behind.

Cade and Lee came up from the tunnels into the middle of a sun-streaked, bustling square. There were plenty of people ready and willing to stare at them.

Lee shook off, from her wet-clumped hair to her squelching feet. She ran, and Cade watched as her legs pumped fast, watched as Lee grew small. But just before she took the corner at full speed and disappeared down an alley, she turned. Ran all the way back to a stunned Cade.

"Come on!" she said. "Let's drain."

Cade had been sure that getting them found out, followed, and almost caught meant she was out of the Express. Done. Without a hope of making it to Xan.

Lee grabbed her arm.

"So you got into a bit of trouble," she said. "Got yourself out of it, too. That makes you one of us."

CHAPTER 8

ACTION AT A DISTANCE In violation of the Principle of Locality, two objects separated in space have an unmediated interaction

It looked like being "one of us" meant letting Lee spill the contents of your stories to anyone who would listen.

"And then she busts into it . . . these notes high and wild . . ."

Rennik raised his already dramatic eyebrows, even though he'd heard this part three times.

"And then the door at the top of the stairs *slams!*" Lee ticked a finger in one direction, then the other. "No, wait. I missed a part."

The three of them stood in Rennik's cabin. He hadn't invited them in, at least not until Lee attacked the door with what she insisted was a secret knock. Rennik's room was small but thick with comforts—blankets made of supersoft wool, little prints of planets done in pale colors, actual books on an actual shelf. Cade didn't know the titles, but the presence of pasteboard and paper and spines was enough to explain his

old-fashioned grasp of English. The room was made for someone tall like Rennik, curved like Rennik. The walls and furni-
ture didn't seem to give a big-bang about straight lines. They
were more interesting and organic than that. When Cade's
arm brushed against the wall she felt it pulse in and out, slow
and shallow — like breathing.

"Then we tore into the tunnels," Lee said. She frowned, her
freckles drooping. "No, wait. I missed another part."

"Of course you didn't," Rennik said. "You're just having
some . . . trouble with the chronological construct."

The blankness of his face made it impossible for Cade to
tell if he was helping Lee out or making fun of her — or both.

"We tore into the tunnels!" Lee cried, committing to it this
time.

The retelling was shined-up and overblown — still, it sent
Cade back to those tight spaces, the heart-stop of dead
ends.

Rennik watched Cade. She could feel his worry even though
his face was resistant to the idea of wrinkling. If he wanted
to say something, he should say it. It made her feel tight and
coiled inside, having to guess. Did the story make him worried for the ship? For Lee? For her? His eyes bore down, and
Cade noticed his double pupils for the first time. A thin ring
of darker black that circled around the first — the difference
between night on a well-lit planet and the pits of space, right
there in his eyes.

"You should have seen Cade tear through those tunnels when she heard the song come back," Lee said. "The

spacesicks knew the whole snugging thing! They pounded it out and—"

"We should find you something to play," Rennik said, looking straight at Cade.

Her heartbeat went soft and shushed and hopeful.

"Like . . . an instrument?"

"*Like* an instrument is precisely what I mean," Rennik said. He reached to the desk and scribbled a few notes to himself—in English. Cade was starting to wonder if he'd tossed his own language out with the spacetrash. "I don't have anything . . . traditional onboard. But we'll see what we can do."

Lee crowded in next to Rennik so she could see his notes, and Cade couldn't see much of anything.

"This is for the Express, right?" Lee asked.

Rennik capped his pen with a liquid-firm click. "Of course."

Cade didn't give one good snug what it was for. She would have something to play. To keep the beat on, to set her voice to, maybe even—if she was lucky—to strum. She lit so pure with happiness that she was sure Xan could feel it.

She tried to hide her wattage from Rennik, even if he had been the one to spark it. If he saw the true force of her feeling and responded with calm, she might burst. In a shards-all-over sort of way.

Rennik edged toward the door. "If you ladies will excuse me, I need to be sure that Renna's on course."

That reminded Cade of something she wanted to ask. She figured she had enough good standing to trade it against one stupid question.

"If you're here with us," she said, "who's flying the ship?"

He put a hand to the wall and laughed. "Renna flies herself for the most part. She would hate to think I took all the credit for her abilities just because I'm the one with the face. Faces are ridiculous, according to Renna. They make you think you know a person when all you know is a few twitching inches of skin." He patted the wall and Cade could feel the room . . . sigh. "I do set the courses. I check bearings, make suggestions."

The wall shuddered a warning.

"Gentle suggestions."

"So if you're not a pilot, what are you?" Cade asked.

"An outlaw," Rennik said. "It's a full-time occupation."

"We should know." Lee cocked a leg up on Rennik's desk chair. She looked half fierce, half adorable.

"I carry goods," Rennik said, "and most of those are legitimate."

"And he carries us, and we're not."

"Yes, my passengers would be the bottom-feeders of the universe, if it had a bottom."

Lee gasped, but her smile was there, firm beneath the outrage. Cade got the feeling that she wasn't bothered by his comment at all.

Cade thought of the two things she'd done with her life —headlining at Club V, and now this. She'd gotten into both because she needed to, and because she was the one who could. There had never been much choice involved.

"How did you get into outlawing?" she asked.

Rennik flashed a look at Lee, and they both went tighter than overtuned strings.

"Long story," Lee said.

"Yes." Rennik leaned over Lee and pretended to whisper. "Even longer than the one you just told me four times."

She pummeled him on his shoulders and arms as he left. As soon as he passed through the door, she shut it.

"So," Lee said, flopping down on top of the soft-blanketed bed. "Boys or girls or both?"

"What?"

Cade's head rang with the question like she was getting reverb.

"This is basic, Cade. You don't need to look at me like I'm ten shades of green. Boys . . . or girls . . . or both?"

Cade sat down at Rennik's desk, in the welcoming palm of the chair.

"Is this because of the kiss-attack on Highlea?"

"No," Lee said, playing a pouncy game with a loose string on one of the blankets. "I'm just curious."

Cade thought through the scene that had just unfolded in front of her. "Is it because of Rennik?"

"Now I hate you," Lee said, "and I'm still curious."

Cade didn't have an answer shined up and ready to go, so she stalled.

"What about you?"

"Both," Lee said with a big, cosmic sigh. "Not that it matters when you work the Express. I can't keep someone waiting for me in every spaceport. Well . . ." She scrunched up her freckles. "I *could*, but I won't. Too much mess, too many appointments to keep. Your turn."

Cade's knowledge of coupling was wobbly at best. She had seen men and women together in different combinations on the streets of Voidvil. She paid less attention to their man-or-woman-liness than to how unhappy they looked — faces puckered and pure-sour when they turned to each other, wide and searching for something better when they turned away. The fans that came on to her at the club were men and women, with an emphasis on men. Most of them were spacesicks, and all of them were fevered-up with wanting her. It had never occurred to Cade to want them back.

Now she wondered if that could change. She was noticing things about people that she'd never noticed before. The sweep of faces, the intricacies of hands. She still didn't want anyone to touch her — and at the same time she did want them to.

Then there was Xan. Cade's feelings for him were strong. Visceral. They touched every part of her and sped through her bloodstream. But he wasn't just a *boy*. It was more basic than that, and more complicated at the same time.

"I haven't had time to think about it, I guess."

Lee had been patient, waiting for Cade's answer, but now she jumped on it and, with a sweet laugh, tore it apart. "You were living in a desert, alone, for five years and you didn't have time to *think* about it?"

"Look," Cade said. All of a sudden the tough girl was back, singing her old standards. "You're abandoned on an ashtray planet as a little girl, you don't see a lot of people. It doesn't come up."

"Didn't you have friends?" Lee looked at Cade with wide and wary eyes, like Cade had changed from a human into a strike-anywhere match.

"No," Cade muttered. "You can be the first. If you're interested in the position."

"What about your family?" Lee asked.

"What about yours?" Cade tossed the questions back to deflect — but she was surprised to find how interested she was in Lee's answers.

Lee put all of her focus into ripping the stray string out of Rennik's blanket. She didn't look like she wanted to say much, but she never dodged a direct question. Cade wondered what it was like, to live that open and honest — not just with one person who'd been planted inside of her head, but with everyone.

The string popped away from the blanket. Lee picked her words with care. "My family is . . . not on the Express anymore."

"Planetbound?" Cade asked.

"Most of them."

"Because of spacesick?"

Lee twisted the string around and around her fingertip. It darkened to a violent purple.

"Most of them."

"I'm a tubie." Cade had never said the word out loud. It sounded strange in her ears. Hollow.

"A tubie with a brother," Lee said, perking up a little bit. "First-class outrageous."

Cade had forgotten that Xan was supposed to be her brother. It had seemed like a harmless lie at the time. But now —when she thought about him—she wasn't so comfortable with it. Her cheeks splashed warm.

"Yeah, well, Xan and I are special."

Lee stood up and closed in, on her toes, like she might tip forward and crash-hug Cade. Lee was sweetness and storm tossed together in equal parts, but whenever the conversation took a turn toward family, her eyes doubled in wideness, and she became—almost—somber. "So this brother who's about to be killed," she said, "he's the one person you have in your life?"

"Well . . . we've . . . never actually . . . met."

Lee laughed and pressed a hand to her forehead.

"Cade, I have seen a lot of strange things in this universe," she said. "But you rank higher every time you open your mouth."

Lee didn't even know the half of it.

Cade thought about telling Lee more than once in the next few days—when they woke up in the same secret bedroom or sat together at lunch after Rennik drained out and Gori sat, not-eating, and stared at Cade for an hour. But no matter how many opportunities she had, she couldn't get herself to say it.

I'm entangled.

My particles are connected on a subatomic level to the particles of someone I haven't seen since I was two, and I need to save him from double-shadowed creatures, so we can change the fate of the human race.

Or something.

Telling Lee before their feet left soil had been her best chance. Her only chance. And she'd missed it. She could see now that it was too late — off-planet, the situation had one possible ending. Lee would stutter some nervous thing, and decide that Cade had gone spacesick.

So she had to keep Xan a secret. It was hard enough when he was busting into her head, sending thoughts and feelings. But now he'd gone radio-silent.

Cade sent messages the same as before — snippets of emotion, flashes of scenes she thought he might like. Once or twice she reached hard and tried to drop him into the moment. But for the first time since the Noise had cleared, Xan wasn't there to answer her call.

What could be so strong, so distracting, so terrible that it could keep him from her?

It made her wild to connect. If Cade's thoughts about Xan had been a rhythm, now the beats blurred into a hum. She couldn't sleep, or muscle down more than three bites of egg-dish in the morning as Lee picked the rest off her plate. All she did was stare at the walls and think of ways to get to him.

And then, on the afternoon of the third day, Cade

remembered. The fight-or-flight connection. The automatic snap that brought them together.

It was time to send Xan a message he couldn't ignore.

Cade couldn't use the bedroom in case Lee came in. The main cabin was too central and the mess was crowded with tables and cookware, and people ate at all hours. Rennik split his time between his cabin and the control room, and sometimes Lee was up there, too, looking out the star glass and chatting to Renna.

No one seemed to use the common area.

Cade slipped in and closed the door behind her. It was a spare and clean space, ringed with cushions and dotted with a few game boards and books that could translate themselves into fourteen languages at the touch of a button.

Cade pulled a cushion to the middle of the room and sat facing the door. She would find Xan. Make sure he was safe. But first she would have to stop the endless Möbius-stripping of her own thoughts.

What did the Unmakers want with them?

She and Xan, and the rest of that batch of babies from First-bloom, could survive better in space than the rest of their kind. But that didn't help anyone else, as far as Cade could see. Was she supposed to be a blueprint for a new generation? The scientists on Firstbloom were dead, and it's not like there were hordes of other humans scientists to pick up where they left off — if it was even right to go on with their blatant baby-altering.

Cade shook her head and rattled out the questions. There

were no answers to be had at that moment, sitting on a cushion in the common room. And there was something she could do.

Check on Xan.

Get to Xan.

Xan.

His name clinked over and over and over.

Cade reached out into the silent space in her head and then past it, to the edges. But she didn't feel him there.

She stood up and ran as many laps around the small room as she could before she felt like a total spacecadet. Her heart rocketed against her skin. She sat down, panting, and the transmission kicked in.

Xan was with her. Nervous, eager. She could feel the strain of him — a chord aching to resolve.

She beamed.

You're here. You're here.

But it wasn't enough. Cade wanted to be sure he was safe, at least for the moment. And while she was at it, she could search for some clues about why the Unmakers hated them so much. To do that, she needed to see what Xan was seeing. She needed him to feel something strong enough that his own transmissions would kick in, too. She had to flip this channel, or make it run both ways.

She looked around the small room, desperate to show Xan something that would put him in an excited state. But cushions and boardgames and books in languages he didn't know weren't going to do it.

Cade dug through her pockets and found three things. The circle-glass. The seven-blade knife. The tip of mirror.

Xan knew that he was entangled, so the shock of the circle-glass was out. That left her with two options, and two ideas, both of which sparked into her head at the same time. It came down to a guess — which one would have more of an effect on his heartbeat.

Blood or skin.

Xan had seen horrible things on Firstbloom. The Unmakers had murdered everyone he knew, unless you counted Cade. His system might run fast and wild at the sight of blood — or he might be almost immune to it. But as a human in a coma for most of his life, and then kidnapped, Xan had missed all of his chances to see skin.

Besides, it seemed like the much nicer shock.

Cade pulled out the tip of mirror and angled it down. Her tan shirt had a high neckline but the buttons slipped their holds without a fuss. Cade couldn't ignore the amped-up crashing of her own blood as she undid the first three — then popped one more for good measure.

She could see the faint underline of her breast where it stretched into the cotton curve of the shirt. Finding a connection to Xan was what mattered. Keeping him safe. But all she could focus on was that line of skin, and the dangerous edge of her feelings. She reached in and brushed a thumb against the dark circle. The touch echoed, first in her fingertips, then farther, chiming through her body.

That seemed to do it.

Cade dropped into the picture of Xan's room.

Something was wrong. She could feel it even before she saw the two Unmakers posted in the corners.

Xan sat on the bed. Not tied or lashed, but he couldn't leave that place. Stuck as fast as a stone in deep sand.

"She's here now," Xan said.

The Unmakers leaned over him, their robes so black they blotted out the rest of the room. Their faces — if they had them — hid in dark folds. Cade focused on the too-small hands that crept out from the dark swirl of sleeves.

Here came voices for the first time. Deeper than wells, deeper than steam pits, the deepest sounds Cade knew.

"Did you tell the girl to come?"

"No," Xan said. His own voice was lower than Cade had expected, and scratchy. But it was nothing compared to the bottomless slide of the Unmakers.

"She's getting smarter," said one, his breath tinged with the smell of metal.

"Too smart," said the other.

"This is how it begins."

Cade sent all of her fighting strength to Xan. But Xan fought back — against her. He pushed down all of her impulses to kick, scratch, and run until the universe ran out. She pushed, and he pushed back, just as strong.

He sent her waves of calm and control. Everything about him said, *Let it go.*

Cade trusted Xan — and she had never trusted anyone. The feeling was new and uncomfortable, like the hand-me-downs she'd worn at the Parentless Center. Itchy and three sizes too big. But there was relief in trusting, too — knowing that when Xan made a choice she could stand by it. Even now she could see that he'd let her calls go unanswered because the Unmakers kept a tight watch.

So Cade let it go. If it was too dangerous to fight, she wouldn't force it. But she wanted the Unmakers to know that they wouldn't have him. That even if he was sitting on a bed in front of them, he belonged with her, half a universe away.

She sent the raw thought to him, hoping he would be able to translate it back into words.

They won't have you. Tell them. I'm coming for you.

Xan put up a struggle against this, too. But Cade insisted.

Tell them.

The Unmakers bent so close now that Cade could feel the warmth of them, the weight of them, and smell their metal breath.

All she could do was send her calm, her strength, her steadiness to Xan.

And he wasn't afraid.

"She wants me to tell you . . ."

Tell them.

"That she'll be here soon. For me."

The Unmakers must have thought he was making it up. A sad little burst of self-defense. They started to laugh and it was like the ground opening up beneath Cade's feet. It was like falling.

"Cade!"

Her name rang out—but it wasn't Xan speaking it, or one of the Unmakers. The voice was flat and warm and familiar.

"Cade!"

Sound ripped into the picture. Blacked it out. And then the world faded to white.

Cade was in the common room, Rennik bounding at her. A strange white object clanked in his hands and a smile claimed most of his face. He stopped short when he saw the wide-open state of Cade's shirt.

She jumped to her feet and spun, so she could button up in something like privacy. Rennik turned and faced the door. They talked in opposite directions, to each other.

"Are you all right?" he asked in the politest tone she'd ever heard. "Your eyes were . . . very far away."

"I'm fine," Cade said, doing her best to keep the snarl out of her voice. It wasn't Rennik's fault she had been sitting half-dressed in the middle of the common room.

"I need a minute."

She stabbed the buttons through thin slits on her shirt. She had to get rid of Rennik and get back to Xan.

"Just . . . getting myself together. I was—"

"What you do with your free time is none of my concern."

She got to the bottom of the shirt only to find that she had one slit left, and no more buttons. All the tugging in the universe wouldn't make the ends line up right—which meant an open flap at the top. But after what had just happened, Cade didn't care if Rennik saw one clumsy stripe of skin.

She turned around, defiant. "What is it, exactly, that you wanted in here?"

"It's just . . ." Rennik still faced the door. Cade wanted him to turn and look at her. She wanted him to leave. "I brought you something."

He spun, and pressed one arm into the space between them.

Rennik was holding a guitar.

"Where did you . . . ?"

Cade's hurry slid off, and she wanted to be in the common room, with that perfect white guitar, for as long as she could.

"It's something I would love to take credit for," Rennik said. "But I can't. Renna wanted you to have it."

Cade could see now that it was made of the same stuff as the walls. A thick, dependable sort of white clayish material. The strings stretched thin and soft, like strands of hair. It was acoustic, which meant Cade couldn't play it in her trademark ear-destroying fashion. But it didn't need a current, which meant she could play it anywhere. From one end of the universe to the other.

"She made this? For me?"

Cade's hands couldn't wait for the answer. She reached for the half-circle of the guitar's neck, caught the body in her other hand. It had a bit of shine and was cool to the touch. Rennik let go with a linger, making sure the instrument didn't fall. But he had nothing to worry about. Cade pulled it to her like a needed breath.

"There aren't any other musicians onboard," Rennik said. "Unless you count Renna. She makes something like music, if you know how to listen. Lee is tone-deaf, and I don't think we'll see Gori bursting out in song anytime soon."

"What about you?" Cade spared his four-knuckled fingers a glance. They thinned to long fingertips, and there was an ease to them, a sureness that made Cade trust they would land in the right places. There was serious potential in those hands.

"So?" she asked.

"I'm afraid not," Rennik said.

But he was smiling. He started out of the room and stopped in the door, turning around with one hand on the frame. He looked up at the ceiling, at the walls, at the whole first-class ship.

"In case you were still wondering . . . this means she likes you."

He closed the door on his way out, leaving Cade with the guitar. She picked it up, touched its thin fretboard and deeply curved side. She rushed her fingers over the strings, made a breathless run through her scales. They sounded like spun silver. All she wanted was to spend hours sinking into this instrument, until her fingers blistered and her mind melted down to music.

But she set the guitar on the softest cushion she could find, and hid it so it wouldn't tempt her, at least not until she was done.

Cade had an entangled boy to get back to.

She closed her eyes to look for Xan again. She didn't get far before something stopped her.

A snap.

The stare of two dark, lashless eyes.

Gori had her own seven-blade knife at her throat.

CHAPTER 9

NON-OBVIOUS CAUSALITY A complicated interplay of factors resulting in a given outcome

Cade was impressed. He picked the right blade and everything.

"Gori . . ."

The tip of the squat, triangular blade nicked the soft patch between her collarbones.

"Look, Gori, whatever you think I did . . ."

His face loomed close, eyes filmy, with crumbs at the corners — like he'd been sitting in a strong wind with his eyelids pinned open.

"The reaching has become *too much*," he whispered. The fingers of his knifeless hand worked the air. "To have you *grasping* at me all the time, it is not to be allowed."

Cade put her palms up to show him that she wasn't reaching for anything.

"Probing, prying, filth-minded human," he said, twisting the blade a bit closer.

Cade didn't jump. Didn't cry sour. She stayed calm.

Maybe it was knowing that Xan would come and help her. Maybe it was enough that Cade knew Gori had her all wrong. She looked down at his short, stout frame, at the robes that clung to the patterns of his shriveled skin.

"I don't want to touch you," she said, with complete honesty and a touch of brass. "I'll keep to myself."

Gori skittered the point of the knife up to her chin.

"This is not a game," he said. "Rules are rules. There is no going back if you break them."

Cade swallowed against the press of the knife-tip.

"Consider them intact."

Gori blinked his dark double spheres. Tossed the knife across the room. "Do this again," he said, "and I will not pretend there is a difference between air and skin. I will let the blade prove it."

As soon as Cade had herself pulled together — knife snapped firm and lodged in her pocket, buttons triple-checked — she pounded up the chute to the control room.

It was one thing to keep a firm head through an attack. It was another to let it blow past and pretend it had never happened. As much as Cade wanted to reach out to Xan again and find out more about the Unmakers, she knew it was best to devote some time to the people on her own ship who might want to kill her.

Mr. Niven had told Cade that she had enemies. Plural.

Maybe the Unmakers weren't alone in hating the entangled. Cade wondered if any of the other babies from that lab on Firstbloom had grown up with the same range of nonhuman troubles, or if she and Xan were special.

In the control room, she found Rennik bent in his usual position, twisting dials. He looked deep into the starglass, studied what he saw there, and made adjustments to a few knobs.

"Rennik," she said, slipping in at his side.

A new tension lit up around him like a forcefield. Cade didn't have time for fallout from the button incident.

"Rennik, I need to know about Gori."

"Gori?" The forcefield weakened, but Rennik kept his eyes trained on the panels. "He's the first Darkrider I've had on-board. I'm still figuring him out myself."

"I don't know a lot about Darkriders." Cade had thought to ask Xan, but he wasn't likely to have picked up much about them in his coma. Sometimes it was hard for Cade to remember that Xan wasn't the best and only person to talk to about everything. But Rennik — a well-traveled Hatchum — seemed like the clear source of information on nonhuman species.

"All I know is that Darkriders don't have a planet," Cade said. "And that they can see dark energy."

"Not . . . see it, exactly," Rennik said, twisting a knob, twisting it back.

"What, then?"

He stepped to the starglass, and waited for Cade to follow.

The darkness circled around them. Rennik looked out past the planets of the system they were traveling through, to the thick white spatter of stars.

"The Darkriders did have a planet once. A fine planet. Home to millions of Gori's kind."

Cade looked into the distance and tried to follow the trail of Rennik's eyes, but her center swam off. There was no up in space, no down. She set her fingertips on Rennik's arm just long enough to get her bearings.

"Gori's planet was pulled apart," Rennik said.

"By . . . ?"

"Dark energy."

Cade focused on the deeps of the starglass, overwhelmed. Not by the vast, sparkling spread of what she could see, but by what she couldn't. Dark matter, dark energy — no matter how much she could point out and name in the starglass, there was so much more to the universe. The powers that held it together and spread it apart.

"I thought dark energy was just another force," Cade said. "Benign."

Rennik nodded. "For the most part. It pushes the universe, speeds its expansion. It doesn't get mixed up with matter. Just shifts the worlds and the suns and space, farther and farther into . . . well, we're not sure what.

"I have a dial to measure it," he said. "There."

He pointed to the far end of a panel. Most of the dials were clear glass and eye-smarting copper. This one was covered in smoked glass, backed in dull black and topped with a shiny black needle. It measured the slow-but-sure rate of the universe's expansion.

"In the case of Gori's planet," Rennik said, "something went wrong. A few believe it was a gathering of dark energy, a whirlpool, a sort of natural disaster. Others think a Darkrider made it happen — by accident or design. Those who survived had the gift of sensing dark energy. They knew what was coming, even when no one believed them. They could move their families to the safety of space before it hit."

This story was about the Darkriders, and some planet Cade had never heard of, but she couldn't help thinking about Earth. Her blue-green mother planet, swirled with clouds and capped in ice. It was hers no matter where she lived. Hers no matter how long-dead.

Cade bullied herself back to thoughts of Gori.

"So the Darkriders don't see dark energy, they sense it," she said. "How?"

Rennik looked up from his star-trance. "Where did all of this sudden curiosity come from, Cade?"

She ran her fingers over the black dial. "Can't a girl ask about the wonders of the universe?"

"It's not a particularly human trait." Here came the flatness again, the simple factual pitch in Rennik's voice that drove Cade a special kind of insane.

"I thought you were pro-human," she said.

Rennik turned his thoughtful eyes on Cade. "I like the individuals I like, regardless of whether they happen to be human."

Cade's voice had the metal edge of a snapped string. "How . . . *advanced* of you."

But she couldn't fluster Rennik. His double pupils didn't flash wide, his smooth skin didn't crease.

She almost told him about Gori and the show he'd put on with her seven-blade knife. That would have gotten some kind of reaction. But it also would have complicated things. As calm as Rennik looked now, she had no way of knowing what he would do with a murderous passenger. She needed information, not more issues.

"So," she prompted. "This sensing that Darkriders do . . ."

"From what I can tell, it's a kind of meditation."

"You mean that rapture state Gori goes into? When he puffs up and gets all gaseous?" Cade remembered the mass of gray skin, the unblinking black eyes. The breathing in, and in, and in some more.

"What's moving through him isn't matter," Rennik said. "We sense him to be larger because our minds can't process what's actually happening."

"Don't make me ask—"

"He's letting dark energy move through him."

Cade nodded. The more she nodded, the more sense it made. The more sense it made, the less she liked it.

"To do that," she said, "does Gori have to open his mind?"

Rennik shrugged. "I would think so."

Cade's breath left in a rush.

"What is it?" Rennik asked.

She pressed her head into her hands. "Gori was right."

Cade *had* been reaching out—but not with her fingers. While she was trying to connect to Xan, she must have bumped against the boundaries of Gori's thoughts and almost breached them.

If she had done that, he would have killed her.

Cade could almost understand—she felt a spot of rage, dark-purple and painful, like Lee's string-throttled finger, when she thought about someone intruding in her head. She had no interest in getting into Gori's.

But what if she couldn't control it?

Cade couldn't go the rest of the way to Hades without transmitting to Xan. But she didn't know if it was safe to tell Gori she was entangled. She didn't know if it was safe to tell anyone. Cade gulped in breath, but none of it reached her brain. She looked down at the dials and the needles danced, unreadable.

"How soon do we get to Hades?" she asked.

"Cade, tell me what's wrong . . ."

She ran back to the starglass. The stars rushed up to meet her, blurring into ragged white strings. They settled back into prettiness, and she looked for Hades again. She still hadn't found it, but it was out there somewhere. A place of negation. A collection of snipped-out bits of space, darker than dark.

What she found was gray and close, and moving toward them. Fast.

"Is that a ship?" she asked.

Rennik stepped in to see what she was seeing. A passenger ship in the shape of a closed palm.

"Cade," he said, "it would be best if you went and found Lee."

Lights blinked yellow and outlined the ship as it flew.

Rennik turned to Cade and put his hands on her shoulders. All his ease slipped off. "Find Lee and get into the human's cabin. Now." He moved down the control panels. "Don't come out until I tell you it's safe."

Cade started to run, was halfway out the door when he said it.

"We're being boarded."

The little room where Cade and Lee slept was bright — too bright.

"What if someone sees the cracks of light around the edges of the panel?"

Lee paced around the square in perfect, crisp lines.

"Good point."

She patted the wall and Renna did her part, sliding the room into a dusky state. "Rennik gets so worried about these boardings," Lee said. "Every time. The exact same amount of too-worried."

But Cade noticed that Lee's hands were shaking.

"Come on." Lee picked up handfuls of clothes from a pile on the floor. The Saea outfit. Cade's old Andanan skirts. Her own spare set of pants and plain shirt. She pressed them into Cade's arms. "Here. Help."

They reached in and plugged the tunnel, so that if someone did open the panel it would look like a storage unit. When that was done, they sat in what seemed a lot like silence, even though Lee stuffed it full of babble.

"We go to Menno next, and that's a nice planet, a fine place. Then Czisk, which has these jungles you won't believe, the colors of it. Purple trees! And then we coast straight past Leiden, no humans there, and we hit the Grestle belt . . ."

Cade pulled her knees to her chest. She made herself as small as possible, but she couldn't keep her fingers from wandering. They reached out to the bunk and stroked the side of her new guitar, which she'd had just enough time to nab from the common room. It sat there, tuned and patient, waiting to be played.

"What's that?" Lee whispered, noticing it for the first time.

Cade held the guitar out — the faint light of it claiming the darkness like a stretch of night sky. It hung between them, and in that one suspended second, it earned a name.

"Moon-White," Cade said. "Renna made it for me."

"Ohh." Lee's eyes took in the instrument with such tender care that Cade decided it would be safe to let her hold it. "Brass." Lee's finger caught on a string and the sound spun out and filled the room. Cade clapped a hand over the thin metal. The note buzzed into her skin.

"Renna is a wonder," Lee whispered.

"Sure is."

Lee held the guitar out to Cade as some kind of proof. "Nothing bad will happen."

Cade cradled Moon-White and dreamed of the songs she would tease out of the strings as soon as the boarding was over. With nothing else to do, Lee's voice limped back to chatting. "So after the Grestle belt, we . . ."

"Shhh."

Cade's ears picked it up first—of course.

Steps coming up the chute.

"And this is our resident Darkrider, Gori," Rennik said, his voice laced with fake-smile. The clothes in the tunnel and the panel muffled things, but Cade could hear well enough.

"And up at the top is the control room," Rennik said.

"We have no interest in the control room," said a new voice —but not entirely new. A known voice. Smooth and deep and as unexpected as the ground opening up.

From the shuffling sounds of their steps, Cade put the Unmakers at four. She could only hear them, but her other senses rose up and filled in with memories. She felt the touch of metallic breath on her face. Saw double-shadows and space-black robes. Smelled smoke.

"Right, then," Rennik said, the strain pressing through his friendly tone. "I can show you the common room, or my cabin—"

"We came for one thing."

"The girl."

Cade's body was a chant.

Heart, muscle, blood.

No, no, no.

But then she looked over at Lee and saw that her long, pinched-tight body was chanting the exact same thing.

Heart, muscle, blood.

Lee thought the Unmakers had come for *her.*

"Have you seen those . . . things before?" Cade asked. No sound, just the careful shaping of lips.

Lee turned her dark-moon eyes on Cade, shining at her in the gloom. "Have *you?*"

"There are no humans on this ship," Rennik said. Announced, really. Cade got the feeling he wanted them to hear from their hiding spot. "There are barely any passengers. My Renna is cargo class, cleared for twenty-two systems and deep space."

"We know the clearances of this ship."

"Yet . . ."

Cade waited for them to say that they'd tracked her — that they knew her thoughts, could hear her heartbeat, sniff out her blood.

"We traced the girl here."

Traced?

"I'm afraid I don't know what you're talking about," Rennik said. Flat. Unhelpful. Hatchum, through and through. For the first time, Cade understood just how useful that maddening calm could be.

"We were sold a tracer code on Andana."

"Andana?" Rennik said, as if he'd just heard of the place. "Yes, I did go to port there last week. But all I picked up were some sand-crusted engine components."

Feet shuffled up and down the chute, paired with a few low murmurs. "The tracer code tells us a different story."

"Those are notoriously easy to tamper with," Rennik said.

"I used them on a shipment of crab fruit once and ended up with ten crates of sawdust. Whoever sold this to you must be a practiced liar."

Cade fitted a hand to one of her faded bruises. They had gone past mottled black, past purple, to the last phase — tooth-rot yellow.

"A tracer?" Lee mouthed. "What are they talking about? I don't have any tracer on me . . ."

"Go back and take it up with your Andanan," Rennik said.

"He is no longer with us."

So the Unmakers had snuffed out Mr. Smithjoneswhite. At first, Cade couldn't tell if she was shaken or thrilled. All she could think of was the slurp of his voice, reminding her that she belonged to him, in name and deed, for the rest of time.

The mourning period was over before it started.

Lee chanced a whisper. "What's happening?"

Cade turned and took in Lee's violent folding and clench-ing. Her fight to keep perfectly still. How fully she was losing it.

The time Cade had spent with her was the closest she'd ever gotten to a real friendship. And now Lee was certain the Unmakers had come for her. Cade couldn't look her in the face and lie about it.

"They want me."

The shine blinked out of Lee's eyes.

"You have a tracer on you," she whispered. "And you knew it. You brought it onto this ship. You brought . . . *them*."

Cade's thoughts shot back to the spaceport on Andana, the last-minute standoff with Mr. Smithjoneswhite. Once she'd shaken free of his slithering hands and cracked that atmosphere she thought she'd never hear about the tracer again. "Look, Lee . . ."

"Shut it."

Her hands flew over Cade's clothes, ripping, searching.

"What are you—"

"You don't grow up on the Express without learning how to take off a tracer. You should have told me straight off. Now shut. your. sour. face."

Cade held her arms out and let herself be searched. Heat flooded her neck, her arms and legs, to the tips of her fingers and toes. Lee's hands slid up the right side of her shirt and stopped at the nipped-in bend of her waist. "It's right here."

"How can you tell?"

Lee looked at her with a sharpness that could have sliced through metal. "The texture of the skin is different. Rough, raised." She held a palm out to Cade. "Knife." Cade pulled it out of her pocket and Lee had it out of her fingers in the same heartbeat.

"This tracer is imprinted in the skin, not underneath. Like a tattoo, but one you can't see under plain light." She clicked through the blades and settled on the long, precise, needlelike one.

"Clamp down on something."

Cade held the edge of the bunk. Her bottom teeth dragged against the top ones as Lee tore into her flesh. She carved out a small, square piece.

With the tracer pinched between two fingers, Lee climbed

to the top left bunk and worked at one of the ceiling panels. She dumped the panel on the bed and hoisted herself, elbows first, into the gap. Cade waited. Lee's head popped back into the room, hair knots first.

"Oh. Please. Make me do all the work."

Cade followed in a kind of trance, perforated by the *stab, stab, stab* of the skinless patch on her side.

Lee reached past her and shifted the ceiling panel back into place. She led Cade down a twist of tunnels, plummeting through the depths of the ship, and opened another panel, this one in the wall of the cargo room.

The Unmakers were one door-slide from seeing them.

"It's a good thing Rennik didn't let me come on that little tour," Lee whispered. "I know the inventory *so well* now."

She crept in and crossed straight to a pile of crates, blew off a thin dusting of sand, and pried the lid off the top one.

"There," she said, dropping in the thin flutter of skin with all the engine parts.

Cade waited in the walls to see what came next.

Lee and Cade pressed together for at least an hour as the Unmakers looked for the tracer and Rennik crashed back and forth between pretending to help and icing them out.

"If that had been a strong tracer code, they would have found us in under a minute," Lee whispered. "Must be old, or used."

Cade sent up a halfhearted thank you to Mr. Smithjoneswhite, for being such a cheap bastard.

The door to the cargo hold flew open and Cade heard the sounds of the little tracer-hunting party. Somewhere deep in her mind, she noticed Xan for the first time that night—even though her body had been humming the End of Times song for two hours straight. Maybe her fear was starting to lose its edge. Or maybe she was just getting used to Xan's company.

"We've been in here before," an Unmaker said.

It was the first time Cade heard a twitch of emotion in one of their voices. Frustration, pure and obvious.

"Yes, but the tracer code . . ." said another.

"Is useless," Rennik said. "Like I told you."

Cade had heard fear claim his throat as she ran out of the control room, but now it sounded like he had a solid grip on his patience. She wondered how often Rennik's composed surface was just that—a surface, with something else beating underneath.

There was a crack of crates being tipped over and the assorted clangs and slumps of cargo hitting the floor.

"Here," Rennik said. "Is this what you're looking for?"

Cade didn't need to see it to know he was holding up the patch of skin with the tracer code. The right side of her waist ached an echo.

"Looks like this girl of yours dropped it at the spaceport," Rennik said. "I watch the crates, of course, but not closely enough to notice . . . this."

And then, without warning, the Unmakers let loose the sound—the beyond-death cry. It went on and on, as Cade's blood hammered out a response. If Xan had been missing for most of the boarding, he was definitely with her now, listening. But there was nothing for him to say, no form of soothing he could send, that would cancel out that sound. Lee pressed so close into Cade's cut side that it flared up with pain, then went numb.

The wail didn't seem to have one shred of an effect on Rennik. "Yes, well, if you're all done here . . ."

Cade could almost see him studying the white-slivered moons of his fingernails. She let a tiny smile slip.

"It would be a simple thing to destroy this ship," one of the Unmakers said.

The smile died. Cade and Lee both put hands out to touch Renna. The walls clenched tight.

"One button," an Unmaker said. "The work of a few moments."

Rennik pushed on, flat-voiced and unimpressed, but Cade heard his breath rise to a new pitch. "If you meant to do that, you would have done it by now. You're afraid the Hatchum will come after you. You're not wrong to be."

The Hatchum were known as relentless fighters, and loyal to the point of triumph, idiocy, or death—whichever came first. Cade wondered if even the Unmakers feared them.

Voices spiraled down until they were more feeling than noise.

"You mistake us."

"We would die here, and know happiness."

"But then there is the girl."

The Unmakers left, their words still troubling the ground.

CHAPTER 10

QUANTUM REALM The nano-scale used to measure quantum effect—which can operate at a macro level

Lee waited another hour before she would open the panel in the wall. She finally emerged, shining and refreckled, into the light of the cargo hold.

"You were . . . amazing," Cade said. "Impossible. You saved my life."

Lee tossed out words—dark as thunderclouds, with twice the rumble. "I saved *all of our lives.*"

It stopped Cade short.

"Yeah," she said softly. "You did it fast and first-class."

She followed Lee up the chute to the control room, wanting to thank her at least eight times a minute. But Lee was silent in a way that warned Cade to be silent, too.

Rennik stood at the panels, not even pretending to steer. He was in almost the same place he'd been when Cade left him. The same dials. His hands clutched to the same knuckle-gleaming white. Cade felt like she could step backwards and land in that moment—nudge time back a bit more, and feel Rennik's hand on her shoulders, where before she'd felt only hollowness, and a hard outline of fear.

"Rennik." Lee crossed to him, pushing time forward. "I need the hailing codes."

Cade hadn't been able to hear the full drain of the act Rennik had put on for the Unmakers, but she could see it now. The skin beneath the double hooks of his cheekbones drawn tight. The corners of his eyes perked to hold the lids up.

"Now?" he asked.

"No," Lee said. "In a thousand light-years."

It should have been a joke, but it was too sharp around the edges. Lee's words stabbed the air. Rennik took them—like he always took the brunt of Lee—and absorbed it without a wince.

He pulled out a thick binder of charts, maps, and time-tables. Started to page through. "Human codes?"

"Yeah," Lee said. "Start hailing anything that bleeds red."

"Are you sure this needs to be done—"

"*Now,* yeah." Lee drummed her fingers on the wall. On Renna.

Cade knew that she should let it go. Lee had saved her from a dark, double-shadowed fate. She'd earned some strange behavior. But this was strange behavior that might steer Cade away from Xan.

"What's the new, can't-wait business?"

Lee pressed her hands against the control panels—splayed them hard into branching lines of bone.

"This isn't about the Express. And you know it."

Lee waited until Rennik turned away, then swiveled and stuck to Cade's side with magnetic force.

"I trusted you," she whispered. At that moment, from that distance, she looked old. Every hatch in her skin, every too-pale inch a bit of proof, and it all added up. Lee was a human girl who'd grown up where no human should.

Her voice changed into something loud, airy, all for show.

"It's Cade. I'd cancel the run for her if I could, but it's too important. So we'll find her a new ride. She needs to get planetbound."

Planetbound?

Cade's nerves crackled and her muscles tightened one full key-turn, like they did when a punch was about to make contact with her gut. "Lee?"

"Don't look at me like that," Lee said. "I'm doing this for your own good." She clapped on her most solemn, honest face, and lied. "We need to get Cade off this ship."

Rennik opened his mouth, but before he could ask — "Yes, *now*," Lee said. "She's spacesick."

Cade dragged Lee out of the control room. Rennik stared, but didn't stop her. Even Lee didn't stop her. She let herself be marched down the chute and shoved into the hidden room. Cade faced her in the thin bar of space between the beds.

"What in the blinked-out stars are you doing?"

Lee answered with a shoulder to the stomach. She drove Cade up, onto her toes and off balance. Cade saw flashes of

white room, flashes of blue shirt, until things came back together around the swing of Lee's fist.

Cade rushed at Lee, forced her to the floor.

"It had to be *them* after you, didn't it," Lee said.

"The Unmakers?"

Cade's torso slanted over Lee's at an uncomfortable angle,
trapped her. Lee went limp under the makeshift cage.

"They don't have names," she said. "I asked on twenty
planets." Lee's chin pitted, trembled. Light brown hair crossed
her face like fine cracks. "It had to be *them*. Of course it
did."

Her wrist jerked to one side, sudden enough that it smashed
through Cade's grip. And then Lee was at her again. Fingernails, knees, whatever she could point at Cade.

Cade fought back.

But she didn't let herself feel it, not fully. She paced her
breath slow in the hopes of muffling her own heart. If she
wasn't careful, the automatic connection to Xan would snap
on, and she didn't want his help. It wouldn't be fair to meet
Lee with doubled-up strength. Cade's own muscles and her
training, courtesy of Club V, should have been enough to
counter Lee's blows, to block and absorb. But Lee swung and
swung and wouldn't stop. She was a glitching machine.

The ground underneath them went full earthquake, and
lurched Cade out of the action. Lee landed in front of the tunnel on the far side of the room. It took Cade a rattled second
to figure out that the disturbance had been Renna breaking up
the fight.

"Thanks," Cade muttered.

"Whose side are you on, anyway?" Lee asked the room, rubbing at her elbow.

Cade sat there, 2 percent of her mind taking stock of her bruises. The other 98 percent narrowed in on Lee's words.

It had to be them.

Cade had brought the Unmakers. The damage Lee could do was nothing compared to what they would have done. And not just to Cade — to everyone who had ever helped her.

"This was my fault." The words came out weak, like the bridge of a song. Something Cade couldn't get right, no matter how hard she tried. She reached a few stiffened fingers and touched Lee's arm.

"I mean it, Lee. I didn't know . . ."

Lee spun on Cade. "Don't." She shook her arm, and Cade's fingers slid off. She was still new to the business of touching, and she didn't have much practice in saying she was sorry, but she got the strong sense she'd done both of them wrong. She was about to try again, but Lee's death-to-traitors stare sent her reeling back to her old ways.

"Don't expect me to grovel," Cade said. "What I did . . ." The voices of the Unmakers grated, low and metal, against her thoughts. "What I did was a mistake. You knew exactly what it meant when you told that lie."

Lee came in close, but this time she kept her fists to herself, attacking Cade with a rasp-edged whisper.

"You're surprised I would lie to get you off this ship? Really?"

Even Cade knew it was the kind of question you didn't actually answer.

"I think that's funny," Lee whispered. "I think that's a first-class *riot*. You brought the worst fate in the universe down on our heads, which never would have happened if you'd bothered to tell me the truth."

Cade dropped to her heels, swept over with nausea — and it had nothing to do with the fight or the exhaustion or even the fact that the room had broken into waves under her feet. Cade was more scared for Xan than she'd ever been.

"The worst fate in the universe?" she repeated.

"You don't even know what you almost did," Lee said. "To the people *I care about.*" She shook her head, hair fallen from its ties and tracing crooked lines almost to her hips. "What's more, it doesn't matter to you. All that does is that brother of yours."

Cade didn't spit out a response — because she had nothing. Lee had scraped too close to the truth. From the second Lee had said the word *planetbound,* Cade had been determined to change it, right her tipped-over plans to get to Xan. Maybe stop Lee from hating her, as an afterthought.

"Why spacesick?"

Lee went back to a whisper. "It's the best way to get Renna and Rennik to set you down. They like you, you know." Lee added a flick of the eyes that said, *I'm sure I don't know why.* "If I tell them to drop you to save their own necks, they won't do it. But if they think it's the only way to help you . . ."

Lee shrugged. "Besides, could be true for all I know. You spend enough time acting like a spacecadet."

If the scientists were right, entanglement and spacesick were mutually exclusive. But even if Cade was immune, no one on the ship knew it. Lee's claim could still ruin her life.

"I don't have time for this," Cade said. "Tell Rennik to stop with the hailing codes."

"Or you'll do what?" Lee asked. "Stick me with your seven-blade knife?" She pulled it out of her own pocket, left there from butchering Cade's side. Cade felt all of her sore spots like the knife had called their name — from the freshly exploded vessels where Lee had hit her to the terrible strains of her missing tooth.

Lee dropped the knife to the floor. Cade picked it up in one clean swipe.

"I'll tell them that you got it wrong," she said. "Prove that I'm not spacesick. Simple as that."

"There is no proof," Lee said. "There's your word, and there's mine." None of their shipmates would take Cade's over Lee's. She didn't even have to say it. "You did make a good run of it, though. Pretending to be one of us."

It was a solid hook, and it landed. But Cade knew all the signs that Lee still had a fight brewing in her. Twitchy fists. Shallow breath. Flashes of anger across her face like heat lightning. It would feel good to clash with that again — lose herself in the landing of a few blows.

But anything Cade started, Lee could use against her. Say

that she was in deep with spacesick, and had gotten to the hands-all-over stage. That she would lash out and not know what she was touching, who she was hurting.

If Cade wanted more, she would have to snare Lee into starting it.

"I hope all of your friends know how fast you'll drop them, when you get scared," she said. "You're still scared, aren't you?"

Lee flew across the room.

This time Renna didn't bother with the floor.

Water burst from the ceiling. Not unsure fingertip-flecks —this was rain. The drops as fast and knowing as a spring storm.

They slicked Cade off her feet and into a newly formed puddle. The water slid over her sore skin and sent calming messages to her overheated muscles. It doused some of Cade's sureness that everything was going to hell.

Cade tipped her face to the ceiling, opened her mouth.

The water tasted silver-perfect, and it went down with a cold burn, the way Cade imagined it would be to swallow a mouthful of stars. But when she looked over at Lee, she was shining with water, stone-faced. She looked like a girl who'd never learned how to smile.

She looked like a stranger.

CHAPTER 11

HIDDEN VARIABLE THEORIES Created to explain how previous definitions of quantum mechanics were incomplete

Lee left, and Cade wasn't sorry to see her go.

The bedroom dried as Renna circulated a hot wind. Now Cade was back in the desert every time she blinked. She crashed onto her bunk. No use wasting energy — she would need all the drops she had left to fuel a connection to Xan.

Cade called out to him with the insistence of her heart, the battering of her breath, all the clamor she'd held back during her fight with Lee. But the automatic connection wouldn't snap on. It didn't help that Gori's little outburst added to Cade's list of concerns. Now she had to be specific, and careful, when she reached for Xan. It felt like a mental tiptoe, when she wanted to sprint.

Cade reached harder, slammed through her own resistance, tested the limits of her mind against unfeeling time and space. She needed to know if Xan was all right. She needed to know that she would be, too.

He didn't come.

Cade squirmed on the inside when Xan didn't tune in to her transmission. It brought up Unmaker-shaped worries, and now those had been sharpened on the edge of Lee's words.

Cade heard the grind of metal against the dock. It sank into her like teeth. The hailing codes had worked, and fast — Rennik had found someone to pick her up and slam her on a new surface. *Planetbound.*

But as the docking eased into smooth clicks and sighs, Cade recalibrated her thoughts. Maybe this wasn't such a bad thing. Lee could kick her into the starry cold; she could null and void Cade's plan with one perfect lie. But no one could stop her from aiming for Hades.

Maybe it *was* time for a new ride.

Cade grabbed Moon-White and chased the sounds of the incoming ship. She didn't think anyone would show up to send her off — but there they all were, in a ragged line facing the dock. Rennik, Gori, Lee, with her jaw set to one side and her hair pressed back into its knots.

"It's not a party," Cade muttered. She didn't trust Lee. In light of their willingness to toss her off the ship, Cade didn't trust any of them — and she didn't have to. Cade had never needed a band to back her up with wilt-wristed drumming and uninspired bass. She went on solo.

Rennik stepped forward and dropped a hand on Cade's shoulder. Nailed the role of the nervous friend. "I want to meet this girl."

"Yeah," Lee said darkly. "Me too."

"I intend to watch that one leave the ship," Gori said, pointing a shriveled excuse for a finger at Cade. "I have no interest in the girl."

"Girl?" Cade asked. "Who is this girl?"

"I spoke with her briefly through the transmitter," Rennik said. "She's a human pilot, traveling alone on a long-distance mission. Everything sounded in order. This is just a precaution."

Cade deadened her eyes. "So you *do* care if the pilot you dump me on is a murderer. That's nice."

Cade meant the words to sting, but Rennik had a severe allergic reaction. His face swelled. His already-long neck stiffened into strings.

"Hey," Cade said. "Are you all right?"

Lee set a hand on Rennik's arm, curling her fingers around the muscle and leaving Cade with nothing to do but drain out.

The door on the other side of the dock swirled open.

The girl who crossed the threshold had the sort of hectic-busy hands and shy feet that Cade had seen only in small children at the market. But she was older than Cade, and more advanced, in obvious areas. Her broad frame burst with curvature. None of the scrappiness Cade was used to — this girl looked like she'd grown up on a planet that boasted better nutrition than cactus milk and rodent stew. She looked like she'd grown up on a planet with hamburgers. She had amberish skin, and dark curls, and her brown eyes were bright — but that could have been a side effect of the curiosity that flew out of her, like sparks.

Cade waited for her to start things.

She tossed out a hand, a flare into darkness. "Ayumi."

"I'm Cade."

"Interesting," Ayumi said, still shaking her hand. "I've never come across that name, attached to a living person or a history. Do you know its origins?"

Firstbloom. It rose in Cade, drenched in white and antiseptic.

"No."

Ten seconds in, and she was already not-telling truths. But Ayumi was too taken with her surroundings to notice. She met the wonders of the main cabin with more eye-sparks and fireworking fingers. When she reached the line of shipmates, she nodded and shook hands, vigorously, collecting the rest of their names.

Ayumi was ankle-deep in a conversation about Hatchum genetics when Cade heard her own voice.

"Let's go."

"*Go?*" Ayumi asked, half turning. "But this is a fascinating ship. And I'd like to speak with all the passengers before we leave. Human ones, in particular. And . . ."

She caught sight of the latest Human Express haul in the cargo hold. Things were out of their crates, which didn't surprise Cade — Lee only seemed to care about inventories when she was mad.

Ayumi ran, her fingers outstretched. "What is this?"

"Those are mine," Lee said. She rushed to the crates and started loading her arms with blankets and papers and books.

"They're human-made." Ayumi touched the items with painstaking care. "Yes. I would stake my ship on it."

"They're little trinkets," Lee said. "Just things I pick up."

Ayumi's eyes could have set the hold on fire. "They're *artifacts*."

Rennik caught up to them and tried to regain control of the conversation. "Where are you headed?" he asked.

"Headed?" Ayumi said. "Nowhere. Or rather, right here."

Lines stamped the skin around Rennik's lips. "You're floating around the universe . . . untethered?"

Ayumi blinked a few too many times, and then said, "No, no, that's not it at all. I'm here for Cade. She needs me and I, as it happens, need her."

Cade cocked an eyebrow.

"I'm from Rembra," Ayumi said. "You've heard of it?"

Rennik, Lee, and Cade shook their heads.

Gori closed his eyes and puffed slightly, all over. "No," he said. "But I can feel its presence."

A clear battle clashed on Ayumi's face — whether to stop and ask Gori a thousand questions, or push on.

"It's one of the last self-sustaining human colonies," she said. "Everyone there has a purpose. Mine is to find, collect, catalog, and understand things related to Earth. And all humans have a relationship to Earth, no matter how old and rickety."

Cade didn't know if she liked the idea of being part of someone's little project. It sounded demanding. She'd hoped they could make it to Hades in silence. Punctuated by Xan.

Still, it wasn't a bad trade, considering she needed a ride to the darkest brink of space.

"Should we . . . ?" Cade asked, pointing toward the dock, all readiness.

Ayumi looked universe-bent on staying where she was.

"I can't help but notice certain clues as to what you're doing here." She focused on Lee and blushed molten-red. "This is the Human Express, isn't it? You're carriers."

"*I'm* a carrier," Lee corrected.

Ayumi turned, unleashing her blush on the rest of them. "And this is your faithful crew."

"Yeah. Well. Minus one."

Lee's stare lodged in Cade — but if Ayumi noticed, she chose to ignore it.

"This is the best hailing," she said, running her fingers through the piles. "I usually pick up stowaways being flushed from various craft because the crews are too soft-hearted or weak-stomached to toss them out of the airlock. Or they don't have an airlock. Or their cultures don't permit murder. But that's about all I get these days — space-rats and traitors."

Lee's stare didn't budge.

"It's time for us to go," Cade said.

She cut through the main cabin and waited at the dock. Ayumi looked confused, but followed. Lee nabbed the girl's arm. Ayumi stared down at Lee's fingers like they were words in another language.

"Look," Lee said. "You seem like a decent person."

"That's a nice, if somewhat hasty and unfounded, opinion."

Cade couldn't speak it — not yet — but a purpose had been forming in her mind, swirling like space-dust until it took on its own roundness, its own gravity. It had collected around the core of Ayumi's words.

What you can do.

Connect. Cade knew how to do that better than any human, because entanglement had changed her.

What you choose to do.

That was her music. The rawness of notes and the hard-caring crowds, the finger-sting of guitars. It was the one thing her mother had left her, and the first thing Cade had chosen for herself.

What needs to be done.

This was stranger, and bigger, and it terrified Cade. There were humans to un-scatter from all over space. There was glass to clear from spacedrunk eyes. And the rest of humanity — she couldn't change all of those lives. But she could do her best to bring them together.

Another flash from the black hole sliced into Cade's thoughts. It was Xan, still confused about where she'd gone. How would she be able to help anyone when she hadn't saved the one person she set out to?

Ayumi sat near Cade's feet, patient, while she worked it out.

Lee came and checked on Cade fourteen times in an hour. Rennik brought her three different lunches, and she ate them all. Renna pulsed her happiness at seeing Cade again, little triplet beats that bubbled underneath Cade's fingertips.

The Unmakers would be after them all soon enough. But for a little while, there would be days like this.

And time. Cade knew what she had to start doing as soon as she was strong enough. But the idea of connecting with someone other than Xan was pure pain. The absolute wrong note.

Still. It would have to be struck.

Cade reached out, and it was like small steps into cold water. So terrible, her teeth rattled. But she found a simple string of notes, and sent it to the people on the ship. Lee, with her loose-fiddled melodies, and Rennik, who didn't sound hushed anymore. Ayumi's mind was laid bare, and it reminded Cade to be brave. Like she had on the verge of the black hole, she reached hard and it was all there, waiting. Bright and clear. The number of minds and their need to be heard overwhelmed her. Then Cade sent out the first notes she'd ever heard her mother play, because she wanted them to be part of the song — and from somewhere, impossibly far, she was sure she heard an echo. And for a moment Cade forgot about the pain. Not because it was gone, but because there was something else to listen to. The people on the ship. And the ones somewhere beyond it — in the wide sea of space, on far planets.

She cracked herself open, and let their music in.

"Fine. Maybe you're a snugging cannibal. Either way, don't let this one talk you into a suicide run."

"What does that mean?"

"Hades." Lee crossed her arms. "If she brings it up, do the iron-stomached thing. Toss her out the airlock."

Cade cracked her knuckles. She would have to do this, *again*, in front of everyone. And this time she wouldn't stop Xan from helping. It was bigger than a grudge now. It was a matter of getting to Xan before he got hurt. Cade couldn't let one knot-haired scrap of a girl stand in the way.

As a bonus, people would come out of this with the truth. What they did with it would be up to them.

Cade threw the first punch.

Rennik was between them, fast, and her fist met the wrong body, square on his rib cage. It didn't shake him.

He turned to Lee. "What is this about?"

"Don't listen to her," Lee said. "I'm doing you a favor." Rennik circled his arms around Lee, but she crashed hard against him. Started to cry. "You have to trust me. Why doesn't anyone here trust me? Why doesn't anyone tell me things I need to know or trust me when I tell them—"

"You lied." But it didn't come out like the swell of triumph Cade thought it would. It sounded small. A technicality.

Lee sank to the floor, and Rennik went with her. She was all broken-down parts and steam. "I'm the honest one here. You want more true things? You want me to tell you all of it?" she babbled, running her hands over and over each other like water.

Cade closed her eyes. Braced herself for something so bad it had melted Lee down to this.

"I had a sister," she said. "The Unmakers killed her."

"Well, this is first-class embarrassing."

Rennik had installed Lee in the narrow bed in his own cabin and then disappeared. Lee looked small, with the covers pulled up to her chin. Cade had followed her in and hadn't gotten herself kicked out. So far.

"What's your pilot doing?" Lee asked.

"Waiting in the mess. Studying our dietary habits."

Lee coughed up a weak-throated chuckle. Cade couldn't even smile back.

"I never wanted to tell you," Lee said. "Or anyone. But I think you need to hear this."

She nodded at the end of the bed, and Cade sat down near the white hills of Lee's feet.

"I used to make runs with my family," Lee said. "Did you know that?"

Cade shook her head. "You never told me."

"I guess we both left a lot of blanks."

Cade didn't know how to answer that, so she let the silence do the work. It had a weight that warped the air around unsaid things.

"Two fathers and a sister," Lee said. "She was five years older than me. So much prettier." Lee's face turned into a dense grid of emotion. "Moira was the sort of perfect where you don't even hate her for it.

"On a run to Wex 12, one of our dads was picked up. Local force. They detained him for forty-two hours in a sonically padded holding cell. Released him for lack of evidence." Her laugh came out strong, but Cade didn't take that as a good sign. "We were on a planet where they still cared about evidence, even when it came to humans. Our other dad had been fighting off spacesick for years, but the glass was starting to come right and regular.

"That was when our parents decided the Express had gotten too dangerous. They wanted me and Moira to join them in retirement on some subtropical disaster of a planet. But we were in love with the Express — addicted to it. We weren't going to spend the best stretch of our careers peeling coconuts and sleeping under somebody else's stars."

Lee stopped talking, and Cade wanted time to stop with her. Ayumi and her ship could wait. Even Xan could wait. Cade had never been patient for someone before, and she wanted to be patient for Lee.

"Moira and I made promises to both retire when I hit twenty. We hugged our parents under the palm trees. Filled our sacks. Left.

"Moira wanted new routes. She said we needed to branch out. There were more people who needed us to carry, and it was our job to find them. She was always like that. Caring too much about people we'd never met, and even more about the ones we had. Well . . . I didn't like the looks of the pilot who picked us up on Sligh, no matter how human he was, no matter how many stories he slung about his nieces back home. He didn't look like he made friends with little girls."

Cade's lungs sent up a sharp knock. She wasn't breathing.

"We got out past the Tirith Belt when we saw the lights. Yellow lights. Boarding. It happens all the time. It was a class of ship we'd never seen before. But there are thousands of models. We had no real reason to be worried. Moira looked at me . . . we had the same eyes, Cade. It's something, to look in your own eyes and face down that much fear."

Cade could see it. Two sets of dark moons. And the Unmakers' ship, coming fast. Lee's words were so strong that Cade could almost climb inside the story and live the rest.

"They didn't ask, and didn't listen. They did terrible things to her. I heard them say . . . she deserved it. Because that's what humans did, hurt each other. Hurt everything they put their hands on. She'd been pretending to be better than that, but she was human, so she couldn't be. So this was the right and honest way to end her. The Unmakers killed Moira before she could say a word. But that doesn't mean they did it fast. It was more like . . . they twisted her out of herself . . . one twist at a time.

"Moira was brave. She wouldn't have begged. The pilot, though, he did. That's how I knew he'd sold our lives. But the Unmakers killed him, all the same. Just a little too fast for him to mention where I was hiding."

Lee put her head down. Pushed out all the breath she hadn't used.

Cade didn't know if she should put an arm around Lee or leave her alone for the rest of time.

"She would have taken you," Lee said. "Back on Andana, when you asked, Moira would have said yes. So that's what I did, too."

Cade wondered if there was more to it, though. She thought back to the story she'd told in the market — about her soon-to-be-killed brother. Lee's face had changed; she had studied Cade so carefully before she said *yes*. In that moment, Lee had decided she and Cade had something in common.

Then the Unmakers showed up, and it turned out they had too much in common.

Lee sank down in the blankets. "Don't get that weird cadet of a pilot killed, okay?" She looked at the square of fabric under her hands. Spoke to the stitches. "Don't get yourself killed."

Lee's face went into shutdown, and sleep couldn't be far behind. So that was it. The end of what Lee had to say to her. Cade stood to go, but something stuck her to the door handle.

"Why did you tell me?" She thought Lee had reached the limit of her caring a good while ago.

Lee shrugged.

"It's a fate I wouldn't wish on enemies, Cade. And you're not that." She closed her eyes and spoke the last words in a once-upon-a-time whisper. "You're no Moira, but we did make a brass team."

Ayumi had made herself at home in the mess. She had also found a way to clatter every dish at the same time.

"What are you doing?" Cade asked, taking in the lit flame

on the stove, the stack of dry goods on the table, the clusters of pots on the floor. Ayumi pressed a steaming cup under her nose.

"Old Earth recipe," she said. "Well, as close as I could get it."

A fresh green smell folded around them.

"It's like . . ."

"Grass," Ayumi said. "I made it for your friend. It should do her good." She ran for the door, turned back with a tea-slosh. "I'll meet you here. We'll leave as soon as she's drained the cup. Even though I'd rather make a full study of this ship and its cargo. We'll go. We'll go. I promise."

Ayumi rushed across the main cabin, dripping tea as she went.

She passed Rennik, who had climbed down the chute and was headed toward the mess. Headed toward Cade. She had never noticed how good he was at moving around the ship, how even in the false-grav he knew how to carve out space. She hadn't spent time with the fact that his eyes made her think of autumn — a season that lasted for all of three days on Andana.

She'd been too busy for that.

But now her minutes on the ship were numbered. She would have to do all of her noticing. Fast.

"I'm sorry," Cade said. The words slipped out this time. Easier than they had with Lee, but they still sounded wrong.

"For what?" he asked.

Choosing Rennik's ship. Getting him almost-killed. Not caring because she had someone else to care about more.

"I punched you."

He looked down at his chest, absently.

"Oh," he said. "I suppose you did."

Rennik sat down in the chair at her side, leaving a slice of space between him and the door, a slice of space between him and Cade. He looked straight ahead, hands twisting over each other, fingers hooking and unhooking, the patterns so close to regular that she could turn them into a beat, anticipate.

Cade kept trying to do that. Make a song out of his hands.

"Look . . ." she said.

Rennik surprised her by having something that he needed to say so much, he cut through her still forming words.

"I don't like the idea of passing you off." He snarled a hand through his hair. Broke his perfect finger-patterns. "It's not right. Once you're a member of this crew, it's final. Renna feels that as much as I do . . . if not more. We don't make these decisions lightly."

We. That one little word hit Cade with asteroid force. Rennik thought of himself as part of a *we* — and ever since Cade had left Andana, she did, too. Which meant Rennik was like her, in a way she'd thought no one was.

She didn't know what to do with that information. So she pushed at a pile of tea leaves on the table.

"You're free to come and go, of course," Rennik said. "But those creatures are after you, Cade. I don't want you on another ship."

Her body blared hot, like it did when the lights at the club hit her all at once, branding their reds and yellows.

"It's not safe," Rennik added.

"Right."

"Of course, you weren't safe here, either," he said, all of the air vacuumed out of the words. "We could have taken better precautions." Rennik was still hurting over something he thought was his fault.

But the boarding was pure Cade. She had crashed into their lives, trailing Unmakers behind her. And now she wanted to do the same thing to Ayumi — draw a line from here to *more* trouble.

"You did what you could." Cade wanted to thank him for the calm he'd shown in the face of the Unmakers. For his unwavering Rennik-ness. Even if that same Rennik-ness did sometimes make her want to set things on fire.

Cade looked for words to hold all of that, but she couldn't find them.

Her fingers dropped to Rennik's wrist, before she could remind them how much she didn't like touching.

Rennik didn't shake her off. But maybe he should have.

"You shouldn't let me do that if I'm spacesick, right?"

"I shouldn't be sitting so close to you, either," he said in those unreadable tones Cade knew so well.

The stage lights were back. Brighter. Cade felt as alive and ready as she had in any of those preshow moments. But she was just sitting in the mess. She willed her body not to pump so much red, to wash down to a cool blue.

Rennik's eyes were patient and told her nothing. She didn't

know if he was protecting himself from her or not—but he should be.

Cade snatched her hand back. Blamed the drawn-out nature of the whole thing on inertia. Stood up.

That was how Cade could say she was sorry. She could leave, and never hurt them again.

Ayumi came back to the door with an empty cup and restless fingers.

"Shall we?"

It was time to leave. But Cade couldn't leave. And she couldn't stay. The things Lee had told her, Moira's fate—she couldn't be the reason that happened, not to anyone.

Now Cade was the one who trailed Ayumi across the main cabin, toward the dock.

"Where to?" Ayumi asked.

"Nearest habitable surface," Cade said. "I need to get planetbound."

CHAPTER 12

ESCAPING AN ATTRACTOR When a particle has excess momentum, it is possible for it to fling itself out into undifferentiated space

Ayumi's ship was like nothing Cade had ever laid her space-sore eyes on.

They passed through a whirring engine room, into a half-lit hold. It brimmed on every surface with more of what Ayumi called *artifacts* — anything and everything that related to Earth. Books that had lost their pages. Pages that had abandoned their books. Tacked-up photographs of an ocean. An old map of somewhere called New Jersey, worn through in places and curled over at the edge.

Ayumi trailed her fingers over the objects and smiled at them like old friends. She led Cade through a low door, into the main room. It held a pilot's chair, a navigator's chair, and two passenger seats, their backs high, fabric slicked down by time and bodies. There was a row of colored buttons and stubby switches, and over that, a central span of glass.

All of it looked standard-issue. But the walls sang out, strange.

Paint covered them, bleeding indigo into purple, purple into black. The colors of night sky and space, an echo of what sat outside the window. But more than that, too. There were planets and moons, small craft careening from one colorful blip to another. Broken white lines trailed the spaceships, forming sharp-angled patterns, like constellations. One whole stretch of the right-hand wall was marbled in blue-green.

"What is this?" Cade asked.

"History," Ayumi said. "Specifically, the end of Earth history and its effects. The artistic merit is questionable." She squinted at an awkward nebula. "The artistic merit is questionable *at best*."

"But it's part of your project?" Cade asked.

Ayumi's face seared with heat. "It's not a project. It's a purpose. And yes."

By the time they settled into the chairs, and Cade struggled her arms through the straps, Ayumi had traded in her crisped pride for a shy smile. "Would you like to learn?"

"Maybe later." Cade needed to put some distance between herself and a ship full of souring memories.

Ayumi nodded. Tried — and failed — to pretend she didn't want to tell Cade all about the end of Earth history and its effects. Then she turned to face the blackness in the window, and her disappointment wiped clean. Ayumi's brown eyes took in space views like fresh water after a drought.

The little ship lifted off with a lurch and a knock—like crashing into nothing. Cade pulled her straps tighter, set her teeth against each other, and gritted out the ride. Minute after bumpy minute. She had gotten used to Renna's easy flight-style.

"I set an auto-course for Hymnia," Ayumi said. "It's the nearest planet with a human settlement, one that isn't basically a prison camp or a work colony. It even has a fountain in the square that sometimes has water in it! And fish! But people tend to spear the fish and eat them. I would take you back to Rembra, but it's a months-long flight in the other direction, and—"

"No," Cade said.

"—you seem to be in a bit of a hurry," Ayumi finished.

Cade fidgeted with the stub of a switch, until she remembered it might be wired to something important.

"I'm not really spacesick."

Ayumi's face, which so far had been as readable as fresh ink, changed. "I didn't think so."

"Is that part of your . . . purpose . . . too?" Cade asked.

"No," Ayumi said, with a tight little smile. "I have an eye for these things."

Cade sat forward in the navigator's chair. Renna was long-gone, but Cade still whipped fast when she caught something roundish in the corner of her eye.

"I'm just glad you didn't need the ride to Hades," Ayumi said. "All of those black holes." She shuddered against the chair straps. "I'm not a bad pilot, mind you, but I do have . . . limitations."

Ayumi looked like she was about to say more, but Cade let her eyes drift closed. She hadn't slept in days. And if she was headed for the crust of some new nowhere-planet, there was no point in getting-to-know-you games.

Cade kept her eyes closed and pretended to sleep, but really she was spending some quality time with her new plan.

Once she reached Hymnia, she would need a ride. One that *didn't* put any good people in danger. She could stow away, or commandeer a ship. If she did stow away, it would mean less chance of the Unmakers finding her — but it also meant she'd never make it to Xan unless she commandeered the ship at the last second. And how would that end? She would tell the pilot what to do, and instead he would take her out to the nearest patch of pitch black and make short work of her.

The one sure way to get to Hades was to learn how to fly, and then find a ship, or steal one. But that would take months.

Xan would be dead before she got to him.

Which left Cade with bottom-of-the-barrel questions. Could she find a new life on Hymnia and forget about him? How many layers of toughness would she need to lacquer on before she didn't feel him anymore? Would she know what happened to him if she never made it to Hades? Would the connection cut if — no, *when* — he died?

Was it time to give up?

Soon it was the only question left. Until the words were a stereo-echo, bouncing in her head.

giveup giveup giveup

And then Xan came for her and her own smile hit her like the rush of space at liftoff and she gasped.

She fell into his room. Fit into his headspace. Cozied up to his emotions.

The fear that she'd grown so used to — the skittering boy-sweat fear — was gone, replaced with a calm. A warm stone at his center, working its warmth outward, filtering through all parts of him.

This was what Xan's confidence felt like.

He stood and stretched until he almost filled the small room. He crossed to the sheet of mirror.

Xan stared at himself. No, his gray eyes were too sharp for that. He stared *into* himself. His skin was still colored like clouds, but the puffs and folds of childhood were gone, thinned down to muscle.

After the threats from Gori, the fight with Lee, the flickers of hesitation when she sat too close to Rennik — this was relief. When she looked at Xan, the things she felt were strong and painful-obvious. He was a strong beat, driven into her in four-four time. Cade needed to feel him, the way first-row spacesicks needed to feel guitar-buzz on their skin. Cade wanted him, like this but closer. Without entanglement and mirrors in the way.

Xan stared out, bruises underlining his eyes. Cade's fingers rose to touch the soft, broken skin, even though it was still so far away. She watched him gather his mouth, all of the muscles tight around the acute slant of his lips. He readied himself to speak to her, out loud, for the first time.

"Cadence."

She had forgotten she wasn't the only one in the universe who knew that name.

It left a little patch of cloud on the mirror, and the cloud grew as he said, "Please."

That one word reached into Cade.

And she snapped back onto the ship. She thrashed, the straps scoring her chest, her arms, her breath down to drowning gasps.

"Are you all right?" Ayumi asked. "Cade?"

"Cadence."

"*Cadence.*" Ayumi closed her eyes and said it again. "Pretty. Do you know its—"

"Origins? No."

Cade just needed to say it. That was her name. Who she really was. She'd gotten to the point where giving up on Xan felt as good as giving up on herself. Her body staged a revolt against the decision to change course. Her mind only agreed with itself half of the time.

"Tell me about that," Cade said, nodding at the paint on the walls. "Earth history. Effects." She was desperate to hear something besides the coming-apart strain inside of her.

"Sure," Ayumi said. "Sure."

She turned from the controls, and Cade almost leapt to grab them. Then she remembered the auto-course.

"You haven't heard, I would guess, of the caves at Lascaux?" Ayumi asked.

Cade searched her thinning-out thoughts. "Is that a planet in the Mann system?"

"No," Ayumi said. "It was a place in a country called France. On Earth. The caves at Lascaux kept a record of human life. I wanted to do the same thing. The story starts here." She pointed one strong finger at the swirled blue-green, that unmistakable sphere. "I'm sure you know the beginning."

"Earth was blinked out," Cade said. "An asteroid." Her breath leveled. Finally. It was easier to talk about the destruction of her home planet than to think about the end of her entanglement.

"That's right," Ayumi said. "But do you know why?"

Human history wasn't the subject of much small talk on Andana.

"No."

"On Earth," Ayumi said, "at the end, humans were more plentiful than we are now. A million times over. And technology kept them ever-so-connected. Across the planet, in an instant, they could transfer voices, thoughts, images."

It sounded like what Cade could do. Maybe not as intense or particle-based as what Cade could do. A primitive form.

And, of course, thinking about that led her back to thinking about Xan.

"So?" Cade asked through a fresh round of pain. "What happened?"

"Everyone knew the asteroid was coming. People had seen

it in their telescopes and done the calculations. They frittered away decades, not-finding a way to save themselves. There was no lack of time, or money, or the resources needed."

Cade reached her hand and touched the blue-green. It should have been warm and firm; it should have grounded her. But under the skin of paint, it was just a wall.

"What happened then?" she asked.

"Nothing."

Cade held herself quiet, sure there was more. She must be missing a note that would tie the song together, make it make sense.

"Some ships were built," Ayumi said, pointing at a line of little gray dabs on the wall. "But it wasn't enough. Not nearly enough. Fighting broke out over who should use them. Corrupt lotteries were drawn. Some of the ships were launched into space close to empty."

Cade followed the lines as they left the safe rings of atmosphere — the harbor of a home planet — and pressed out into space. The distances between them grew and grew.

"A million humans," Ayumi said. "That's the top estimate. Instead of banding together, they fought. And then came the Scattering." Even Cade, on her concrete island in an endless sea of sand, had heard about the Scattering. "Small groups of humans headed into the wide universe, alone."

"And that's how they stayed," Cade said.

"For a thousand years," Ayumi finished.

Until the entangled.

Cade and Xan weren't alone — not like the other humans

living in space. Their connection stretched across light-years. A bridge to span the impossible distances.

Mr. Niven had made it clear that Xan had to be saved because entanglement was important. When Cade went after him, she did it for her own reasons — but there were all of these other reasons, lurking behind hers. Would she keep turning away from what entanglement could mean — to the scattered and the spacesick, to the people she'd wanted to call her friends — all because some old hologram brought it up first?

And then there was Xan. Still sitting in a cell in Hades. Still beating a question through her bloodstream.

Asking her not to give up.

The dark in front of the little ship was pushed up and up by the wide rim of a new planet. Its atmosphere spun thick with strands of dark and storm-ridden clouds. The surface showed underneath, pale.

"There she is," Ayumi said. "Hymnia. Now, before we get any farther, there's something you sh —"

But she didn't finish. Ayumi stared out into white — and white came back to frost her eyes.

She was glassed-and-gone.

CHAPTER 13

CRITICAL FLUCTUATIONS A marked increase in variability just before a phase transition

"You're spacesick?"

Nothing came from Ayumi's wilted lips — which was all the answer Cade needed.

"Dregs."

This time, she did leap and grab the controls. The fact that they were on an auto-course didn't make her feel safer.

The planet swirled its storm clouds at her. The ship blinked its buttons. Cade flashed one hand in front of Ayumi's face, raised and dropped her arms to test muscle slackness.

The pilot was in a state of complete disconnect. It gave Cade the perfect reason to turn around — and no way to do it.

"Ayumi," she whispered. "Ayumi, *come on.*"

The glass shined on another coat. If Cade was going to redirect the ship, she would have to do it herself.

She searched the buttons and switches for a hailing signal. Nothing looked the same as it did in Renna's control room.

And she got no help from the ship—no warm flash or small rumble—to let her know that she was getting close.

At the far end of the panel, Cade found a black-hatched circle that reminded her of a microphone. Next to it was a finger-worn number pad and a red button. She tested the button and heard static.

Static was a start.

But she needed Renna's hailing code. She fluttered through every loose scrap of paper, slammed through every binder, hoping Ayumi had scribbled it down somewhere.

At the same time, she reached out for Xan.

The hailing code, she thought. *I need the hailing code of the ship the Unmakers boarded. The hailing code. The hailing code.*

Cade didn't know how Xan would be able to get it. She knew that however he did, it would be dangerous. But that's what she had figured out, in the second when Ayumi glassed and left her for some star-flecked inner void.

Trust was a dangerous thing.

Cade had thought it would be safe to trust a ride from the girl slumped against the pilot's chair. She'd thought it would be safe not to tell Lee that the Unmakers were following her. It was never safe. It wasn't even a *question* of safe. It was how much you knew, and how much you were willing to risk.

Cade had played the whole thing wrong. And she had lost her best—her only—real chance of getting to Hades.

Her fingers jumped against the number pad. She had the digits punched in before her mind processed them.

340426.

She didn't have time to ask Xan how he'd gotten that number so fast. She felt a single drip of worry, like a bead of sweat.

Cade pushed the red button.

"Ayumi?" Rennik's voice crackled and split, but it was his. "Come in, Ayumi."

"It's Cadence," she said. "Cade. Look, I need to get back to you."

She waited for the well-reasoned, perfectly worded Rennik-style argument, but he didn't make one.

"I'm on an auto-course for Hymnia," she said.

The planet loomed larger and whiter as Cade shed important minutes. They peeled off behind the ship, dark and too fast.

"What happened to—"

"Later!" Cade said. "Right now, I need to end up *not* fried to atmosphere or crash-landed on an ice cube."

She pulled out maps and charts. Numbers blurred, lines wavered. Cade wasn't even sure if she was holding the pages the right way.

"I don't know our coordinates . . ." Xan was there with her, trying to read the charts, but he didn't know how to do it, either.

Rennik's words were calm and certain. "I have a lock on you."

"How did you do that so fast?"

"I had to be sure the Unmakers didn't follow when you broke off from us."

A hard sigh dropped out of Cade.

"First-class."

Cade flattened the charts to one side and set her hands against the alien geography of the controls.

"Here's the other problem. I don't know how to fly."

"At all?"

She wondered if Rennik could hear the shutting of her sudden-dried throat, the failed swallow.

"Uh . . ."

Another crackle.

"Pulling up specs on the ship model," Lee said. "What did you get yourself into this time?"

Cade glanced at Ayumi's low-swung head, a thin trail of spit running from her lips to her shirt.

"A minor catastrophe."

"You need to find a square of four lit buttons," Lee said, "and push all but the top right one. That should turn off the auto-course."

"Don't you think I should learn a few simple maneuvers before I turn off the —"

"You're about to breach atmosphere," Rennik said. "There's no time."

"Maybe I should let the ship land itself and wait —"

Voices jumped out of the transmitter, swelled to a pitch that cramped the small cabin.

"No!"

Rennik pushed on, smoothing over the show of fear. "It's

not safe to land a ship without a pilot, no matter how carefully the auto-course is set."

"And you just told us you're no sort of pilot," Lee added.

Cade set her fingers against the cluster of buttons — and pushed.

The ship, which had hurtled on a steady course, slowed to a sickening float. For a moment, everything went loose and still. It reminded Cade of the look on Ayumi's face when she glassed out — the look that lived thick on her skin. That unnatural calm.

"What comes next?" Cade asked.

"Renna will fly at top speed in your direction," Rennik said, "but you need to come toward us. You'll get picked up if you linger in a shipping lane."

"Picked up or smashed into," Lee muttered.

Cade spread her fingers. Said goodbye to one more terrible planet, and the life she might have lived there.

"Let's go."

Rennik and Lee pounded out a string of directions. Press this button. Jam those switches to the right.

Xan wanted to help, too. As Cade worked, he nudged her muscles in what he must have thought were helpful directions. Cade tried to hold him back — how much could he know about flying a ship? He'd been coma-soured and bedridden his whole life.

"Steer clear of all orbits and fly straight," Rennik said.

"Don't answer hailing codes," Lee added. "Just in case."

Faster, Xan told her. *Clamp down and don't let go.*

The little ship clunked around in a wide arc and cut into open space. Bits of trash clung and cluttered the flight path, and, with Lee's help, Cade fixed the blast-wipers. Broke up the problems. She followed instructions, but barely — she felt like the ship kept leaping ahead of her as soon as she caught up. Which meant there were seconds, whole lurching minutes, when Cade didn't have control. Planets and moons and other ships crowded on all sides — and with two voices stuffed in her ears and one inside of her head, Cade's mind hit maximum capacity.

So she tried not-listening. Banished all other input — and within thirty seconds, found herself wrestling the orbit of some rogue moon. The cabin slapped on another layer of distraction. The glare of sirens and a bright-red beat.

"So what you need to do is . . ." Lee said.

Xan twitched her fingers to a set of switches that calmed the lights and the sirens.

"Don't worry," Rennik said. "Those are just warning levels. You're going to be fine as long as you bear down and left."

Cade did want their help. As much as she could get. But there were too many strands of sound and feeling, and she couldn't pick them apart and find what she needed and process it in time to make the right call.

She would have to learn how to channel all of it at once.

Fast.

She balanced the input, like the levels on speakers, so she

could hear the information coming in from Rennik, the instructions from Lee, feel the deep tug of Xan in her body, and add her own instinct, too — trust her fingers to unlock the secrets of the console and her muscles to find the rhythms of the ship.

She needed all of it. The full band.

Cade dialed voices in and out, funneled the words down to action. Her hands reached and slid.

The ship slammed forward.

She wasn't good at it. She wasn't in the same galaxy as good.

The sight of an asteroid field set every one of her nerves on their shattered ends. She didn't know how to play an asteroid field.

It was time to improvise.

A massive rock swam up close, showed its underside. Cade held the course. Let her fingers find the button to throw them vertical at the right moment and fling them free. Clusters of space-rock spread beneath the little ship like false land, but the holes that gaped between the rocks showed the truth — that space was dark and forever-deep.

There, on the other side of the field, smaller than the smallest asteroid, round and perfect and headed their way —

"Renna." Cade sang it again, to the transmitter. "Renna. I have you in sight." Cade sailed close, and Renna threw out a burst of false-grav. The little ship surrendered. Let itself be sucked in.

The transmitter crackled and cut out. Xan retreated. Cade's adrenaline levels crashed like a Voidvil slummer after a long Saturday night.

Something stirred and shifted next to Cade. The lump in the pilot's chair was coming back to life.

"Nice timing, spacecadet."

Ayumi's brown eyes flutter-blinked, and her curls flew in ten different directions as she looked around. "Where are we?"

"Back with Renna." Cade couldn't hide the sag of relief in her voice.

"But that's fantastic! I was hoping to make a full study of . . ." Ayumi wiped the corner of her lip. Pulled herself up straight against the chair. "Did I . . ."

Cade sighed.

"Yeah. You did. In a real way." She offered Ayumi a hand. The girl walked like she'd just figured out what legs were for.

"It's our last chance to catch this ride," Cade said. "Try to keep it together."

The homecoming was less than Cade hoped for.

Rennik and Lee straggled into the main cabin. They had worked feverish-hard to get Cade back, and now they were treating her like a biohazard. Rennik wavered on his feet. Lee kept a meaningful distance. Renna was taut and silent, waiting it out until Cade's place on the ship was sorted. Gori stared down at the whole thing from his bunk.

"What happened?" Rennik asked.

"Ayumi . . ." Cade waited as the girl stumbled across the dock. "We got clipped by the thruster of another ship, took a bad rattle. She passed out."

Ayumi's step bobbled deep, and she almost fell.

"You lost consciousness while flying?" Rennik asked, rushing to help. He laced an arm under Ayumi's and led her to the bottom of the chute, where he helped her sit while he frowned at her head.

"Oh, utterly," Ayumi said, catching on to Cade's game and playing it with all the enthusiasm of a bad liar. "But it's nothing to worry about. All reversible damage. Not *even* damage! Nondamage. I'm entirely to blame. I kept Cadence busy talking when I should have kept an eye on the shipping lane. I checked and double-checked and triple-checked the course, but incoming ships can move so fast and—"

Cade cleared her throat. Now that Ayumi had gummed the air with words, Cade remembered how much she needed to say. It had all been building in her since she faced the white of Hymnia.

She crossed to Lee, took her by the shoulders, and started with the truth.

"I was never lying when I told you there's someone I need to save. But he's not my brother. He and I are . . ." Cade didn't know how to say it except to say it. There was only one word for this in the whole universe—no translation.

"He and I are entangled."

That was what she owed Lee. Not a string of apologies like that same flat note blasted over and over. The truth, in all of its shining complicated harmonies. It was the one thing she'd owed Lee — and anyone she wanted to call a friend — from the start. She could only hope that saying it now would be enough.

Her words met a wall of blankness. Everyone stared at her. No one seemed to know what to say.

"Entangled?" Lee asked, with a steep double-eyebrow spike. "Is that some prettified way of saying you and this boy are . . .?"

"No." Cade lost a bit of her measured cool and fired up, cheeks first. "No, no. We're *quantum* entangled — it means we're connected to each other, particle for particle. It was done when we were babies. In a lab."

Lee's eyebrows spiked higher.

Cade's voice — and her sureness — faltered. She needed to explain all of it better than she was now.

"The Unmakers are our enemies," she said, using Mr. Niven's words. "They want to stop us from what we're meant to do."

"And what's that?"

"I wasn't sure for a long time. When Ayumi told me about Earth, that helped." Cade still didn't understand it completely, and when she thought about the hugeness of it, she could hear the blood in her ears. Cade knelt down to refocus, fingertips to the floor. The coolness of Renna infused her with calm. "I think the scientists who created entanglement want us to reverse what happened to the human race. The Scattering. Spacesick."

Lee bolted her arms across her chest. It was impressive —how tight she could hold on to a grudge. She had told Cade about her sister, worked to make sure she flew safe. But not wanting someone to die and letting that someone back into their lives were two different things, with a universe between them.

"The scientists . . ." Cade said. "They talked about hope. For the future. For something more than survival."

She reached into her pocket and tightened her fingers around the facets of the circle-glass.

"I'll show you."

Cade led them all to the control room.

"Rennik, do you have a projection lamp?" she asked.

"We should," he said. "There was a stretch of a few months when Renna liked to have old slides of Hatch projected on her walls. She goes through phases. But we won't talk about those. She might teach us a lesson by turning the gravity off." He headed to a far corner of the room, but Cade heard him mutter, "Again."

He came back with a tall, slender projection lamp and set it on the control panel. It was dim, but filled with the potential for shine. Cade tamped the circle-glass into it and pointed the whole thing toward the back wall.

"Hello," boomed a voice. "Welcome to Project QE."

Babies invaded the wall, oversized and toddling at each other. This time, Cade sorted them quickly. She found her- self—the one at the center of the crowd, holding her small hands in her lap while the others flailed. She knew the cloud-skinned boy, crawling at her.

Xan was perfect. Xan was the point.

Cade watched the crew watching the film. Rennik studied it with his customary sweep of the eyes — calm and quick. Ayumi was enthralled. She inched closer to the picture every time a new pair of puffed cheeks came into view. Lee followed along, mouthing the narrator's words, committing them to memory like a good carrier. Gori was the same old Gori. Silent. Unmoving.

Cade felt like she had pinned back her chest and showed them all her hard-drumming heart.

" . . . this batch of standard human children will undergo the process of quantum entanglement."

A hot second of white. Cade had forgotten about those splices.

It came to the part with two babies facing each other, and Ayumi broke into Cade's thoughts with a yelp.

"That's you!"

Everyone drew closer to the screen, to see if it was true. Ayumi ran to the wall and traced the line of Baby Cadence's arm with one finger.

"That really is you," she whispered.

"These two are optimally suited for entanglement," the announcer said. "Our greatest hope lies with them."

The film spliced again — Rennik winced at the searing.

Then it was the same two babies but later, then bouncing circles, then babies again, and fade to white.

"That's entanglement," Cade said. "In five minutes or less."

She held her breath.

The universe inched outward.

Rennik stood up in front of the lamp, absorbing the beam of light with his bent-over body. "That explains quite a bit," he said. "Do you mind if I take a look at this?" He touched the rim of the circle-glass with a finger.

"Sure," Cade said.

He ran his long fingers over the glass ridges. "I'm glad you made it back, Cadence."

He was gone before she could say anything—turning the slow build of warmth in Cade to an outraged fizz.

"Nice to see you, too," she called after him.

Gori crossed the room and circled Cade, eyes leveled directly at her brain. He breathed in once, twice, and let the air out in a rusty hiss. It wasn't exactly pleasant, but the lack of a knife tickling the base of Cade's throat seemed like a leap in the right direction.

Gori went off—to his bunk, or to expand into a dark energy balloon.

"Cadence!"

She spun just in time to see Ayumi collapse into yet another pilot's chair. Cade rushed to the armrest and looked down to find a pair of glass-free brown eyes. In fact, they were lively and ticking all over the place.

"Are you all right?" Cade asked.

"Notebooks!" Ayumi cried. "I need all of my notebooks. I need to write down all of this. And cross-index it. Right away."

She jumped up, adding as she ran, "If I had left you on that planet, Cadence, I never would have forgiven myself. Of course, I never would have known not to forgive myself. Which would have made it *even worse* . . . whether I knew it or not."

Cade spun again and found herself almost alone. Renna gently rumbled the floor under her feet to get her attention. Cade put one hand to the ground and smiled as Renna picked out the beat of Cade's heart and played it back to her.

Not bad, for a *welcome back.*

It was down to Cade and Lee — Lee, who had been strangely quiet and soft around the edges since about halfway through the filmstrip. Now she floated toward Cade like she was in a dream state. "Is it true?" she asked, all of the bluster and brass gone out of her voice. "Is it true you can't get spacesick? . . . *Ever?* I know people on the Express who would give their left leg for that. And the ones stranded on all those planets? If they didn't have to be so afraid all the time? That's first-class, Cade. I mean, that's, that's . . . important."

Lee reached out and circled Cade's wrist with her thin fingers.

"It could change everything."

Cade had heard those words before, she had even thought them herself — but somehow when Lee said them, they were worth more.

"So what do we do now?" Lee paced the room, slipping into the brisk business mode she used when she collected for the Express.

"We?"

Lee pressed a hand to the sharp line of her collarbone. "You think you're going to change the fate of the human race without us?"

Cade shook her head carefully.

"Snugging right you're not!"

Lee nodded once and headed out. "I'm going to make us all an egg dish and think about this."

Cade had the control room to herself. But instead of looking out at the stars, she wandered to the top of the chute and watched as people crossed and recrossed the main cabin, calling out to each other. The whole place hummed with work being done. Three humans, two nonhumans, and one ship, on the same course. Cade thrilled to the sound of it. Her life had been the same stale chorus over and over, and this was a welcome new verse.

She sent the good news to Xan — and tried to leave out the one sour note that kept coming back to trouble her.

If trust was a dangerous thing, they were all in it, deep.

CHAPTER 14

ECONICHE The unique subset of the environment for which evolution has prepared a particular species

Wherever Cade went the next day, it seemed like Ayumi was always there, waiting with a notebook and a comet-bright smile.

"I hope you don't mind . . ." she said. "Just a *few* questions."

After Cade had slept and washed up and eaten twice, after she consulted Rennik and Lee on the course, after she unstiffened her fingers on some scales and tested the timbre of Moon-White's strings, she said, "All right, all right."

They sat in the control room—or really, Cade sat in the pilot's chair and Ayumi hovered, her pen flashing wide arcs before Cade even started talking. She thought Ayumi would start with entanglement, but she wanted everything.

"It's a history," Ayumi said. "For the sake of current and future generations, don't leave out a single detail."

Cade stammered through a few sentences about her bunker

on Andana, about the sandstorms that had kept her company. Ayumi sifted through Cade's memories, asking about one detail or another, always wanting more. She was worse than the fans who stumbled backstage, uninvited.

"There's nothing good to tell," Cade said.

"Then give me the nongood," Ayumi said. "I don't need sunshine and miracles, Cadence."

Ayumi's notebook, with its cracked cover and flimsy pages, didn't look like much of a home for the history of humankind.

But maybe she was right. Maybe it did matter.

Cade sent herself back through the space-black, to her best-forgotten planet, and hit a memory.

An old, stale night at Club V. Sweat, the batter of crowds, a drink she wasn't supposed to have burning a hot trail down her throat. It had been handed to her by some asteroid of a man who was clearly hoping for a full-body thank-you. She shoved him away from the edge of the stage and took her place at the center. Hung her head over the fretboard and fitted her finger-grooves to the strings. The lights shone hot on her back. The spacesicks at the front of the stage reached for her feet, lapped at her like waves. She pounded out chords for them and felt nothing. She pounded harder and felt less.

"Right," Ayumi said, scribbling and scribbling, "but you had a life before the club. What about that?"

"The Parentless Center? Basic home for sand-brats. Parents all dead, run-off, or spacesick." Cade studied Ayumi's reaction to the word — or rather, the smoothness where her reaction should have been. "You don't want to know about that."

Ayumi shook her head like Cade was a small child and didn't understand the rules of the game they were playing.

So Cade told all of it. She told the rotten food and the every-where-smell of piss. She told the fights with the other sand-brats, the drained eyes of the adults. And after all of that, she unearthed one good memory.

The first time she'd seen a guitar. She was nine years old, and an older boy had smuggled it in. A tatty old acoustic, but when the boy put his fingers to those strings and played one of the two chords he knew, Cade could hear that this was a sound to beat back the Noise.

She wanted to stay in that moment a while — wait for the slide of the wood under her hands, the glue-and-sawdust smell, the first press of the strings, the buzz and stumble of notes, the smile of the boy.

But Ayumi pressed in close with her notebook. "What about before that?"

"I don't know," Cade said. "It's the Firstbloom scientists you want to ask. But they're dead." She thought of the Niven-pile on the floor of the dressing room. "Of course, sometimes that doesn't stop them."

Ayumi nodded and started to wander the room. Cade won-dered if she was being given up on. Without someone stand-ing so close, she had time and space to think herself back, and back, farther than she'd ever thought before.

It came to her in white shards, mostly — the edge of a crib, the egg-bright glare of overhead lights. The sharp coats of the scientists. Faces came in different variations, but all of the features were the same—mouths firm and muscles set, eyes the grimmest Cade had ever seen. She even caught a glimpse of a much-younger Niven, proving that he'd been a person before he was a projection.

Firstbloom. Cade didn't even know she *had* memories of Firstbloom.

She made out the forms of other babies, crawling or clapping their little hands or crying. The more Cade flipped through moments, the more the babies seemed to be crying.

In one small chip of memory, she saw a woman in a pale blue dress with white flowers on it, standing in a corner. She was crying, too.

Then came Xan.

He stared out at Cade with those steady gray eyes, and things made sense. Things felt right. Some of them even felt easier. No wonder the Noise had been so unwelcome in her head. It had a lot to measure up to.

"Hey, Ayumi," Cade said. "I think I found . . ."

Cade turned and caught her in the false deeps of the star-glass.

" . . . what you were looking for."

Ayumi was swathed in space and suns and planets, her fingers spread and pulsing, her eyes thick with shine.

"Isn't it this wild, perfect thing?" she asked, looking out. "Don't you want it to . . . just . . . swallow you?"

Cade grabbed Ayumi's wrist and tugged. "Come on." But the girl was pasted to the stars. "Come on. We need to go."

"Where?"

"Somewhere we can be alone. No galaxies. No nebulae. No endless, meaningless black. Just the two of us."

Ayumi's arm went limp. She let herself be led out of the control room, but she kept her eyes trained on the starglass until it was out of sight.

Cade hurried Ayumi down the chute, and dropped her on the first crate in the cargo hold.

"Now I need to ask *you* some questions." Cade grabbed Ayumi's notebook and held her hand out for the pen. Ayumi winced but handed it over — she knew the rules of the game, and she played along.

"How long have you been spacesick?" Cade asked.

Ayumi twisted her fingers. "A little less than a year," she whispered.

"But you keep flying."

"That's not, technically, a question —"

"Why do you keep flying, when you know it could get you killed?" Cade left out the part about getting other people killed.

"What I'm doing, the information I'm gathering, it holds such importance," Ayumi said. "I can't stop because there are risks."

Cade had snatched Ayumi's notebook for show, but she found herself writing those words in her harsh, slow lettering.

I can't stop because there are risks.

If Ayumi had gambled on Cade understanding the concept, it worked.

"There's more to it, though," Ayumi said. "Earth has been

my life for as long as I can remember. Space was just the way to get what I needed at first. It was dark and it was necessary. But the more I flew, the more I . . . loved it. I can't explain this if it's something you've never felt. But I love it."

Cade sat down on a crate across from Ayumi and inspected her, from the tips of her dark curls to the curves of her feet. Her eyes were lit up, warm. She was one of the most alive people Cade had ever met. Ayumi *couldn't* be spacesick. But, of course, any human could—that was the point. The number-one reason the human race was still strung out across a hundred planets in thirty different systems, a thousand years after the Scattering.

"Isn't spacesick what happens when you can't stand it?" Cade asked. "When your mind and body check themselves out and never come back?"

"That's the very common, very wrong explanation," Ayumi said. "The truth is easier to see if you know a little more about the origins of spacesick. About Earth."

A flick of nerves set off a chain reaction up Cade's spine. "So what am I missing?"

"Space euphoria."

"Is that more sick babble or—"

"No!" Ayumi's face pulled tight, so pained and *there* that Cade was relieved. "Space euphoria is ancient. The name for one of the first stages of spacesick . . . although people on Earth didn't know it at the time. It started when Earth pilots, not even space pilots, just atmosphere muckers, punched through enough layers to feel the disconnect. They were flooded with a strange delight. The same one" — she closed her eyes and breathed in through her nose like she was inhaling half the universe — "the same one I feel with liftoff.

"The normal bonds . . . to people, to planets . . . all of it breaks."

Cade could see that becoming a problem, fast.

Words from the spacesick bay floated across blackness and time. "Space is beautiful," Cade said, "but it doesn't give a dreg."

Ayumi's smile disappeared. She raked her fingers on the surface of her crate. "There's no way to face it forever as this flawed little speck. There's no right perspective, now that we don't have our planet. So people give in to it. Lose all traces of themselves. Some of them . . ."

Cade could fill in the blanks on this one. "Suicide?"

"Sacrifice," Ayumi corrected. "But only in space. They go back to the birthplace of all things."

"But the planetbound I met didn't love space at all. When I asked them how to leave Andana, they *hissed*."

"They're fighting it," Ayumi said, and the flinch in her eyes let Cade know that the fight was real, and it hurt, and it was probably happening inside Ayumi at that moment. "It's easier to keep it back when you can't see the flash and perfection of the stars, don't have constant reminders of how small, how *nothing* you are in the face of it. We're all fighting it, Cadence. It helps that I have these facts about Earth. I've even dreamt about Earth." She smiled, and sailed off into that beautiful thought — then came crashing back. "It's not enough. That's where the touching comes in."

The mention of it electrified Cade's skin. She felt it against her clothes, the crates, the air.

"You must think it's some depraved act," Ayumi said. "But that touching is the body's last effort to feel human."

Cade shifted back, recalibrated her breath. Ayumi stared off into the distance, unchanged.

"You're so calm about all of this," Cade said. "Like you don't care if it happens to you."

"It's *in* me," Ayumi said. "It's in all of us."

Cade wasn't sure why, but she needed Ayumi to be wrong. Ayumi *was* wrong. Cade was the proof.

"But what about me? I'm entangled and —"

"And you're one of how many?"

Cade couldn't give her a number, but she knew it was a small one. How many of those babies from the filmstrip had made it as far as she and Xan had? How many had been hunted down by the Unmakers? How many pairs were alive, and awake, and together?

Cade's thoughts dead-ended when Ayumi's hand met her knee. But this wasn't a sudden, empty spacesick touch. It was urgent.

"I have to ask, you, Cadence . . . I've found the Express, and the idea of entanglement, all of it at once. There's so much here I need to know. Please don't tell the others about me. Lee . . ." Ayumi blushed, and full-eclipsed her face with her hands. "Lee would want me to leave, I know she would."

Cade had seen that scenario acted out. It would be useless to argue.

It would do no good to have a spacesick onboard, and it would do even less to have a secret spacesick that no one else knew about. It would mean keeping one eye on Ayumi at all times, constant worries and glass-checks. But when Cade opened her mouth to say *drain out,* the words didn't come.

She knew what it meant to be banished from the ship, and she couldn't do that to Ayumi, send her back to a drifting alone-state.

"We'll be in Hades soon," Cade said. "It's a rough place. If this gets worse, you have to go home."

Ayumi put out her hand to shake.

"That's fair," she said. "But, you know . . . you use that word, *home,* incorrectly. Earth was home. We lost the one place we were made for, Cadence. And space wants us back."

Cade left Ayumi in the hold, up to her elbows in Human Express cargo, safe from the siren wail of space. Cade couldn't talk about all that emptiness anymore. She needed to feel something.

She stopped in the mess and stuffed herself with whatever Rennik had been planning to transform into dinner. Sheets of crackers and heels of bread and ropes of salty dried meat. She went at the shelves with abandon and stepped back, so over-full she lurched in the false-grav. But the food didn't make a dent in what she was not-feeling. She headed up the chute again, through the square tunnel, and into the furtive little bedroom.

Moon-White was just where Cade had left her.

She picked up the guitar and struck it without thinking, without planning, big careless sounds that spread into a song. The notes were so close to perfect that Cade could have pushed them to it, but it didn't seem to matter. She had gotten too used to an audience. Even when she thought she didn't want them at Club V they had been there, caring when she couldn't.

She tossed the guitar on the bed and curled herself around it. She pulled the sheets up and tucked in close to the wall.

Then she remembered Renna.

She put one hand on the wall and plucked an open chord. Renna found the beat and gave it back to her in little bursts. Cade strummed and strummed until her fingertips blistered.

It was the best conversation she'd had all day.

Cade couldn't get herself out of the pale desert between asleep and awake. Her arms hung loose around Moon-White, but she hadn't played in hours. Lee twitched and snored in the top bunk.

Cade walked on soft feet, slid through the tunnel that connected her to the ship's open spaces.

She headed up the chute to the control room, where she found the pilot's chair empty and the panels dimmed, the brass needles sliding along their dials. The starglass beckoned.

Cade stood in its light-flecked embrace and turned in circles. The first time she could pick out stars from space, but after that it became a blur of black and white, black and white, until the universe went gray. She didn't stop until she hit a patch of black so pure that it almost shone.

Cade stepped toward it and reached out a careful hand — as if even from this distance, her fingertips would be able to feel the desperate pull that waited inside of that black.

Hades.

Cade sent it in a flash to Xan. The word, and its twin — the vision in the starglass. In that moment between seeing and thinking — the moment of understanding — she reached for him.

And what she found was more than comfort, although he sent her that. It was more than a firework of eagerness, although he sent that, too.

When Cade and Xan had first connected on Andana, she'd been overwhelmed by these sensations, the Xan-feelings in her head. But now she was alive to what the connection did to *her* — the amplification of her feelings, the reception of her body, the trembling possibilities of her mind.

Cade sent flashes of Hades, flashes of the brave stars clustered around it, flashes of the ship. He sent her a strong, unbroken line of pulses, to let her know that he could see it all, and that the view was fine. Each moment that passed back and forth between them centered and grounded her.

I missed you, Cade thought.

But this was more than a simple missing. The lack of him had set her adrift.

Cade had been sending flashes. Now she asked Xan to come and spend a minute on the ship.

See what I see, she thought. *Leave the Unmakers and come to me.*

Even before she reached him, she could be his escape.

She steadied herself against the panels and closed her eyes. When she blinked them open, Xan was with her.

And all of a sudden, she couldn't be still. She ran down the chute, through the night-stilled cabins, past the crates in the cargo hold, past the closed doors. Her muscles stretched wide, her throat opened and released an unfamiliar sound. Cade leapt and rushed, running her hands along the walls and floors as she did, drumming Renna out of her half-sleep, so Xan could feel the racket of life against Cade's fingers. But it wasn't enough. She could feel them both, wanting more. She shed clothes as she went, so he could have the touch of nighttime on her skin. She ran her hands down her arms and sides and stomach, so he could have that, too. Xan pushed her whole body toward wildness, and Cade didn't hold back. He'd been captive for too long. And so had she—on the wrong planets, with the Noise, on ships that never sailed fast enough. So she ran, Xan streaming in her, air hard against her, as she twisted back up the chute to the starglass.

She stared out at Hades and for the first time knew she was looking at him.

Cade woke up to thousands of stars and her whole body warm against the floor. It felt softer than a floor had any right to be.

"Thanks," she mumbled to Renna. She curled up tighter and sighed and almost went back to sleep.

But a firm hand on her shoulder put a stop to that.

"Cadence."

She looked up and saw Rennik on the other side of the starglass, his arm broken through the black, his four-knuckled fingers resting on her shoulder, just below the curve of her neck.

"Cadence?"

Rennik's hand felt nice, so she let it rest there, his thumb anchored across her collarbone — until she looked past that thumb to the rest of her almost-naked self. Cade bolted to sitting. In one quick-strewn flash, she remembered the trail of clothes she'd left up and down the chute.

"Damp hell." Cade went so all-over red that she was glad the thin curtain of the starglass stood between them to mute the shade. A thick vein of anger ran through her embarrassment, even though she knew that wasn't fair — Rennik had every right to wake her up if she was sleeping in the middle of his control room.

He knelt across from her, his lips in a ready shape, like there were words he might have to say at any moment. His eyes full-open so the double pupils showed. Cade had to admit that Rennik's predictable face had settled on a new expression. But it was one she didn't have the translation for.

Cade had lost her dignity along with her clothes, but she would have given the last shred — of the dignity, at least — to connect with Rennik in a way that would help her understand him. Give her answers to the questions that she could never seem to crack the surface of. Did he miss his home, or did Hatch not mean home to him? Why did he slog humans all over the universe? Did he ever regret taking Cade onboard? Was he regretting it right now?

Cade curved her back and set her chin to her knees, so he was mostly seeing her face and the short double lines of her shins.

"I promise you won't find me running around again in any state of undress." She flashed back to the button incident, and added, "Ever."

Cade got up and scrambled out of the far side of the starglass, so there were two coats of darkness and a thick layer of starshine between them.

"It's not that," Rennik said, dusting his knees as he stood. Cade watched him closely. "Well, you should probably deal with that, but . . . as soon as you do . . . I have something to show you."

"Now?" she asked, spotting the nearest piece of clothing — a sock — at the top of the chute.

Rennik cut wide around the starglass, picked up the sock, and tossed it to her in an easy white arc.

"I think you'll want to see this, yes."

Cade struggled the flimsy bit of cotton as far up her calf as it would go. Now she was almost-naked except for a sock. Perfect. Her instinct was to get clear, avoid Rennik until — forever. But there was a first-class reason to stick around. The last time Rennik wanted to show her something, it had been Moon-White.

"Is it a bass?" she asked.

"No."

"Drums?"

"You need to see it," Rennik repeated. His calm made her want to put fingers to metal and shred chords into little tiny pieces. If it wasn't music, and it wasn't Xan, how much would she care about what he wanted to show her? But Rennik's face turned urgent and his hands spread eager, and Cade wanted to know all over again.

"Fine."

She ran ahead and gathered her clothes, one item at a time, slinging them on in the order she found them. Rennik gave her a healthy lead. After a minute he followed her down to the main cabin and nodded her into his room.

They fit too neatly in the small space. It was hard not to think about how recently all that skin had been exposed.

"Please sit," Rennik said, pointing at the desk.

She took the curved chair. He sat on the bed.

"I've been looking at this." Rennik reached into his pocket and held out the circle-glass. "Where it splices, there are bits missing from the playback. Did you know that? At first I thought they'd been cut, but that's not right. They weren't taken out at all. They're still in here, but someone pinched them."

"Pinched?" Cade forgot her skin and its recent state and leaned in, over the shine-washed facets of the circle-glass. "What else is in there?"

She had always known there must be more to her story — what it meant to be entangled. But she had been so fixed on finding a way to Xan that the rest of it tended to slide when she wasn't looking.

"I haven't been able to restore it all," Rennik said.

"But . . . some of it?" Cade asked, a hoarse shred of hope in her voice. She wondered if Rennik heard it — or if the great crashing symphony of her human emotions was as bewildering to him as his one-note Hatchum face was to her.

"There's a section . . ." he said, reaching past her to the desk to pick up the projection lamp. "A section I managed to restore to its full length." Rennick palmed the circle-glass. It looked at home in his hand as he turned it.

"I haven't gone through it," Rennik said. "It felt wrong to watch it without you."

Cade nodded.

Renna dimmed the lights and the room grew quiet. Rennik fitted the circle-glass to the lamp and it threw a square of gold onto the wall, which turned into a scene.

A familiar scene. Cadence and Xan, diapered and crib-bound. "These two are optimally suited for entanglement. Our greatest hope lies with them."

A new stretch of film sprang up where before there'd been a hot white scar. Scientists at work in another part of the lab, surrounded by the most delicate possible equipment — petri dishes and glass droppers and splinter-thin vials.

"Xan is part of our control group — designed and conceived for the purposes of Project QE. All genetic material has been configured for optimal space resistance and entanglement potential."

A lab-coated man with close-shaven hair and perfectly square teeth held up a petri dish and smiled.

"Cadence, on the other hand, is from the organic group. These children have biological origins. They were planet-born, with no influence or assistance from Firstbloom. More impressively, Cadence's genetic material comes to us from the spacesick subset. Her biological father was a pilot out of the Tirith belt. He flew for an almost unheard-of twelve years before experiencing the first symptoms."

A picture flashed. Dark hair. Light brown skin. Green eyes. A scowl to beat back the sunrise. Cade's father, through and through.

"He died on a routine run during a sudden fit of spacesick."

Cade heard the words, but she didn't feel them. She couldn't not have a father one second, have one the next second, and then lose him again. He washed over her like an unbroken wave.

"Cadence is Project QE's greatest success," the filmstrip pushed on, "and its greatest surprise. Perhaps her father's resistance to spacesick has something to do with her aptitude for entanglement.

"Or perhaps the answer lies with Cadence's mother."

The woman on the wall—Cade knew her and she didn't. The little white flowers on the blue dress, sky-bright against her skin. That image was captured on the day the woman visited Firstbloom. The day she stood in a corner and cried. The day she gave up her daughter.

CHAPTER 15

LONG-TERM POTENTIATION A lasting
enhancement in signal transmission between
neurons, with implications for learning and
memory

It happened in a Firstbloom nursery.

The people stood out against a painful shade of white. Cade inspected the cribs, found the little pale smudge most likely to be Xan. A scientist scuttled back and forth, rocking cribs with one hand and taking notes with the other.

And then there was the woman. Blue dress, white flowers. Her eyes so glassy you couldn't see their color. Her steps loose, muscles limp. She carried Cadence in her arms. Almost dropped her twice.

A white-coated woman with a comfortable manner eased the baby out of her arms. A stocky man smiled and told her that they'd take good care of her little girl.

Cade could have reached back in time and punched that smile to pulp.

But her mother just nodded, up and down, up and down,

too many times. Until the scientists told her she could leave.

That's when Cade found out one of her memories was wrong. When her mother stepped back to the corner of the nursery, she didn't cry.

Cadence did.

Wailed in her crib, face red with the welling of blood under her skin, reaching for her mother with too-small hands.

"As you can see, Cadence was saved from a life with a mother in the advanced stages of—"

The voice cut out. The picture disappeared.

Cade lost the next ten minutes of her life.

Her head went as white as the now blank wall. She stood up, knocked the chair back, collapsed into a heap on the bed. Rennik sprang up and asked her something—asked her what? She could see the deep curves of his lips in motion, could see the concern sunk into his steady expression, but that was it. The silence inside of her was complete. She waded through shock without moving.

"He never told me," Cade said. "He never told me . . ."

Rennik took a careful seat on the far end of the bed and spoke to her in soft tones. "Who?"

"Mr. Niven. When they sent him to find me. He never told me about . . . her."

Rennik turned the circle-glass over and over in his hands. "It's possible he didn't know."

The silence stirred. Underneath it, anger expanded, pushing into the vacuum where Cade's feelings should be.

"He knew," Cade said. She remembered the lie now, in crisp detail. "Told me he was there on the night I was born. He kept her from me, because he was afraid I might take off after her instead."

Rennik studied her from his perch at the end of the bed. "Would you have done that?"

It was such an unfair question. The amount of heat it generated inside of her could have kept a small sun burning for years.

"Yes," Cade said. "No. I don't know." She settled on the answer. "No. She's been spacesick for years — if she's even alive — and I need to get to Xan. He needs me." It was the chant that drew her on, past the planets, past the stars, toward black holes.

"He needs me."

And for the first time, she hated Xan for it.

This was too much to need, and she had never asked for him. She had hoped for a mother, but she had never been brave or foolish enough to ask for one. And now a mother had been given to her in ten seconds of unpinched film.

After too much space, the nondays and nonnights, the blue of her mother's dress flooded Cade like morning.

She stood up and filled the small room. "I have to know if she's out there."

Cade expected Rennik to say something reasonable and useless, about charting courses and distances to and from Hades and how many people there were out there on how many planets and how they would never, ever find her.

Instead he looked up at her, his eyes so steady, she didn't need to be planetbound to feel grounded.

"Of course."

Surprise stopped Cade's whole body for a beat. There was something in that answer, something about Rennik, that she didn't understand. But there was no time to untangle it.

"I can't change the course," she said. "I still have to get to Xan."

"Right."

"Stop agreeing with me," Cade said. "It's making me nervous."

Rennik smiled, and Cade — somehow — laughed.

Rennik put the circle-glass on the bed. "You care about them," he said. "Both of them."

Cade ran a finger along one of the facets of the glass. "The scientists thought I was some kind of wonder child. So I'll do what can't be done. I'll find them both."

After a few bites of breakfast, Cade put whatever scraps of a plan she had into action. First, she enlisted Lee and Ayumi, who were in the cargo hold sorting Human Express deliveries. Lee named items and checked them off a long list. Ayumi reached for each one with a fresh-ignited fire. Cade would have felt bad interrupting if she didn't know Ayumi had seen all of it at least four times by now.

"We're going to find my mother," Cade said.

Ayumi dropped an armful of fluttery papers. "I didn't think you had a—"

"Neither did I."

"But this changes your story!" Ayumi said. "I'll have to write it down. There are endless ramifications—"

"Which we're not going to talk about right now." Ramifications threaded through Cade's mind on an endless loop. She didn't need help on that count.

Lee shrugged. "I'm getting used to the strange revelations," she said. "But if you're a sand-slug pretending to be a girl who's *pretending* to be entangled, you should tell me right now."

"Where are we going?" Ayumi asked. She tensed from fingers to toes and flicked a glance toward the dock where her little ship waited.

"Not space," Cade said. "Here. On the ship."

"Can't get into too much trouble on the ship," Lee said. "Can we?"

The ground rippled underneath them, unsettling their feet. That was Renna, telling a joke.

Cade led Ayumi and Lee through the main cabin. They didn't have far to go, and there was only one preparation to make.

Cade checked her pocket for the seven-blade knife, snapped and safe in its little cloth bed.

"Meet our guide," she said, as they rounded the second twist in the chute.

Lee's lips pinched together on one side, unimpressed.

"Gori?"

He was stretched out on his bunk, head propped up on pillows, not sleeping.

"Right," Cade said. "Gori."

He didn't look up from his musings on his own feet.

"Gori," Cade tried again. "Hey. Gori? Darkrider?"

This was an interesting turn. Ever since Cade set foot on the ship all Gori had done was stare at her. While she was eating, talking, passing by. He pinned those glossy eyes on her and didn't let up. Stared without stopping, without shame, without a *Sorry for all of that staring.* And now that she needed him to look up, he couldn't be bothered.

"What happened before, with us, was an accident," Cade said. "I guess I never got the chance to tell you that."

Gori didn't budge. He wasn't even noticeably breathing.

Lee elbowed her way to the bunk. Crossed her arms and took up as much space as possible — short of puffing herself out in a rapture state. "Look. Cade here wants to talk to you. She's doing you the favor of making it out loud and not in your head, so listen up."

Gori's eyes rose slightly. He spoke to his kneecaps.

"If the girl breaches the mind of a Darkrider, she has to be killed."

"That's a lovely sentiment," Lee said. "But that's not what the girl . . . what Cade . . . wants to do."

"Look," Cade said. "The more I know about my . . . abilities, the more I can control them, the less likely I am to go barging into your brainspace, right?"

Gori stared at her.

"That's more like it," Cade muttered.

But now that she had Gori's attention, she wasn't quite sure how to handle it — it was a delicate thing, and a dangerous one — glass that could crack at the simplest touch. Cade fumbled for words to keep the moment intact.

She would never have guessed Ayumi would be the one to step forward and break the silence.

"Cadence has a purpose," she said. "One that's still forming. But she needs a guide. The universe won't mind if you take a minute away from admiring it. The universe will be here when you get back."

Gori took a break from staring at Cade to stare at Ayumi. She held up well under his scrutiny, drawing herself tall, holding her shoulders back like she might sprout wings. She must have said something that made sense in Gori's differently wired brain, because he nodded and shuffled out of his bunk.

The four of them settled into the common room — not Cade's favorite place, but it was quiet and out of the way. Of Rennik, in particular. Cade wanted to give him time to work on the circle-glass. See what else he could recover.

Gori looked over at Ayumi as she piled up pillows to sit on. "How does she need to be guided?"

"I'm glad you're such great friends now," Cade said, "but you can talk to me."

Gori blinked at Cade and didn't hide the frustration in his snapping lids. "How do you need to be guided?"

"You told me once that I reached out to you, and almost entered your mind," Cade said. "I want to do that on purpose.

To someone else. I need to find someone." She used the word *someone* instead of *mother*, because *mother* was too new. Not a word she was ready to give away.

"You want to find a human?" Gori asked. "One human?"

Cade knew that she should only care about finding Xan —in her mind or out in the universe. And not just because the Unmakers had him. She got the feeling that other people weren't supposed to matter as much once you were entangled. But she couldn't forget the picture of her mother huddled in a corner of Firstbloom.

"Yeah, that's right," Cade said in small tones, but not backing away from the words. "I have one human to find."

Gori turned to Ayumi again, his blinks speeding in tempo. "You see how this is useless."

"I would beg to differ," Ayumi said. "You don't know what she's capable of. There's nothing useless about Cadence."

"Cadence can hear you," she said. "Cadence feels much more useful when you *talk to her.*"

Gori sighed and looked at Cade. Or maybe he had never looked *at* her, even with all of that staring. Maybe he looked near her. His eyes reminded her of two flies, dark and impatient, searching for a place to land.

"At least she's listening," Gori said. "Now listen to this: be careful."

A friendly reminder that if their lesson soured, he might be forced to slit her throat.

Gori took a breath so deep that it seemed to reshape the

room, suck in the walls. Cade watched for the first sign of the expansion that would turn Gori into a mountain of dark energy. His arms lifted and his chest inched out. His wrinkles filled in like dried-out riverbanks, flooding.

"To begin connecting is to open," Gori said. "To open yourself is a task. You have to set yourself to this task as often as you can, in order to relearn the borders between self and not-self."

"Cade's not exactly a novice at this," Lee said, bristling with borrowed pride. "She's entangled."

"Yes," Gori said. "I, too, saw the little movie."

"So shouldn't this be easy?" Cade asked.

"There is easy and there is possible." He breathed in, puffed out. "Entanglement is a matter of particles. It is a collapse. All space is one space. All time is one time. Entangled particles know that."

"But we don't live that way," Lee said. "We'd all be on top of each other, for one thing." A shiver worked its way up her shoulders. "Squishy."

"The human with the knotted head is right," Gori said. "For all particles to exist in such a state at all times, there would be no universe as we know it. So we have selves and we have boundaries and we have your mind and we have this other mind."

He waved his ballooning hand at Cade. "The girl —"

"Cadence," Ayumi said.

Gori stared at her, perfectly still.

Ayumi's curls shivered, but she stood her ground. "If you know the names of all the stars in the universe, you can learn one more."

Gori moved on. "Cadence has grown used to a quick and direct channel . . . a shortcut . . . that connects her to a single human. But to find another, she has to leave the safety of the channel. She has to be open to all."

"But I only want one," Cade said.

The woman in the blue dress.

Cade had a mother, and that fact could knock her down at any moment. Capsize her. She had to push it deep in a safe place just so she could see straight, just so she could walk. But even then, she felt different. Knowing that her mother was real, and might be out there, had tipped her inner balance.

"So this is how I find her?" Cade asked. "By finding . . . everyone?"

It sounded like the opposite of what she meant to do. It sounded like crossing the deserts on Andana and getting lost on purpose, in order to find your way. You'd end up dead of thirst or, at the least, scraped so raw with sand you'd never be able to look at a grain of it without screaming.

"Give it a try," Ayumi said.

Gori nodded and breathed and grew.

Cade settled into her pillows. "One little thing," she said. "How do I open myself?"

"Whatever you were doing last time will be a start," Gori said.

Cade closed her eyes. Last time, she had been reaching for

Xan. She had been wanting to get to him. She had been un-buttoning her shirt, too, but she hoped that wasn't an impor-tant part of the equation.

Cade breathed deep. She tried to hold it in, the way Gori did, but the air sat in her lungs and weighed them down like stones. So she breathed normally. Picked a point across the room. She let everything else melt around it, in the strange but simple way that harmonies bend themselves around the strength of a melody.

Cade was afraid that if she reached for Xan, that's exactly who she would find. So instead she reached — and *didn't* look for him. Just reached. Like stretching a muscle she didn't know she had. Soon she was straining and dripping, hot and sweaty-cold at the same time. The harmonies grew thick, and pushing out into the air was like walking through music.

Then, a new song.

Fierce and bright, with bursting high notes, sudden plunges, and the wild, sliding rhythms of a fiddle.

She could tell, somehow, that this was Lee.

It wasn't music, really, but that's what it sounded like to Cade. This was raw thought, the kind she'd first heard on An-dana. Thought without words, thought without laid-on form.

And then another song. Harmonies that spread and then weaved themselves back together, flecked with warmth.

Ayumi.

Cade could hear both of them at the same time. She could move from one to the other, dial in and out. She could get close — but she couldn't go farther than that. She didn't have access to them the way she did with Xan. She couldn't drop into their minds and make herself at home in their bodies. Lee and Ayumi were sealed rooms, and she was listening through their windows.

Something else trembled at the edge of what she could hear.

It started with a shiver of sound and then broke wide, symphonic, all the colors of the sky, all the shades of light and dark, night and day, notes streaming through her body like wind.

Gori.

Snug. Gori.

Cade pulled back, but it was too late. He came at her across the room, still puffed out to mountain size. She grabbed the seven-blade knife and waved it around with vague aim. Lee leapt at the Darkrider and took him to the floor, landing them both on pillows. Ayumi stood back, all overwhelmed eyes and alarm, but at the last second she jumped in and twisted one of Gori's arms. He condensed to his smaller state in two blinks.

"Now, what do you have to say for yourself?" Lee asked, sitting on his back to keep him down.

Gori wrenched his neck to look up at Cade, eyes dark as a bitter-cold night without stars.

"The girl came too close."

But Cade hadn't gone far enough. Her mind hadn't left the ship. It hadn't even left the *room.* She would never find her mother at that rate.

She backed out of the common area, through the main

cabin, into the cargo hold. She wasn't sure what she was doing there — not being in the common room, for one thing. At some point, Gori was going to stop with the threats and start with the slicing.

Cade planted herself in the cargo hold and watched as the others drained out one by one. Gori first, up the chute and back to his bunk. Lee crossed the main cabin to the mess, covered in feathers from the explosion of pillows.

Ayumi headed out last, and Cade followed.

The inside of the little ship looked the same as Cade remembered it. Bathed in suns, moons, and space. Ayumi crouched on the pilot's seat with her legs tucked underneath. She looked out the window at the real, streaking-by stars.

"Hey," Cade said.

Ayumi smiled without looking up.

"Cadence," she said. "It's nice of you to visit."

"You said, in there, that I have a purpose, that it's still forming. What did you mean?"

Ayumi kept her eyes on the dust of a distant nebula.

"We live according to a purpose. At least, on Rembra we do." Her eyes warmed with the delights of explanation. "Lee has the Express. Rennik seems to have tasked himself with helping humans." She scanned Cade up and down as if a purpose was something that could hide in her eyes, or shine out through her skin. "You have one, too. I'm sure of it."

Ayumi turned back to the window. A bit of spark went out of her eyes, traded in for glass.

"Hey," Cade said. "Look at me." She turned up the volume.

"Ayumi." Maybe if she blasted her words as loud as her music, Ayumi could be bullied back into herself.

"Look at me!"

Ayumi's hands sat loose on the panels, fingers slack against buttons. Cade's voice wasn't enough to snap her out of her infinite space-love and back to the human scale.

Ayumi had spoken words in the cargo hold that came back to Cade now, clear as the thin window that shielded their skin from space. Words about touch. About the body reminding itself to be human.

"Dregs," Cade muttered.

Since she'd connected to Xan, the idea of touching had gotten an upgrade — from unwanted to complicated. What she did with him felt like touching, and more than touching, and not-enough, all at once. She had started to like the fact of fingers on her skin, but the time between thought and touch-down made her sick, and the sensations lit her up like a hard-dragged match.

Cade claimed the arm of the navigator's chair and leaned in, cut the distance in half.

"Ayumi," she said, voice dialed all the way down. "Hey."

Cade patted her shoulder. She ran her fingers down the grain of Ayumi's sleeve until it hit softness at the elbow, then trailed down her forearm to the wrist. She fit her other hand to the blank curve of Ayumi's face.

She looked up, gasping, face drawn wide with hurt. "What are you doing?"

Cade had torn her Ayumi away from something she loved — and it showed.

"Sorry," Cade muttered. But she wasn't sorry for keeping Ayumi from her precious void. She wasn't even sorry for the pain.

One blink at a time, Ayumi traveled all the way back to herself. But there was still the uncomfortable fact — Cade had promised that she would send the girl home if her spacesick went into overdrive. The moment had come, and Cade paced away from it.

"So how do I figure out this purpose?"

Ayumi swung around in her chair so she faced Cade, blocking out the stars. She seemed grateful for the change of subject, pleased to leave the bout of spacesick behind them, untouched.

"This is how we understand it where I'm from," she said. "A purpose is three things, in roughly equal parts. What you can do, what you choose to do, and what needs to be done."

Ayumi held up her notebooks. They still looked flimsy to Cade, but Ayumi treated them better than treasure. "What I can do is read, and write, and fly. I've always liked people, so I chose something that meant people . . . learning about them, being around them." Cade couldn't imagine choosing that, not in a thousand blinked-out years. "What Rembra needed was a new Earth keeper. We've always had one. Put all of that together, and you have a purpose."

Ayumi made it sound natural. Easy. But Cade had too many

things to do and no idea if any of them *could* be done. She ticked the tasks off in her head.

Rescue Xan. Find her mother. Change the fate of the human race.

She looked out the scroll of window into the black, and for the first time the untouchable hugeness of it didn't make her feel small. It only made her itch. Cade couldn't help feeling that she would lose everything to it, even if she was entangled and — supposedly — strong. Space could keep her apart from Xan for too long. It had claimed her parents. It would claim her friends.

"I need your ship," Cade said. "For the mission."

This was why she couldn't send Ayumi home, even though she knew it was the right thing to do. For a while, the splinter of an idea had been working its way deep into Cade's mind. There was no way she could ask Lee and the others to face the Unmakers again — they had risked too much. But this would be a clean trade. As long as she could keep Ayumi conscious.

"I thought I told you I couldn't fly —"

"Into Hades. I know."

Ayumi shifted to inner-battle mode. "I want so much to help, Cadence, but —"

"I know it's a lot of black holes. But the boy waiting for us on the other side? You could fill a whole notebook with him."

Ayumi clutched the frayed stack to her chest.

Cade banged on Rennik's door, then banged again in the pattern of Lee's so-called secret knock.

Rennik pulled the door open and smiled when he saw Cade. She remembered when she'd first boarded and was sure he'd never cast one of those smiles anywhere near her.

"Progress?" she asked.

He shook his head and shifted to the side so Cade could stop jittering and step into the little room. He must have been able to read her signs better than she could read his.

She honed in on the circle-glass sitting on the desk. One of its facets was hinged and Rennik had swung it open, making a tiny door. She touched the thin edge like secrets might spring out.

"How does it work?"

"The material is threaded in intricate shapes and calcified into crystals, which undergo a chemical change during the playback," he said. "The pinched sections are stuck, unchangeable. Here," he said, centering the circle-glass on the desk. "If you hold it still and I have both hands to work, things might move along better."

Cade nodded and leaned over the desk. Rennik leaned in from another angle, face lowered as he worked. His fingers brushed up against hers over and over in their little motions.

"Why are you doing this?" she asked.

Rennik snatched his hands back, and Cade lit up with a certain kind of triumph. She'd finally managed to get a rise out of him. But he just pushed his fingertips together and arched his palms. Then he stretched his neck — the stiffness released as a low, hollow crack. He'd been at it for hours.

"The tech is interesting," he said. "Renna and I are fascinated."

"I meant this," Cade said. "All of it. Helping me. And Lee. Helping—"

"Humans?"

Rennik returned to the desk, but he didn't touch the circle-glass. He ran a finger along the spines of his books. "Sometimes I feel more human than Hatchum," he said. "I've always been quite . . . different."

That fit with what Lee had told Cade when they first boarded the ship. Rennik wasn't like other Hatchum. Cade could understand that. Different From Your Kind. It was a tune she knew forwards and backwards.

"Well," she said. "Thanks."

But the ground under Cade's feet came alive and shuddered with a sort of warning. Cade could read Renna's signs well enough to know—either Rennik was lying, or he was leaving something out.

Cade studied Rennik's face. The soft-molded skin around his eyes. It was hard to imagine him telling a lie. But Cade didn't think he had a hidden stockpile of secrets, either. There was something he wasn't telling her because it was easier not to say.

"Renna thinks there's more."

Rennik lowered his head again, and went back to the minute workings of the circle-glass.

"Does she." It wasn't a question.

Cade put a hand to the wall for backup. "I agree."

Even with his face pointed down, Cade could see that Rennik had gone back to his standard lack-of-expression.

"Lee told you about Moira."

Moira. Cade hadn't been expecting that name. "I know that she was . . ." Cade stopped herself short of saying *killed by the Unmakers*. "She was part of the Human Express. I know that you sometimes flew them, Lee and Moira."

"Yes," he said, "but there's more to that story."

Cade held the circle-glass still, the edges sunk into her fingertips.

"I was different from other Hatchum," he said. "Always. Only a little, but it was enough that others noticed. My parents were the first to point it out and name it. Do you want to know how they could tell I was different?"

Cade nodded.

"I loved them too much."

Rennik's answer was full orbits away from what Cade would have guessed. He suffered from an excess of emotion — at least, in Hatchum terms. So he was the opposite of what Cade had been — moving through most of her life not-getting-too-close as a point, not-getting-too-close because it was what came to her as smooth and obvious as breathing.

"Hatchum are loyal to the group," he said. "Always. Creating a bond with one that could be stronger than the bond with any other is treasonous."

Cade remembered what Lee had said a long time ago, when they first met, about the ship that blinked its black eyes, rolled out a scratchy pink tongue.

"But you did make strong bonds," Cade said. "Renna."

"Right." Rennik lit up at her name. "She kept growing

because I paid her more attention, cared for her more than I was supposed to. I talked to her, taught her languages, read her stories at night. But she had to be hidden, so others wouldn't know.

"And then Moira came," he said. "Then there was no hiding it."

There were two things now — the story, and the fact that Rennik was touching her as he told it. His hands nudging into hers, without comment, as he worked on the circle-glass. Cade was aware of these things, like two melodies played at the same time. Clashing at one moment, complementing each other the next.

Either way — distracting.

"I had taken to flying with Renna," he said, "at night of course, so we wouldn't be seen . . . making short runs from Hatch to the nearby planets. I took passengers out of curiosity. We carried Wexians and Highleans, Toths, even Andanans. Lee and Moira were the first humans I took on. Lee had always wanted to see a Hatchum, and I guess I didn't disappoint."

Rennik's hands canted at a strange angle — Cade spun the circle-glass so he could get to what he needed.

"Lee was mostly scraped knees when I met her. And Moira . . . Moira was beautiful." Rennik's whole body shifted, like the word was a note and he was tuning himself to it. "You hear humans talk about beauty, and it makes no sense. All Hatchum are beautiful, in the sense that they're well constructed, strong, with fine features. But Moira was less than that, and more at the same time. Imperfect. Fierce. In love with too much."

Cade couldn't see his eyes now; they were turned away. All she could do was hold tight to the circle-glass.

"You loved her."

An echo of a long-gone snatch of gossip.

Hatchum don't snug humans.

Rennik looked straight at Cade. "It would have happened either way. But the fact of being with a human made the whole thing worse." He redoubled his attack on the circle-glass. "I was sent away from Hatch when my family found out, but they were saving me, in a way. If the Hatch Consortium knew, they wouldn't have been so kind as to let me keep my freedom, my orbital, and four working limbs."

Cade lined her words up with care, still working it out. "A human was important to you once, so you keep humans safe?"

"Something like that."

Renna grumbled under her feet again, but another sound caught Cade's attention—

The insides of the circle-glass clicked.

"Here," Rennik said. "Cadence, look . . ."

He grabbed the projection lamp and she grabbed the circle-glass and they landed on the bed at the same time. Cade told herself it was just the best angle for watching a picture on the wall. Rennik fitted the circle-glass to the lamp, but she pulled the whole thing out of his hands, too impatient to wait for him to light it up.

The voice lurched in first, picking up where it left off.

" . . . spacesick. In her life before that, Cadence's mother was a musician. The effects of music treatment have been studied on spacesicks for over a hundred years but found to be insufficient in curing even the mildest cases on a permanent basis. Still, the fact of Cadence's entanglement could give us reason to reexamine this connection."

The picture caught up—small and grainy, less than a square foot on the wall. The woman in the blue dress was there, but this time in white. A summer dress. Outdoors on some forest planet. This was old footage, not from Firstbloom, spliced in from somewhere else. It was her mother, but she looked young—not Cade's age, but not much older. Her hair was a wild mess of braids and more of it trailed down, almost kissing the ground when she sat. She had an acoustic guitar in her lap and a harmonica strapped in front of her chin.

She was going to play.

Cade watched—her mouth dropped and her heart swollen. The song was sweetness and pain and it meant so many things to Cade that she could only begin to sift through them, sort them out. Her mother had lips just like hers and when they opened, her voice was a signal, a call across a crowded room. There were no words—just notes. It was the sort of song that Cade loved most. Made up on the spot. A song that seemed to wander instead of heading in a straight line, with threads that came back to remind you of the best parts.

Cade had always thought her music was a knee-jerk reaction to the Noise. But here was her own mother, to tell her she'd been wrong.

Cade wondered if she should be sharing all of this with Xan. But she couldn't imagine he'd take comfort in a few grainy frames of a woman he didn't know. And the fact that she was Cade's mother snarled things up even more. Xan didn't have a mother. If the filmstrip had told the truth this time, he never would. Once Cade shared this, it would open a new tract of space between them.

The footage died out where the cut would have been. Rennik bent over the projection lamp.

It wouldn't be so hard not to tell. Cade had gotten the sense, more than once, that Xan knew or felt more than he was letting on. And if Rennik had proved one thing, it was that he could help the people he wanted to help, even with a secret.

She reached out for Xan and told him, *I'm almost to Hades.* She told him, *I'm getting close.*

She let her mother go unsaid.

Cade holed up in the bedroom with Moon-White. She was going to teach herself her mother's song if it split her fingertips wide open.

"That's nice." Lee's voice drifted down from the top bunk.

"It's more than nice," Cade said. "It's the best song I know."

"Yeah," Lee said, her fingers dancing in the air above Cade's head. "It's pretty close to perfect."

Lee sat up in her bunk and started to dance. She worked her shoulders back and closed her eyes and when a strong note crested, she tossed her head. Lee wasn't a dancer — she and the beat were passing acquaintances at best.

But it made Cade miss Club V. Not the wince of strong drinks or the armpit smells or the dressing room after the show. The audience. She thought back to them — their wild arms and their hardworking legs, all moving in their own ways, all moving together. And the spacesicks, always in the front rows, crushed in close. How much they cared about her music. How hard they were fighting to connect to it.

It all came to her in one downbeat.

The spacesicks, using her music to connect to something that wasn't nothingness. The song. Her mother. Music and spacesicks. Raw thought, how much like music it sounded. How much she needed to get to Xan, get to her mother, get to everyone. Reaching and opening at the same time.

"Yeah," she mumbled. "Perfect."

She kept playing. Lee kept dancing. But now Cade let herself go to that focused place where everything melted to music. She reached out and opened herself to whoever might be listening.

Lee gasped and hit her head on the ceiling.

"Cade," she said. "What did you just . . . ?"

Lee rubbed her head with one hand and grabbed the edge of the bunk with the other so she could lean over the side.

Cade stared her down, daring her to believe it.

There was a knock at the panel. Cade rushed to pull it

aside. It was Ayumi, her eyes wide — and so brown that there was no other word to describe them but Earth.

"Cadence . . . did you just play music inside my head?"

"Yeah," she said. "I think I did."

The three of them looked at each other, and Cade heard echoes of the song. Lee touched her temple. Ayumi's smile cracked so wide, it could have split the room in half.

"Brass."

CHAPTER 16

MIXED STATE An ensemble composed of several quantum states

From that moment, Cade and Moon-White couldn't be torn apart. One day left until the ship hit Hades, and she planned to spend the whole thing with her guitar strapped on, sending music to anyone who would listen.

Renna was the first one she added to her audience. After a few more minutes of her mother's song, Cade sensed a low thrum past Lee's mind and Ayumi's mind and all around. It didn't move to the same beat as the human thoughts. It was lower, steadier, with a tidelike swish and thump.

Cade modulated down a few keys and tried to play something Renna would like, but it was hard to know what a living, breathing ship would like. Cade did her best, imitating the rhythms of Renna's flight and sprinkling them with the pulses she sometimes felt in the walls.

Sudden knocks sharpened the air. Like applause.

She wondered if that was why Renna had given her the guitar in the first place.

Cade ran up to the control room with Moon-White, Lee marching behind her, Ayumi following them with a dancelike shuffle.

Cade found Rennik studying a chart of Hades, as old as dust and about to flutter to pieces. She didn't wait for him to look up before she launched into her topic of choice.

"Hey," she said. "When we first met on Andana. Do you think Renna could have known something about me that I didn't? Something that I just now figured out?"

Rennik rolled the chart enough that Cade couldn't see it. "Renna understands some things that I don't, and I understand some things she doesn't. But don't—"

"Tell her that," Cade said. "I know."

Rennik finished rolling the chart, stepped away from the control panels. "What did you figure out?"

Lee ran forward and grabbed him by the shoulders. "Listen up," she said. "I mean *really snugging listen.*"

Cade focused and found his thoughts—a constant, calming hum, laced with strange rhythms. Fainter than it should have been for someone standing so close.

She moved her hands fast against the tug of Moon-White's strings, built up a neat little intro, and—

—smacked the downbeat. Double-hard.

Rennik tipped his head down and shook it like he needed to dump water out of his ear.

"That's . . . nice."

"Nice?" she said. She wanted *fantastic, first-class, impossible.* She wanted anything but . . . *nice.*

"Did you hear it?" Cade asked. "I mean, I know that you heard it. But . . ." she touched his temple. "Here?"

Rennik nodded and sidestepped down the panels. "Interesting. Very interesting. But I'm not human, remember, Cade? A great deal of what makes music appealing is based on species."

"What is that supposed to mean?" she asked, following him as he drifted.

"The songs that sound best to you," he said. "Do you know why you like them?"

The tough girl showed up for the first time in days, crossing Cade's arms, pursing Cade's lips. She didn't need to know what she liked about music. Wasn't it enough that she liked *something?* That there was at least one thing worth liking in the whole senseless universe?

Cade thought tough girl had settled in for a long stay, but Rennik threw her off when he started to sing. In a well-pitched voice, he hummed a note and then another note above it — a fifth.

The sound hit Cade in all the right places. She picked it up on Moon-White.

"That," Rennik said, "sounds pleasant to you because it mimics the sound humans make when they're happy. And this" — he hummed two trembling notes, a minor third — "means sadness because it mimics the sound of human grief. Do you know why you like songs that repeat with slight variation? So do your bio-rhythms."

"All right, all right," Cade said. Rennik's little lesson would have been first-class intolerable if it wasn't so fascinating.

Cade thought of the special music she'd played for Renna. Maybe she had to do the same thing for Rennik. So she left her mother's song behind. This called for a strict time signature, finger-picking. She worked out something that sounded calm, but wasn't — like the rush of water under a skin of ice.

Rennik listened politely, but it was clear from the slight lean toward the control panel that he wanted to get back to his charts.

"I did fine with Renna," Cade muttered. "Do you even *like* music?"

Rennik shrugged. Even his shrug was graceful. "Maybe I don't."

"Yeah," said Lee, reverting to her ancient tendency to be on Rennik's side. "Maybe he doesn't."

But the faint, far-off hum of his thoughts told Cade a different story. Maybe Rennik cared for music, and maybe he didn't. But she could feel one thing for sure. He wasn't open to it.

Lee was a good listener, but it was Ayumi who loved the songs most, who sat and tuned in through dinner instead of eating, eyes closed and spoon trailing between her bowl and her mouth. She followed Cade from the mess to the hold and back again. She asked for more as Cade's fingers flared to match-tips. She asked again long after they'd gone numb.

It felt so good to be listened to like that; Cade went on for hours. She dropped into the bunk and didn't reach for Xan before she passed out cold.

Cade dreamed of mountains. Which didn't make sense, because for days, for weeks, she'd dreamed of Xan or nothing at all. But now she faced down thick-veined slabs, heart-spiking peaks, and sheer drops.

She woke to gray all around. Gray walled her into the bed. It took a few seconds of peering through the thin dark to figure out that the walls were Gori, puffed to the extremes of his rapture state.

Cade tried to slide out of the bunk in three different directions, but Gori's bulk stopped her every time. Her hands flew to her sides, but her fingers remembered a nanosecond before her mind caught up — she'd dropped the seven-blade knife in a pile of dirty clothes. Cade had gotten comfortable and stopped being smart.

"Lee." She couldn't see the other bunks, but at least she knew she wasn't alone. "Lee! Ayumi!"

"The other humans are not here." Gori's voice drifted down to her from somewhere near the ceiling. "I informed them of a rare celestial event, and the Ayumi and the human with the knotted head were consumed with the need to see it. I told them you would be along."

"You thought of everything, didn't you," Cade muttered.

She blinked — and there he was at the side of the bed. The

smaller version of Gori, more negative wrinkle-space than solid matter. He stood between the bunks with his back to her.

"I needed to speak with you."

Cade checked his hands. No weapon. Of course, his robe offered a universe of folds if he wanted to hide one.

"When you say speak, you mean words, right?" Cade asked. "Not the language of knives or pain or something like that?"

Gori turned to face her. If his body was a rock-cluster, his eyes had true bottomless-pit qualities. "There is one way that, even with all of your reaching, I might not have to kill you."

"And that is?" Cade asked—not wanting to get herself into something worse.

"In place of a breach, there is a path. A true, narrow path to be traveled." Gori drew himself as tall as he could in his current state, and gathered a twist of robe over his chest in a formal gesture. "I invite you."

The words reached Cade first, and then a minute later, their meaning screeched into place.

"You came here, in the middle of the night, to my bedroom, while I was sleeping, to invite me to share your rapture state?"

"You touched me again," Gori said. "The need became urgent."

Cade almost laughed at the Darkrider's choice of words, but she didn't think it would help her chances of survival. "This is not the middle-of-the-night visit most girls dream about," Cade said. "But I do wonder what goes on in that wrinkle-scaped head of yours." She pushed to the edge of the bed, lined her knees up to one side of Gori's, locked on to his dark eyes.

"Will this path help me find my mother?"

"It will alter your relationship to the universe."

Cade's breath hammered thin. Leave it to Gori to give her a nonanswer.

"What do you *do* when you're rapturing?"

"I feel."

Cade nodded, but it was a shallow nod. Something inside of her didn't want to snap the cord and fall into trusting him.

"Is it dangerous?"

"To open yourself to everything?" Gori asked. "To let the universe, seen and unseen, known and unknown, reclaim its rightful place inside you, streaming through cells, threatening to burst them? To—"

"I get it, I get it," Cade said.

"No." Gori closed his eyes. "But soon enough you will."

Cade closed her eyes, too, and did a mental tiptoe. When she reached the shores of Gori's mind, that thin line, as clear and penetrable as water, she kept moving. Didn't let herself hesitate, because she would have turned back.

The universe slammed into her with the strength of a thousand songs, carried on a thousand winds that tore her open. And the songs were played with notes Cade didn't know, in keys she'd never heard. There was light and dark, but this was no day-light and night-dark. This dark was most of the universe, living inside the songs, pulsing them out—it was the air they filled and the wind they flew on, and it crept and shivered through Cade. All beginnings sprang from that dark, and all endings. It could have crushed her, but instead it brought her songs.

Cade washed up on the shore of the bedroom, full and emptied at the same time. And tired. So tired.

She tipped onto her back, met the simple cool of the sheets. Gori stood over her like a dark post. "So you just sit around and . . . feel that? All day?"

"Most days. To bear witness is no small task." Cade thought Gori was done, he stood there so long without talking. Without moving. Just the faint swirl of his robes in the dark.

"There were times when I chose to do more."

"Tell me about those," Cade said.

She thought Gori would duck the question. Scuttle out of the room. Or worse — decide that this was another kind of breach, this asking. But he sat down on the bed across from her and folded his hands into a small pile. "There are Darkriders who believe we should observe the forces and do nothing. That we should cause no changes, large or small, for fear of the terrible consequence." Earth rose in Cade's head, in all of its blue-green lushness — and another planet, its shadow-twin. Gori's home. "There is wisdom in what those Darkriders say. But there is more fear. I don't find it an acceptable balance." Gori nodded to the chute, and the rest of the ship. "There is a reason I travel in the company of outlaws."

"I thought it was because you were so handy with a knife."

He blinked down at Cade. Blinked. Again.

"Are there rules against Darkriders laughing?" she asked.

"No," he said. "I find your attempts at humor unconvincing."

And for some reason — maybe the press of exhaustion — Cade thought it was the funniest thing she'd ever heard. At some point, Gori stood up and left. At some point, Cade's laughter shaded into sleep.

The bedroom came to her in a white fog. Lee stood over Cade — the back of her hand too close to Cade's face to be doing anything but checking for breath.

"How long was I out?" Cade asked, her voice the guttering of a low string.

"A full day," Lee said.

"And nobody tried to kill me?" It seemed like the longest stretch she'd gone since leaving Andana without a knife pressed to her skin, or a fight on her hands, or a good solid threat.

Lee shrugged. "I rattled you for snoring once."

"Where's Ayumi?"

"She strapped herself down in the cargo hold," Lee said. "I told her it wouldn't do, so she went back to her ship to bunk down. She has a strange spin on her particles, that girl."

Cade almost asked why Ayumi hadn't claimed one of the two empty beds in the room she shared with Lee. But then she thought of Ayumi's condition. The girl clearly wasn't at the stage of spacesick where her hands would invade the nearest patch of skin, but it didn't hurt to be careful.

"What's the story with our new shipmate, do you think?" Lee asked.

"I think she's . . . she's . . ."

The secret wasn't Cade's to tell. And promises had been made.

"She's strange." The lie came like a fumbled beat, sticking-out and obvious. "You said it yourself."

Lee shrugged and leapt off the bed. "Come on," she said as she hoisted herself into the tunnel. She flashed toothy-white brilliance at Cade before she turned and went to work on the panel. "We're close."

"Close?"

It seemed impossible. So many light-years, so much black had existed between Cade and Xan when this started. And now she was close.

Hades.

Cade could almost feel the hole-suck.

She scrambled through the tunnel. She hit the main cabin with Lee. Rennik waited at the top of the chute, twisting the circle-glass around in his hands, looking nervous and pleased. Cade couldn't tell if she was getting better at seeing the flow of emotions underneath the flat surface, or if he was getting better at showing them to her.

"We're putting down in ten," he said.

Lee nodded as if that wasn't ridiculous.

"Putting down?" Cade asked. "Hades isn't a place to stop and get leisurely."

"We're not in Hades," Rennik said, a twitch of pride in his voice. "Renna changed the course."

"Renna . . . wait . . . *what?*"

Cade felt herself stiffen — hands, stomach, throat — until she was locked tight and creaking out words.

"What are you talking about?"

"She came up with the most fantastic flight plan, Cadence. It takes us back to the brink of Hades in two days."

"Back?"

Lee planted herself in front of Cade and got in her face, set and certain.

"It all fits together. We needed time to come up with a plan. The Unmakers know you're coming, and they'll have their traps set. Do you really think you can sail into Hades without them noticing?"

Cade looked for an answer to fling at Lee, but all she had was the sketchiest of ideas — bursting into Hades in Ayumi's little ship and using her entanglement — somehow — to find Xan.

Ayumi crossed the dock with a canvas sack and a thick stack of notebooks, looking refreshed and sleep-scrubbed and anything but spacesick. Anger thrummed out of Cade so hard, it stopped Ayumi in her tracks.

"What's happening?" she asked.

When Cade spoke, she had to press down on each word to keep it from exploding. "That's a very good question."

"Firstbloom," Lee said. "We made it to Firstbloom."

Cade felt a floating, and a fear that spread out from the

center of it. Like the moment she looked out of the starglass —when up and down and right and left, morning and night, stopped meaning anything.

"And no one thought to wake me up and . . . tell me about this?"

Ayumi looked at Lee and then down at the floor. "We were so sure you'd want to see it."

"Why?"

"To figure out what all of this means!" Ayumi burst.

"Everything we know about entanglement comes from a four-minute filmstrip," Lee said. "Do you understand how big this could be? No more spacesick? No more scatter? You're the one hope left for all of us, Cade. Doesn't that merit a pit stop?"

"It's not your call," Cade said.

Rennik headed down the chute to meet Cade. He folded his hands over hers and when he pulled them back, she was holding the circle-glass. "There's one more splice here, Cadence. I can restore it, but not with simple means. It will take the original tech."

And the tech was on Firstbloom.

"The place has been attacked!" Cade said.

"It still shows up on scans and updated flight maps. Which means it's still there."

"It's a mobile lab station," Lee tossed in. "Independent. No one will have come to claim the equipment."

"Or the bodies," Cade muttered.

"There's so much we could learn," Ayumi said, shuffling her notebook stack. "So much that we need."

"I see you've got it all figured out." Cade managed one step at a time until she was in Rennik's face. "This can't be the course. I need to get to Xan."

Lee slid herself into the bare inch of space between Rennik and Cade. "We know he's in trouble. But so are all the humans who can't do more than live and die, scattered on horrible planets, treated like spacetrash. I've seen more of it than anyone, and I'm telling you, things are getting dire for our kind. If you can do something to change that . . ."

Cade didn't know if she would be able to make a difference in a problem as wide as the skies. She didn't care about it half as much as she cared about rescuing Xan. But Firstbloom held the secrets of entanglement. Cade's story was one of those secrets.

She'd thought the hope of knowing who she was had come and gone with Mr. Niven, crumpled on the ground in the pile of his old-man clothes. She'd thought that Xan was the one thing she'd ever know about herself — the single, about-to-be-snapped connection to her past.

But the circle-glass had proven her wrong. Her mother had been pinched down to nothing, almost lost.

What else was there to find?

Cade needed to know, for herself — and for Lee, who wanted to be part of the mission, who believed in it even when Cade didn't. For Rennik, who helped Cade over and over when other nonhumans would have showed her the airlock. For Ayumi, who tried to hide a soft flinch in her stare — who focused on what happened to Cade, even as she fought her own battle against all of space.

Since the moment she left Andana, Cade had put Xan first. She had tucked her own cares into his, lied to her shipmates, cared less about them because there wasn't room for it as long as Xan needed her so much. Now, to turn her back on Firstbloom, she would have to put him in front of herself, her friends, and the rest of the human race. Again.

She reached out to Xan and told him where she was headed.

White, clean, sharp as a seven-blade knife.

Firstbloom.

Xan's adrenaline hit her even before his thoughts, and those thoughts were simple. He would be glad to help her punch the guts, blacken the eyes, and sour the organs of everyone on that ship until she had it turned around and pointed at Hades.

Cade didn't want to hurt anyone. What's more, she didn't want to turn around. Renna and the others had been right. It was time to know more about what it actually meant to be entangled.

Xan disagreed.

Violently.

He kept sending her signals to take all of them down. Kept flooding her with help she didn't want. There were no blows, no knives, but this hurt more than the other fights she'd gotten into, because it felt like Cade was fighting herself. Shredding her insides. Bashing her thoughts back. She threw herself to the ground, so she wouldn't collapse.

Cade curled into a ball, holding her muscles in perfect tension. "Two days," she muttered. "Just two days."

Hoping Xan could hear it. Hoping he would understand.

Cade caught Firstbloom in the starglass as it swam up at the edge of an asteroid field. It was shinier than the dull chunks of space-rock around it — a group of three irregular orbs connected by thin tubes that Cade guessed were bridges. The whole thing looked like a colony of little moons with no planet.

Cade's floating homeland.

Landing would be difficult, because they already had Ayumi's ship on the main dock and there was no one to answer their call and open Firstbloom's hatch. Rennik did the whole thing manually, including a spacewalk in a pressure suit to force the hatch open.

Cade waited at the secondary dock off the cargo hold, with Lee on one side and Ayumi on the other, and Renna sending them regular pulses to let them know Rennik was all right.

The hatch hissed open. The towering door of the dock slid up. Cade stepped through a short spur of walkway and into the lab.

The stillness was the first thing. It was thick and all around, and had settled over the surfaces — the long white tables, the scattered white coats, the hulking white machines — like sheets. The overhead lights were on, content to glare into the distant future, but one in the far corner had given in to a flicker that would sooner or later end in the blink-out. It thrashed in its little glass case.

CHAPTER 17

SUPERPOSITION The tendency of a quantum
system to exist in all possible theoretical
states, until observed

The crib creaked.

Or Cade thought it did. But then the sound came again, and Cade placed it behind her.

She had the seven-blade knife out and unsnapped by the time she turned. But it was just Rennik, clunking in his pressure suit, the helmet off and the rest of it shrugged around his body. He looked out of place in the lab — too tall for the low ceilings, too curved for the sharp corners. Sometimes Cade forgot that he wasn't human. But here, in a place where everything was human-made, he stood out like a smashed thumb.

"Anything yet?" he asked.

Cade shook her head. She hadn't expected answers about entanglement to leap out from behind corners. But so far there was equipment and cribs, dust and silence.

"I found something," Ayumi called from across the lab. "I mean. Someone."

Cade ran over to where Ayumi had stopped in front of a long desk. A little placard that read INFORMATION sat on top of it, undisturbed. Behind it, flickers of light gathered, sparking into something larger and shaped like a person. Arms and a torso pulled themselves together. The head came last, flickering in and out before it snapped into a smile. This projection didn't have a proper body, something elaborate and costumed like Mr. Niven — it was a thin scrap of color and light. At the same time, it was human.

A woman. Middle-aged, with thick dark hair wrapped around her head, a white coat over her patterned dress, and a little brass pin with her name on it.

Andrea.

Cade fought the urge to say hello.

Andrea smiled so thin and tight that at first Cade worried she was about to go spacecadet right in front of them. But no. Andrea leaned forward and folded her transparent hands on the surface of the desk and started to speak in a pleasant, well-modulated tone.

"Hello, and welcome to Firstbloom. We're so glad you came. Firstbloom is the only mobile lab station dedicated to the study of human possibility. Please disregard the current state of our labs. If you are here to consider an investment or conduct an experiment in our research facilities, we invite you to have a look around." Her face wavered — and it wasn't just the light. Andrea was fighting to sink reassurance into each syllable of each word, but she was losing. "And remember.

No matter the setbacks, Firstbloom will continue to . . . press forward into the . . . bright human future."

She pushed the edges of her smile out into new, painful territory. Cade heard a scream — not Andrea's — and then she blinked out.

"She made a projection," Cade said. "Just like Niven. Right before the Unmakers raided."

Cade couldn't believe what she had just seen. A woman saying a polite *sorry* for the fact that she was about to be killed, and asking future visitors to gloss over it so they could focus on research.

Lee stared at Cade. She had no idea what to say.

But Ayumi had a word for it.

"Ghosts."

Another old Earth notion. Suddenly Lee and Rennik didn't seem as in love with their little plan to explore Firstbloom. Rennik started to wander the enormous lab, looking for the tech to repair the circle-glass.

Lee suckered her fingers onto Cade's arm. "Let's find that machine and get the damp hell out of here."

But the more they looked, the more ghostlike projections they found. It was like tripping a wire — one of them would step over a patch of air that hadn't been troubled since the raid, and another memory of a person would appear.

The bald man who explained his work with such calm and precision that Cade would have guessed he made the recording on a particularly boring Tuesday.

The girl — not a day older than Cade — who did her best to look chipper as she pointed out the various parts of the lab.

The woman who screamed and screamed as she watched whatever was coming through the door.

Cade noticed that not a single one of these people said goodbye to mothers or fathers, children or best friends, wives, husbands, lovers. They didn't even try to sneak the words in around their other, more official, messages. Cade hadn't given a lot of thought to her last moments, but she hoped there was more to them than a recital of mess modules or a blank-faced declaration of fear.

"Look," Lee said, tugging Cade to a machine that sat in one of the far corners, behind a plastic door.

As soon as Lee's foot slid over the threshold, a woman with a head of wild red curls flickered into false life in front of them. Cade couldn't help but notice she'd been beautiful. Couldn't help but see the nimbleness of the woman's eyes, the breakable nature of her small hands. Couldn't help but wonder what the woman's singing voice had sounded like.

But when it came to last words, hers were even less inspired than the others.

"This is the editing room . . . This is the editing room . . . This is the editing room . . ." on a forever-loop.

Cade passed the woman and let her voice fade to a single, ringing bell in the background. She waved Rennik over to the monstrous beige machine that took up most of the room.

"It's this, I think."

Rennik looked it over once and nodded. Cade ran the flat

blade of her knife along a seam in the metal until she found a spot to dig in. The cover pried off in one sheet. The machine spat dust, clearly angry that Cade wanted to wake it up from its elaborate plans to not do anything for the rest of time.

The inner workings were spare and dark. Cade noticed a small emptiness, about the size and shape of the circle-glass. She tamped it down and the whole machine lit up.

"I think that means we're getting to the heart of it," Rennik said.

"Or at least we turned it on," Lee muttered.

The room flared with sudden light and crisp color, and the projection leapt to life, plumping the air with babies.

"Welcome to Project QE."

The words were almost a comfort to Cade at this point. She settled in to watch one more time — to fill in her blanks.

"You might wonder why you're looking at a room full of infants."

But Cade wasn't looking at infants, or anything else.

Her head went blank. To black.

The words of the filmstrip became a nightmare soundtrack, pounding underneath what came next. Cade landed in Xan's little room, the failsafe connection snapped on to full strength. She didn't have time to orient herself to Xan's feelings. A rush of sensations hit her first. The Unmakers pulled Xan out of the room by his shoulders, his feet, his hair, whatever they could get their hands on as he struggled. Cade felt some of the pain, but it was a shadow-pain — quick to fade.

The Unmakers dragged him down a stripped-bare hallway

with doors lining both sides. Cade tried to help Xan, send him some of her fight, but all he could manage were a few loose slaps. He felt sluggish, like his limbs had been hollowed out and filled with sand. Xan had been drugged.

The room the Unmakers shoved him into was small, a cell with an unfinished floor — Cade felt the grit on her cheek when Xan hit. She tried to send him strength, to wake him up, but he was slow and fogged as the Unmakers tied him up with lengths of strong rubber cord.

Then they started to torture him.

Cuts, shocks, small but adding up to a great, swallowing pain. The impulses shot into Cade and lodged themselves, even though her skin went untouched. Xan's head rolled forward. He almost blacked out. Blinked hard, back into the cell. Almost blacked out again.

Cade sent him strength, strength, strength.

But it wasn't enough.

They were hurting him and there was nothing Cade could do to stop it. A-touch-more-than-human wasn't the same as invincible. Cade remembered that with each little slice.

"Now?" one of the Unmakers asked, his fingers crushed against Xan's throat. Cade smelled dust and metal and ached to breathe.

"No," another one said. "Let him feel it."

The fingers eased an inch. Cade's throat limped to catch up to the desperate pull of her lungs.

"One more day," the first Unmaker said.

And the others agreed.

"One more day."

Cade snapped back to Firstbloom.

She was on the floor, Lee and Ayumi crouched over her, Rennik farther away, hovering over them.

"What happened?" Lee asked. Cade rubbed her arms, her face, nursing the phantom cuts.

"She must have heard what was hidden by the splice," Lee said, "and reacted."

Ayumi fluttered her hands over various pulse points. Neck to wrists and back again. When she leaned down to check Cade's pupils, Cade scanned Ayumi's eyes for glass and gave her own all-clear. She wanted to wave Ayumi off, on the grounds that a girl with spacesick shouldn't be in charge of health and safety.

Rennik leaned down and the others made room. "Cade, did you see the footage?" Cade shook her head.

"What did you see?"

"Xan," she said. "I heard . . . they're going to kill him."

Cade's decision to turn her back on Hades for two days clamped down, tightened each breath. She'd made the wrong call, and Xan had paid for it. Unless she could get to him in a single day, he would die for it.

"We have to turn back."

Rennik nodded, but there was hesitation in it.

"What?" Cade asked.

"Do you want to go back and watch again?"

"No." Now that Cade knew it was happening, that Xan was being tortured, her head kept pounding two words.

No time, no time.

"Just tell me, please."

Rennik put out a hand in the air between them. Didn't touch her. Just let his hand wait there, in case she needed it.

"The rest of the children," Rennik said. "The ones in the other pairs." Cade felt the sick at the back of her throat, the hot acid pulse she'd been holding down. "They didn't take to quantum entanglement. When the experiment narrowed down from a full room to just two . . . the others weren't sent home. Or raised in the lab or even sent planetside to grow up.

"They died, Cadence."

For the first time, she liked the flatness of Rennik's voice. How it anchored the wild pitch of what she felt.

"Take it back." The words came out whispered, then shouted. "That's not what you saw."

The crawling babies. Every one that hadn't been Cade or Xan. A room full of life. Perfect, soft, still forming.

Gone.

"We're the last two," Cade said.

Her feet touched down onboard Renna. Whatever happened between the floor of Firstbloom and the dock was lost. Cade looked backwards for it, but her mind acted like the pinched film inside the circle-glass — skipped over what it didn't want her to see. This must have been her body protecting itself.

She was marooned with a rage so enormous that even to trouble the edges of it felt dangerous. If she'd had to look at the smooth glass instruments of Firstbloom, the smug white walls, the abandoned crib, she would have bashed the whole lab to pieces.

"We're the last two," Cade said, "and I left him in Hades. I left him to die."

Lee and Rennik held out arms to steady her as she headed up the chute. Ayumi disappeared for a minute, then chased behind them with a steaming green mug of tea. Renna rippled the surface of the chute underneath them in a soothing motion.

But being surrounded by good people who wanted to help her only made Cade feel worse.

Xan was alone. He was alone because Cade had left him. And to do what? Learn that the scientists who had entangled them were even worse than she had imagined?

She stormed the control room and planted herself in the pilot's chair. Lee, Rennik, and Ayumi stood back and watched as she clutched the armrests and set her teeth and chose her words.

"Renna," she said. "I know the course to Hades takes two days. We need to be there in one."

The ship broke into a consuming roar as Renna threw herself into new drive states. She shot forward at such a speed that the white points in the starglass flew up to meet them.

Rennik ran to the control panels, his hands on the dials, his body twisted back toward Cade. "This is Renna's maximum flightspeed," he said. "She can't operate for a full day at this speed."

"That's for her to decide," Lee said — taking someone else's side against Rennik for what was probably the first time in her life.

Renna roared even louder.

"She would do this for you," Cade said. "There are people you would have done it for, too."

She didn't use Moira's name. Judging by the sudden tightness of Rennik's skin, and the visible force of the emotions rushing under it, she didn't have to.

"There's still no plan," Rennik said. "You can't go into Hades without one. They'll be waiting."

The Unmakers. That was why Rennik and Lee cared so much about Cade having a plan — they didn't want to lose another member of their crew to the Unmakers. But Cade didn't have the option of caring. Even if it was a trap — which it had to be — she would fly straight into it and snatch Xan out.

Lee marched over. "We're not going to let them have her." She pushed her hair back and stared up into Rennik's freshly iced-over features.

"You say that as though we'll have a choice. We hardly kept them back on our own ship . . . If they have the advantage . . ."

Cade broke away from Rennik and Lee's standoff and their talk of plans that, in the end, only mattered if they got her to

Xan. "I need to do this," she said. "It will never be smart, and you still have to let me."

Rennik stepped back.

Cade smoothed her hands across the panels and shouted to Renna over the new din.

"Hold the course."

Cade sat in the pilot's chair, pretended to eat the food Lee brought for her, tried — and failed — to sleep. Blame streamed through her mind, as constant as the stars. Blame for the Unmakers, the Firstbloom scientists, herself.

As if that wasn't enough, Cade dropped back into Xan's head for another round of pain.

The automatic connection snapped on and Cade found herself in Xan's cell. She suffocated inside of his head, his thoughts wrapped in a warm fog — one part drugs, two parts ache.

He wasn't being tortured this time, just nursing his wounds. Bruised to a rainbow of colors, not just black. Rot-purple and yellow, the green shine of meat gone bad.

Everything hurt.

Cade held on to the fact — true, but dissonant — that hurt meant hope. Hurt meant he was still alive.

Hours later, and the control room sat empty except for Cade and the roar of Renna's speed. Ayumi tiptoed in with Moon-White, looking small and pale, which was strange because she wasn't really either. Maybe it was just the sheen from the starglass caught on her skin. She held the guitar out—it claimed the icy light and turned it into brilliance. But Cade had no interest in strings or frets.

"I thought you might want to . . ."

Ayumi pushed Moon-White so close that chords started calling out to Cade's fingers.

"I didn't think tea would do the trick this time," Ayumi said. "But this . . . I suspected it was the only thing in the universe that would make you feel better."

Cade didn't deserve to feel better. Until she reached Hades, all she deserved was her share of Xan's pain.

"No," Cade said. "Thanks."

Ayumi turned to leave, Moon-White a little too loose in her grip. Her steps lilted in a way that Cade didn't like.

"Wait."

Ayumi's black curls flashed a circle as she turned, eyes clear and stuck fast on Cade.

"Would it make *you* feel better?" Cade asked.

Her shoulders pressed up in a small shrug. But Cade remembered now—how hard Ayumi had fallen for Moon-White's music. Once Cade started to play, not one speck of glass had snuck into her eyes. Her arms and legs hadn't wandered, disjointed.

Cade grabbed the guitar, moved so fast that Moon-White swung on the strap around her neck.

"Come here."

Cade rushed Ayumi to the starglass. "Look out there."

"You want me to—"

"Just look."

Ayumi watched the stars, and Cade watched her. She stood outside the circle of perforated dark, strumming Moon-White and waiting for the change—the moment when Ayumi would slip out of herself and into the wide body of space. She strummed and waited. Waited and strummed.

It didn't come.

Cade thought of her mother and the music that hadn't been enough to cure spacesicks. It hadn't been enough to save her from a glassed-and-gone fate. But Cade was different. Entangled.

"Do you think . . . ?"

The words were too huge to say out loud. *Do you think I can cure you? Do you think I can cure other spacesicks? What if the scientists were right about the entangled? What if we can change life in the black?*

Cade knew that spacesicks detached from themselves in the face of the endless and the edgeless. Cade's entanglement brought her into contact with Xan, but it also kept her tethered to herself—and that kept space from seeping into her cracks and settling down. What if this kind of connection could be opened up, shared somehow? What if it could bring people back to themselves?

Instead of speaking, Cade worked to push these thoughts into music, with notes rising loose at the end like question marks.

Ayumi looked over. She didn't tear herself from the star-glass. She didn't shudder.

"Beautiful, isn't it?" Ayumi's face sparked brighter than stars.

"Yeah," Cade said. "It is."

Cade slid out of the pilot's chair eighteen hours into the hard-driven flight. She touched the control panel where the needles on Renna's dials pressed to the limits.

Cade tried to climb back into the chair, but Renna tightened up and turned it lump-hard and unbearable.

She was telling Cade it was time for bed.

"If you're going to work this hard to get me to Hades," Cade said, "I want to stay up with you."

The ground underneath her flashed so hot, she worried that the soles of her shoes would melt.

"All right," Cade said, too tired to fight an entire ship. "All right."

Cade headed down the chute. As she reached the panel, Ayumi crashed in from the dock with an armful of blankets and a toothbrush.

She was moving in.

Cade helped her settle into the other bottom bunk. Lee slept on the top, swimming through her dreams. Cade sat on the edge of her own bed and rested Moon-White across her knees. She picked out a quiet song that wouldn't stir Lee. Ayumi stared at Cade, tuned in, awake. She strummed until the night felt deep, until she couldn't see where it had started or where it might end.

"I can't play until dawn." Cade scraped a hoarse laugh at her own joke. There was no dawn.

"That will be enough," Ayumi said.

She sounded so sure that Cade believed it. Moon-White went under the bunk. But Cade let the notes stretch on in her mind—and she felt Ayumi's mind, still open to her.

"Can you hear that?" Cade whispered, without breaking the cord of sound between them.

Ayumi's breaths were soft and fit in the space between beats.

"I hear that."

And for once, Ayumi didn't leap forward to talk about how important this could be. She didn't use the word *ramifications*. She was too perfectly tuned in. Cade stared across the space that separated their bunks. Lined her eyes up with the brown eyes across the room. Thought music at Ayumi until she fell asleep.

Then Cade got up and walked the quiet ship. Her bare feet against the smoothness of the floors. She stepped with care, in case Renna decided to boil the ground and send her back to bed.

Cade ended up in front of the starglass again. Hades sat in the distance, a nest of coiled dark.

Xan waited out there, needing her as much as he ever had. For the first time, Cade felt like she was bringing him something more than a rescue. More than survival—a hope for what came after.

She sent music, long strands of it that she sailed to him. He listened, and sent nothing back.

The border of Hades looked a lot like the rest of space.

Open, black, silent.

"How can you be sure this is it?" Cade asked. She'd slept three hours but she was up again, staring out from the brink of the control room. Rennik, Lee, Ayumi, even Gori stood lined up along the panels.

"This is where we start to navigate around the black holes," Rennik said. "Their gravity will drag us. With a field like this, we'll be pulled in ten or twenty different directions, no matter how hard we work to stay the course."

He brought out a chart, three times as big as any chart Cade had ever seen, crammed with penciled calculations.

"What's that?"

Rennik pushed it across the panels until it sat under Cade's nose. "The course." This time, she didn't even have to look up to know what Rennik felt under all of that steadiness and calm. He sounded proud, with a shiver of nervousness at the edges.

"All we need is Xan's location and we'll be prepared," Rennik said. "Or as much as we can be, going into Hades."

Cade touched the dense, inked-in swirls on the chart and looked up at the space that stretched out in front of Renna. Still normal. Still empty. These things didn't add up.

"You're not coming with me."

Three pairs of eyes swiveled to Cade. She could even feel

Renna press some attention her way. The panel under her fingers flushed cold. Only Gori was the same as always — not staring when it actually made sense, staring the rest of the time. Lee shuffled her place with Rennik's so she stood next to Cade. A skinny arm wrapped around her shoulders.

"Of course we're coming."

"The deal we made was a ride to Hades. I thought —"

"You thought what? That we'd strand you on the doorstep of the most dangerous part of space?" Lee's pale skin went the much-paler shade that only showed when things got serious. "Three things. One, that's not even possible. I mean, we can't force you out of the hatch and let you float the rest of the way."

"There's Ayumi's ship," Cade said, and Ayumi nodded. "That's the plan. She and I have a —"

"Two," Lee chimed in. "That's no plan at all. If the Unmakers are waiting, which they are, and they have more than a handful of ships, which they do, there's no way one tiny blip of tech is going to shake off their entire fleet."

Ayumi stood fast, but the rate of her blinking rose. She clamped her hands tight to keep her fingers from sparking.

Lee pointed to the chart, and Cade noticed the two ships drawn in. One small and quick, darting around the gravity of the black holes. The other round and familiar, dotted with small dark eyes.

"If you have another ship, a bigger one, not to mention one the Unmakers have boarded, to pull the interest, draw the fire . . . now that's a plan."

"Three," Lee said. *"Of course we're coming."*

That should have been the easiest point to argue. It was no point at all. For most of Cade's life, she would have wanted to go into Hades on her own, because on her own was how she did things. But she had a new reason. A better one.

"I can't let you," she said. "Too dangerous."

"We all picked danger a long time ago," Lee said. "What's one extra helping?"

"But Lee . . . the Unmakers." She didn't have to hand the story of Lee's sister back to her. It was always there, tucked in the space between them. "I would never ask you to face them."

"The last time I checked, you weren't asking. I was telling." Lee pulled Cade in close. "Come on. You go in alone you have . . . you. Go in with us, you have two brass pilots, a ship that adores you, a best friend who won't leave your side. And a secret weapon."

"A . . . what?" Renna wasn't outfitted with weapons.

"Gori."

All heads swiveled in a new direction.

"I have agreed to help," he said. "With the navigation."

"He has a direct line to dark energy," Lee said. "And dark energy expands the universe. If we get too close to a black hole, he can push it in a helpful direction."

Cade was the one who stared at him now, unblinking.

"I know you said you could do *more* with dark energy, but . . . ." It felt absurd to even think it. "You can move a black hole?"

Lee leaned in and said, "He can nudge it."

Gori inclined his head.

Cade was amazed. That Gori could do it, and that Gori would do it for *her*. She must have gained a degree of respect when he invited her into his mind.

Cade looked down the line of people, human and not-so-human, who were ready to face the underworld so she could make it out alive. She felt all of her arguments slipping from her on a long fade-out.

"All right," she said. "We go in together."

CHAPTER 18

EQUIFINALITY A given end state or outcome approached through many different paths

Cade sat in the pilot's seat, her connection with Xan so open that sometimes she couldn't tell whose skin was whose, if she was in his little room or the control room or both.

Xan breathed easier now, his bruises faded, his mind eased by her presence. She did her best to soothe him, like a hand at the small of the back. She didn't tell him when she saw the first of the palm-shaped ships.

Now that she was so close to Xan, she'd been expecting some kind of pull to manifest — an undeniable force that would drag her to him like a magnet over this last reach of space.

Instead, he gave her coordinates.

Long strings of numbers that she didn't understand, but which she fed to Rennik. He stood in the starglass with the chart in one hand and a pencil in the other, turning to face this black hole or that black hole to calculate their distance, their diameter, their pull. Ayumi stood at the control panels, dialing. Her fingers sure, her steps balanced. Cade had poured music — loud music — into Ayumi's ears for as long she could before they both had to take their stations.

The plan was for Renna to charge straight for wherever Xan was being held, while Ayumi flew a trickier, more roundabout route and came up on him from another angle. Now that Cade knew she had ammunition against Ayumi's spacesick, that part of the plan felt a lot firmer under her feet. Renna, Lee, and Rennik would keep most of the Unmakers occupied, and Ayumi would be able to brush off the few ships on her tail.

In theory.

"Cadence, do you see that?" Ayumi asked, nodding out the starglass at the ship.

And then it turned into ten ships, twenty ships, fifty. She and Ayumi should have broken off by now. A fleet of the Unmakers sailed up to them from three sides and then a string pulled around the back, flanking them. Two ships locked them in above and below, for good measure.

Cade burrowed deep into the connection with Xan. But she wasn't safe there, either. Not with Unmakers posted outside the door. Xan's fear had drained away a long time ago, but Cade's was fresh and bright, like blood from a bitten lip.

Lights blinked on all of the ships — tiny, yellow, out of time with each other.

The Unmakers wanted to board.

"We can't let them," Cade said.

She was too close. Entanglement had gotten her off Andana,

263

through troubles, into more troubles, out of them again. She had risked herself and cracked open her mind and stretched her life to fit the new people she needed, like fingers reaching for an impossible chord.

"We try to deny them, they blow us up," Lee said. "We try to scamper away, they blow us up."

"Those are armed ships," Rennik said.

"*Heavily* armed ships," Lee said.

Ayumi called back from her place at the dials, the needles flying under her hands. "I would have to advise that we stick to the plan."

But the coordinates were still flooding Cade's brain, and Ayumi's ship sat on Renna's far side, trapped.

How much more? she tried to ask Xan.

But he was so intent on getting her there that he didn't listen. He thought numbers at her with a fury. She knew what those numbers meant.

Get here. Now. Get here. Now.

The ships moved in close — they lobbed themselves at Renna in quick, obvious jolts. Renna wasn't armed, and even if she was, the fight would be fifty to one.

"We'll have to face them," Rennik said.

Lee sprang out from the corner where she'd been standing with Gori. "Face them how? They come in, they kill us, end of story." Lee knew that ending perfectly. Rennik's skin went to ash.

"Ayumi's right," Cade said. "We stick to the plan."

The ship rocked with the first of the boardings. The

Unmakers had latched one of their craft to the secondary dock and would come in through the cargo hold. Which meant that no one could head down the chute without slamming into them.

But when the ship rocked a second time, that's just what Ayumi did.

"No time like the present!" she cried.

Rennik rushed from the starglass to the control panels. Gori stayed put in his corner. Lee ran for Cade, her legs stretching, body electrified.

"Cade." Lee took the last of the room in one long stride, her arm shooting out to grab Cade's wrist. "Listen!" Her dark-moon eyes swelled with twin oceans. "You're not allowed to die."

Cade grabbed Lee's hand, pulsed a message. A *right-back-at-you*. And she ran down the chute.

"Cadence!" Rennik's voice followed her, but he stayed at the panels. There was no way to engineer a goodbye. If his hands left the dials, the whole ship might spin into a black hole before he could right the course.

Cade didn't have time to think about that lost moment, but she could feel the lack of it, like the ache of her missing tooth.

The Unmakers had already stormed the main cabin — a dozen, and more behind them. Cade was so focused on the incoming swirl of space-black robes that it took her a few seconds to find Ayumi. Her dark curls cut a path down the chute. She was still much too far from the dock when an Unmaker caught up.

The floor around Cade grumbled and shook, but the patch she was standing on didn't obey the same rules. The Unmakers groaned to the floor one by one until Cade and Ayumi were the only ones left standing, stuck to their spots.

Cade pressed a palm to the wall and sent Renna some serious thanks. The ship wasn't armed, but she could fight.

The Unmakers found their footing and started up the pitch-and-roll of the chute toward Ayumi.

She was trying to talk the monsters back. She cast words into the fray like faint knife-jabs. "It's possible you think humans are your enemies because you don't know enough . . . enough . . . about us," she stammered. "There are a lot of untruths about the human race that have spread . . . I'd be happy to dispel those . . . and give you a more complete picture of . . ."

The Unmakers closed a half-circle on one side of her.

Cade ran at Ayumi, full-tilt, from the top of the chute. Xan sent all the speed he'd stored over weeks of sitting, body spoiling. Cade remembered running with him through the ship at night — how fast they'd gone. She felt her muscles tighten, her feet arch and pound, arch and pound. She snatched Ayumi's hand and started to run them both up in the direction of the control room. She hoped they could take the tunnels through Renna's center, find some other path to the little ship. The first set of Unmakers pressed tight on their heels, trundling up the chute.

No one made it to the top.

Cade's feet floated away from the ground. Her feet, and

everything above them. She turned to find that Ayumi had lifted off the ground beside her. The air was full of Unmakers.

Renna had turned off the gravity.

It was a good thing Cade had a first-class grip on Ayumi's hand. "Hold on to me."

Ayumi nodded. Her curls bobbed and streamed above her head.

Cade and Ayumi wilted in the no-grav, but the Unmakers were worse. Their small hands clutched the air, frantic. The rest of their bodies hung motionless. The main cabin filled with constellations of loose arms and splayed legs.

Cade and Ayumi hit a wall and sprang off, legs forcing them in at least two different directions. Their crudely knotted fingers kept them from drifting, but all their feet could agree on was where *not* to aim.

Ayumi nodded at the dock. The Unmakers hadn't claimed it yet — there was still a chance. Cade sent Xan hope. The most she'd felt since she'd set eyes on the spaceport on Andana.

She hit the wall a second after Ayumi. Two sets of knees bent deep and sent them shooting through the unbound air.

Gloved hands reached for Cade. The wails of Unmakers sounded thin in her ears. One last push against the wall, and she crossed the dock without looking back. Later — if there was a later — Cade would have to measure and mourn what she had left behind.

The little ship was untouched by the madness of the cabin. The Unmakers tried to recalibrate their paths and come after Cade and Ayumi, but the loose, unwieldy air slowed them too much. Ayumi sealed the door and flipped a few switches. Gravity rushed back, slamming them down. Cade hit the floor just behind the navigator's chair; Ayumi scrambled for the controls.

"Go go go go go go," Cade said.

But Ayumi was already gone.

She was flying before she hit the seat, before she strapped in, before she breathed out. Her flightstyle was still a symphony of clunk-and-clatter, but this time Ayumi poured all her certainty into it, worked the panels with such a confidence that Cade flushed to watch it. Ayumi didn't notice. She didn't have eyes for anything but space, and for the first time Cade wasn't going to get in the way.

They shot into an open field and shook off the unwanted ships like rain. Ayumi rolled, twisted, tumbled them.

"I've never actually had a reason to use half these tricks," she said under her breath as she slammed buttons.

She dropped in a sudden dive, turned her broad side to a black hole, and shook off another three ships. It was breath-stealing, life-bending to watch. Cade shot forward against the straps of her seat so she could see all of it.

So this was what it was like to be the audience.

Cade would have loved the ride, except for two things. There were still ships on their backside — only two, but they were the fastest, meanest two, the ones that forced Ayumi into trickier and trickier evasions.

Also, Xan.

The Unmakers that swarmed into his room this time didn't

bother to drag him down the hallway. They breathed such staleness into his face that Cade's stomach puckered. And then, the pain. Whatever they'd held back during their other visits, they unleashed it now. Knives were drawn, stitches groaned open, bruises burst under stretched-tight skin. Blood spoiled the sheets, slicked the floor, collected in Xan's mouth.

Cade sent everything she had—strength, hope, a steady beat, the knowledge that she would be there soon.

He sent her numbers and agony.

Cade spat the incoming coordinates at Ayumi.

"Cadence," she said, eyes sliding from the controls to Cade's face and back again. "Are you okay?"

Cade clutched herself where the shadow-pains hurt worst. Ayumi translated Xan's numbers into a course and punched it into the ship.

But things switched in the space of one shallow breath, and now Ayumi was the not-okay one. Her eyes glassed. Her fingers wavered. Her chin drooped low, over the controls.

"No," Cade said. "Stay here. Stay with me."

But Ayumi was already gone.

Cade could do only one thing—and it meant taking some of her mind off Xan. She had to make a choice—and the black holes were starting to pull, spinning the ship toward event horizons. Behind them, the Unmakers had almost caught up. Cade felt the rumble of much larger ships.

Unless Ayumi shook this fit of spacesick, they would be lost.

Cade had to fight fast, with every weapon she had. She

unstrapped and climbed out of the navigator's seat so she could sling her arms around Ayumi and fasten them tight. She shivered her hands over Ayumi's upper arms. Pressed her face to the side of Ayumi's face.

She didn't look out the window at the blackness and nothing that was calling their names. She looked at Ayumi — the broadness of her cheek, the stretches of soft skin under her eyes, the strong line of her neck. All the parts that would add up to the girl she knew — if Cade could call her back.

She reached out with her mind and found Ayumi's thoughts, low and muffled. Pumped music into her, tried to shore her against the indifference of space. Cade didn't have time for anything fancy. She thumped a reliable double-beat.

In a little room somewhere else in Cade's mind, the Unmakers drained out. Xan was fading.

She sent as much noise as she could, as much of herself as she could, to both of them.

Ayumi's hands shot out and she gasped her way back to the controls. She swerved out of the pull of a black hole and slid a last-second dive past one of the Unmakers' ships, so close they must have felt the heat from her thrusters.

Cade let out a wild cheer — and kept driving the beat to Xan.

But he was almost gone. The corners of his mind inked with darkness. It crept inwards, spotting the room until there were only pinholes of color and light.

And then nothing.

Into Cade's head — a crash of sound, a flood of chaotic

volume, a thousand notes like crossed wires, the heart-curdling smash of static. Cade had no hope of sending music now. Xan had been knocked out cold.

The Noise was back.

Cade put her head down between her knees. When she came back up for air, the Noise was still there. Ayumi had glassed out again — her fingers dangled limp on a switch.

With so much static between her ears, Cade couldn't reach out and help her.

The little ship lurched and tipped in a new direction, under the influence of the nearest black hole. Cade reached for the controls, but couldn't even pretend she knew where to start. The Noise had no help to offer, nothing but interference in a hundred different keys. Outside the window, a complete, consuming blackness.

The fall toward it sped up and up and up.

One of the Unmakers' ships snatched them back from the edge, and Cade almost sighed.

Almost.

CHAPTER 19

EXPECTATION VALUE The predicted mean value of the results of an experiment

Dark, robe-shadowed nonfaces. Small hands and metal-breath, touching and breathing and in her space.

Out, Cade thought.

But she couldn't be sure she was saying it. The Noise hammered so loud that when she moved her lips, she didn't know if the words pushed past them, into the needle-cold, antiseptic air.

Unmakers milled around Cade. They could see a broken doll of a girl in tattered clothes, but they couldn't hear what had smashed her. A fresh round of coma static. Cade wanted to broadcast the bursting, crackling, mess. Get it *out, out, out.*

The Unmakers shuffled a step back from Cade's bedside.

So she *was* talking.

The space-black robes hovered over her for minutes or hours. When the Unmakers drained out, Cade looked over the room—not a simple task for eyes tenderly connected to a rasping brain. The fact that she'd seen a matching room in the confines of her own head made it easier to know what she was looking at. A rectangle of windowless walls. A narrow bed that barely fit the width of her hips. A sheet of mirror. Strange. Mirror. How many times had she seen it in Xan's room without wondering—why would the Unmakers have a mirror? Cade had been so sure that nonhumans didn't use it. So why a perfect, uncracked sheet of it, why here? So humans would feel more at home in their cells? So they could stare at their bodies, scan the bone-molded, skin-papered landscapes of their emotions, search for their souls one more time before they were unmade?

Something tapped at the door—more than a scratch but less than a knock. Cade tried to get up but her muscles were paste. Another tap. She wondered if someone had come to help—Lee, Rennik, Ayumi without the glass. Maybe even Xan.

But no, that made no sense, because Cade still had the Noise in her head. If Xan came out of his coma, the Noise would dissolve into silence. And at the door—that was a draft from an overhead vent, that was the rattle of a rogue hinge, that was no one. Cade had the Noise, and Cade had no one. She was alone. The same absolute alone she'd been on Andana.

She had no idea how she'd survived it before.

The Unmakers came in with long shiny needles that stopped her thoughts and brought on sleep.

• • •

In fits between dead stretches of black, Cade did her best to focus her mind and reach out.

For Xan, but he was passed out in his own little cell. For Ayumi, but she was deep in space-rapture somewhere. For Rennik, but he'd never been listening hard enough. For Gori, but he might kill her if she made it through this alive. For Renna, but she was off skirmishing with black holes. For Lee, but—

Cade didn't know who she was fooling. The Noise was the real reason she couldn't connect. All of those other reasons were part of a mean little game she made up to distract herself. The No-One-Ever-Cared-So-Let-It-Go game. Twenty or thirty rounds in, and she was getting good.

But somewhere deep, past the sting of the points she kept scoring against herself, Cade knew that the Noise was to blame. It had splintered her connection with Ayumi at the most important moment. She tried to push through bursts of Noise, wrench aside heavy gray-white curtains of static. In one wild moment, she used the song from the pinched circle-glass to reach for her mother, reached so hard that she feared her mind would snap like a stretched-too-far rubber band.

And it did. Snap.

Cade came back to herself screaming. Her arms and legs slashed at the sheets. Now the sound in her head was also pain, each note a blade into the soft parts of her brain. She held her head in her hands, and all she heard was Noise, Noise, Noise, and her fingers were covered in tears.

Cade cried. Maybe for the first time since her mother left

her on Firstbloom. There was nothing to dull the torn edges of her sobs, not even the soft pulse of a wall under her fingertips. Putting a hand out was second nature now, but this ship was not a friend. This ship was a cold, dead nothing. A shined-up set of bones.

The Unmakers came. Cade spat in their nonfaces. She screamed and they were silent.

"Take me to Xan," she said.

The Unmakers didn't move.

Cade lunged at them, fingernails first, all sweat and spent muscles. The Unmakers pinned her to walls, to the bed, to the cold of the floor. She didn't have the strength of two humans anymore. She didn't have the strength of one.

"Take me to Xan," Cade screamed.

The Unmakers held her down.

"Take me!"

The Unmakers lifted her with their small hands and slammed her back on the bed.

"Take me to Xan," she said in a stubborn whisper, "Take me to Xan," so many times the words were just a shape, a sound, their meaning scooped out.

Cade waited until she was alone. No. That was wrong — alone was her state of being now. She waited until the Unmakers drained out. She tested her toes against the floor, half expecting her knees to crumple and bones to crack down their softened lengths. She had been in bed too long, dripped out on universe-knows-what.

But Cade's jellied muscles tensed. Her bones held. She

made it across the room in two steps and tapped the door open with a knuckle.

Metal breath. A slam. Cade was closed in with one of them.

She squared off with the largest Unmaker she'd ever seen. Cade stepped backwards until her legs hit the bed, and the force of it folded her down to sitting. The Unmaker started to remove robes in tissue-thin layers. They pooled on the floor until there was nothing left but a cling of fabric on a gruesome frame.

So there would be no slicing for Cade. No torture. This was something worse. She would have to look at the stripped-bare body of one of these monsters. Come face to face with a creature that chose life in the underworld — and fight off whatever it wanted to do to her.

Cade's hand went to her pocket. No knife. Of course no knife. Her strength — the strength of the entangled — could have made it an even match, but she was drained and disconnected. And knifeless.

The Unmaker's hands reached in, and it started to dismantle itself, piece by piece — the bits of it coming out of the last thin pulp of dark fabric. Lengths of metal and plastic, a little metal voicebox, a light kit complicated enough to cast a double shadow, clipped to a firm plastic collar. The small hands peeled off gloves, unwound more fabric.

Underneath it — a smooth, breakable stretch of skin. A frame that might as well have been glass, a fusion of weakness and beauty. A face that would have been at home on Earth.

Cade's body was a chant.

Heart, muscle, blood.

No, no, no.

"You're . . . human?"

The woman who was an Unmaker shrugged off the last of her elaborate costume, black robe unspooling from her hips. Underneath, she wore a white undershirt, tight-fitting dark pants. She was beautiful, with long curls of red hair and a fine-boned face, a gathering storm of wrinkles. This woman must have been around the age Cade's mother was, wherever she was. Even though none of their features matched, the connection of their ages and something else — a calm set to their faces — struck Cade.

"Everyone on this ship is human, Cadence," the woman said, sitting on the end of the bed.

"Don't call me . . ."

"Cadence?" She cocked her head. "That's your name, isn't it?"

Cade gathered her knees to her chest and made herself small at the head of the bed. She had no intention of sharing the details of herself with this woman who was, after all, an Unmaker. One of the people who had killed Lee's sister. Who had taken Xan. Tortured him.

"Tell me *your* name."

"I don't have one," the woman said. "Not anymore. I gave it up."

She let the words leave her mouth without fuss, each one a small plink, unweighted by loss. This woman had discarded her name. Clipped it off like a toenail.

"What do people call you?" Cade asked.

The woman shifted on the blanket and said nothing. Cade couldn't tell if that was an evasion, or if that was the answer — she was called nothing. Unmaker was just a title Cade had come up with a long time ago, in the billows of the smoke from her bunker. As far as she knew, as far as Lee had known, the whole tribe of them went nameless.

"Well, I'm going to call you *something*," Cade said. "You see, I sort of have to. It's what humans do."

The woman shifted and creased the thin sheets. "Please don't."

Cade worried that this wouldn't end well. So she let the name business go, but in her head she labeled the woman. The one who was the same age as her mother and had the same air about her. Redder hair, finer bones. But still. Cade started to wonder if the Unmakers knew about her mother, and had sent this woman to activate Cade's memories, render her enemies un-hateable.

This woman who sat at the end of the bed, looking at her with infinite care, was not her mother. No matter that the blue of her eyes matched the blue of that Firstbloom dress. This was not her mother. There were no familiar songs stored in those soft-lined hands. Not. Her. Mother. The name almost created itself.

Unmother.

"A lot of us didn't want to tell you the truth," Unmother said. "Not all of it. We worked out partial truths that might have been more . . . palatable. But Xan insisted that you would be open to —"

"Xan." Cade's palms burst out sweating. "Where is he?"

"He's mending," Unmother said, her voice coated thick with patience.

"The things you did to him," Cade said. "You tortured him. Broke him. And when you did that to him, you did it to me."

"We did nothing to Xan that he didn't agree to. Some of it he suggested himself."

"So he politely *asked* you to knock him unconscious?"

"That was an oversight." Unmother waved Cade's words off with one of her soft hands. "Xan overestimated his strength and healing abilities. He'll be fine. Our best medical team is attending to him."

The confusion Cade felt in that moment climbed into her head and rivaled the Noise. It made no sense, and that fact pounded on a loop, threaded through with static and random sound.

Nosensenosensenosense.

"But you stole him . . ."

"The place we took him from wasn't his home, Cadence. It was a laboratory where he was brutally experimented on." Unmother's lips tightened, her volume kicked down a few notches. "You, of all people, must understand that."

Cade thought back to a screen full of crawling babies. She didn't need a lecture on how the Firstbloom scientists were less-than-perfect.

"Still . . ." She grabbed for words. "Why would Xan want you to hurt him?"

"It was desperate, Cadence, but we needed you to get here." She stood up and paced. "Xan is an intelligent, receptive young man. He figured out within the space of a few hours that we were human."

Cade flushed, sour-faced, embarassed. She had come half-way across the universe without an inkling. But Unmother didn't seem to care about that. She had a story to tell, and she wasn't letting Cade's emotions get in the way.

"Xan asked our aims, and we found that there was a great deal we could agree on. But all of our plans hinged on you, Cadence. Teams were sent to recover you, of course." The attack on Renna. The Unmakers who had come to find her, following Mr. Smithjoneswhite's tracer code. The howls that reached for her through the walls. "There were difficulties and delays, moments when we thought you wouldn't come.

"He was the one who came up with the idea," Unmother said, getting animated now, laying it out for Cade like she was letting her in on the secret plan. "He set out the thresholds of our actions. He was never in mortal danger. Flesh wounds, strategic bruises. We made things look more dire than they were."

Unmother nodded at the pile of creature on the floor — metal and plastic, molded and bound. "We have some experience with theatrics."

So the costumes were a twisted bit of playacting. But the pain—that had been real. For fleeting moments it had torn at Cade's skin, churned her insides. She clutched herself across the middle, remembering.

"Why?"

Unmother cocked her head. "Perhaps I didn't explain it well enough."

"No," Cade said. She nodded at the little room, the costume parts, the ship. "Why . . . all of it?"

Unmother sighed. She stopped her pacing in front of the mirror, blocking out its silver-glint.

"So it will never happen again."

"But no one has ever been entangled before," Cade said. "Xan and I are the first."

"Yes," Unmother said. "But the human race has been connected before. And nothing good came of it. When humans flourished on their own planet, they had technologies that kept people as connected as could be imagined. Do you know what happened, Cadence? Wars, terrible violence. I'm sure you know that Earth blinked out, but did you know that it was all but destroyed at that point? The soil, air, even the oceans. Tainted with chemicals. Choked with trash. Ruined."

Cade knocked against the wall, her breath gone, her thoughts boiled down to a whimper. She had been allowed to think, her whole life, that Earth was a perfect, untouched blue-green paradise she couldn't be a part of because some asteroid said otherwise. Now it was another nonplace, like the black holes — sucking in her hope and thoughts like light, giving nothing back.

"That was why humans looked to space," Unmother said. "To escape from the messes they had made, and start making them all over again on some new planet. The Scattering was the best thing that happened to humans, and to the rest of the universe. Apart, humans are weak. Together, they are a great force — used for destruction."

It didn't escape Cade's blunt-edged sense of irony that she was being told this by an Unmaker.

"You do a bit of destruction yourselves."

"We work hard, yes . . . fight . . . to make sure nothing like that ever happens again." Unmother thought what she was saying was noble and true. Cade thought it was a jumble of noise, added to the Noise in her head.

"What was done by the scientists on Firstbloom has to be undone. If you and Xan live, the path to a new age will be clear. And we can't let that happen, Cadence. We're sworn against it. For the good of all."

"You're going to murder us," Cade said.

"We're not as brutal as you'd like to think." Unmother's soft hands, soft voice, inched Cade toward believing it — but everything she knew about the Unmakers tore her in the other direction. "We do things to intimidate, to keep people safe — which means keeping them apart. Yes, there have been times when we've used violence, but those few times have stemmed a tide so much greater." Unmother leaned in and put a hand to Cade's hair. Cade twitched away. "There is no need for us to hurt you, if you can see the reason in what we're saying."

Cade slammed into her wild, blinding fear of the Unmakers. This woman was willing to do horrible things to Xan. The reasons didn't matter. Xan mattered. And because Cade still had to save him, first she needed to know what she was up against.

"If I do agree with you?" Cade asked. "What then?"

"An act of pure selflessness." A new gleam captured Unmother's eyes, made her whole body sing bright. "A sacrifice."

"Sacrifice." The word soured in Cade's mouth. "I can tell you right now, I'm not going to volunteer to be murdered."

"You should see Xan, before you decide anything," Unmother said as she gathered up her robes and her thin metal bones, the pieces of her other self. "You did come all this way."

The woman left Cade on the crumpled sheets, back pressed to the wall.

CHAPTER 20

CHAOS A deterministic system, such as
a quantum system, which is nonetheless
impossible to predict

Cade sat forward on the bed. She could hear a single pair of
footsteps, heading down the hall.

The next person she saw would be Xan. Cade was sure of it.

Whether he came to her or she went to him, whether they
were thrown together by the Unmakers or the simple fact of
their own small but important gravities, collapsing into each
other. Cade would meet him soon.

She had been fed so many strange, hopeless ideas by Unmother, but she hadn't lost one drop of her faith in Xan. He
had seen through the Unmakers' disguises. He must have
been able to see through their elaborate reasoning, too. He
wouldn't have been taken in. And if Xan *was* working with
the Unmakers, he couldn't have held all of that back from
Cade when they were connected — could he?

No. Cade was sure of that. She was sure of him. But she felt a new tremor underneath what she was sure of—a thrum that wandered up and down her spine and shot into her fingertips, electrified her awareness. So when the door flew open and Cade was sure it would be Xan—and it wasn't him at all, it was Rennik with his head high and his hands tied behind his back—the thrum gathered. Grew.

"Yes, thank you," Rennik said to the Unmakers guarding the door. "I won't be a minute."

The Unmakers shut him in. Rennik turned to face Cade, and strain broke through in a hundred small ways—the setting of his forehead, the leap of a vein, the crunch of fingers into a ready fist.

"Lee?" she asked. "Ayumi? Renna?" Even, "Gori?"

"All fine," Rennik said.

Cade sighed. After the first wave of fear passed, a new one bobbed up. "You're prisoners."

"Oh, this?" Rennik tossed a backwards nod at the ties on his wrists. "We were captured, but the bonds are a formality. Renna is cleared for deep space, so I have every right to be in Hades, and the Unmakers don't care to start a war. Not with the Hatchum, at least."

"But I thought you were"—her voice swam to a low note—"*an outlaw.*"

"Yes, but I don't go around telling that to people who capture me."

"What about the others?" Cade asked. "None of them are Hatchum. How are we getting them out of here?"

"I made it clear to our hosts that I was holding the humans in custody, and that the confiscation of Hatchum prisoners would also result in war."

Cade's first sigh was thin with relief. The second was curt, almost a laugh. "They don't care about the others," she said. "Just me."

Rennik's whole noble bearing collapsed.

"You . . . were not negotiable."

Cade's throat closed, full-stop. She had to work it open to ask, "So how did you get in here?"

"I made up a story about intelligence you're carrying that only I can extract. I made you out as a rat who stowed aboard the ship, a rat I only recently flushed out — and the canny leader of a human resistance." Rennik couldn't seem to fight down the smile that spread across his face. "They were all too eager to believe me."

"Easier to believe that lie than the truth," Cade said. "That a Hatchum could be neck-deep in helping humans."

Rennik held out his bound wrists. "I have five minutes. It's enough time to prove them wrong, Cadence."

She looked up, tracing the lines of his arms, the concerned face, the urgent eyes.

"Cadence?" he asked again.

Unmother had called her that. The scientists on Firstbloom, too. But it was the name Cade's mother had given her, once, and she still loved to hear it coming from the right mouths. Rennik had been using it ever since she got back from the shipping lanes of Hymnia. She hadn't noticed until now, when her name was the only thing in a too-small room.

It sounded right.

"We need to leave," Rennik said. "Lee is in a cell down the hall. They would have left her onboard the ship with Gori, but she resisted surrender." Cade couldn't help it — she laughed at the thought of Lee turning her explosive combinations of curse words on the Unmakers. "We'll collect her on our way back to Renna."

Cade shook her head. An escape plan had crash-landed in her lap, but she couldn't take it. Not without Xan.

"Rennik, you have to go," she said. "You all have to go."

"Renna would be offended by that, to say the least. She's attached to you. And I . . ." Rennik shifted from one foot to the other, and back. "I said I was coming to Hades with you. I won't leave unless you're onboard."

Cade grabbed his wrists.

"Let me get to work on this."

Rennik sat at the perfect edge of the bed, facing away from Cade. Her fingers lighted on the ties. She tried not to look too hard at the impossible knots. She focused on Rennik's wide back, the sharp scrawl of his profile.

"She was killed by . . . *them,*" Rennik said.

Cade hadn't wanted Lee to face the Unmakers for her sake. But it was just as bad for Rennik — in a different way.

Cade pried free a strand of the knot on Rennik's left hand. There were still at least ten strands on each. She worked a nail in. The muscles that rivered down Rennik's back tightened as he started to speak.

"It happened after the banishment. Renna had been space-worthy for years, and I had been running passengers, so I kept running passengers. But without the proper connections and the expected paperwork, I could only get the worst clearance on the seediest planets. And I couldn't take Lee and Moira everywhere they needed to go for the Express, not without putting them in more danger. It sounds ridiculous when I say it now." Rennik laughed — an uncorked sound — so loud that Cade worried about the guards. But he wasn't afraid. He was safe in the folds of another time, a story-space where the pain was in the past.

"I was the one who arranged that flight from Sligh," Rennik said. "I was the one who told her it would be safe."

Cade's hands went numb on the ties. She rubbed across her knuckles, got them working, and watched Rennik's face as sadness and panic shot under it like flickers of fire.

"It's happening again," he said.

Cade couldn't see his eyes now, they were turned away. All she could do was redouble her attack on the knots.

"You didn't fail her," Cade said. "I know that you swore —"

"To help humans," Rennik said. "I do that where I can, Cadence. But it's not just that. Not all humans remind me of her."

One of the knots came undone.

"And I do?"

"Of course."

Cade swore quietly. Her fingers scraped along a row of three small knots underneath the one she'd picked loose.

"Sit tight," Cade said.

But something inside of her wouldn't be still. She tried to call up the precise words Rennik had used to describe Moira. *Fierce, imperfect, in love with too much.* Fierce, Cade could understand. Imperfect — that was as obvious as sweat under the noon sun. But she had never been compared to someone who cared too much.

She worked at the small knots.

"You really are just like her," Rennik said. "You're scowling back there, I can feel it. All those knots. She would have scowled, too."

Rennik shone at the memory of this girl who was gone, and Cade could see that Moira wasn't really gone — not for him. The connection was live, and Rennik used it to steer him through his days.

Cade rested her hands on his upturned wrists. When she talked, the words went over his shoulder. "The knots are too much," she said. "I can't undo them. So you're going to have to tell me if you want me to stop."

Before he could say something too reasonable and ruin it, Cade swung to Rennik's side and centered his face between her numb hands. The distance between them was inches, or galaxies. She stared at him for less than a second. More than an unraveled light-year. Scale made no sense. Time lost the firmness of its hold. Now Rennik's calm was not a Hatchum oddity. His eyes coded their signs in a language Cade could read. He filled them with patience. Steadiness. A *yes* that wouldn't make her flinch, or alter the course.

The distance between them was impossible.

Then it was gone.

Time and the solidness of things rushed back up to meet them as soon as Cade reached the high curve of Rennik's mouth. Her hands slid down his face, down the front of him like glass. Her lips took a few moments to find the pulse of this specific kiss — slow, with a linger on the upbeat. And then it was warmth and softness in matched rhythms. Over much too fast.

"Why did you do that?" Rennik asked, looking at her at a much closer range than anyone had before. She couldn't take in his whole face at once, so she focused on the outside crease of his left eye.

"Because I might die. Because of Moira. I don't know."

Rennik nodded as if that made perfect sense. But his legs shook, even under the light pressure of her hands.

"It's time," he said. "We have to go."

Cade shook her head. "I need to get to Xan." His name chased off the moment, and Cade landed back in a cold cell on a dangerous ship in a vast stretch of nowhere. "I came all the way here, Rennik. I can't leave without him."

"We'll find him on our way out," Rennik said, and he was on his feet, headed for the door.

"It's not that simple," Cade said. "He might be working

with the Unmakers." She didn't believe it, but she had to be ready in case it turned out to be true.

"If he's on their side, don't trust him," Rennik said. "Don't even look at him, if it can be avoided."

But her connection to Xan would never let her rest until he was conscious, until she saw him, until he was safe.

A knock sounded in the thick metal door.

Rennik slumped, and in the soft white light, tired and etched, he looked exactly human. "We have to get Lee and get out of this place. If you think we can find him in time . . ."

Another knock, and a kick at the door.

"I can do it," Cade said.

Rennik braced a shoulder against the metal, ready in case the Unmakers decided to slam it in.

"What now?" he asked.

Cade stood up with a mattress-creak. Crossed the room to the mirror. The mirror that all of a sudden made sense — because the Unmakers who'd put it there had been human this whole time. Cade wanted to tell Rennik, but their minutes were up. She tipped the mirror, and it shattered on the cold white floor.

The Unmakers were in the room in less than ten seconds.

In that time, Cade grabbed a shard of cracked mirror, sliced the ties off Rennik's wrists, stooped again for a handful of mirror dust.

She stuck the shard in the swirled robes of the first Unmaker and wrenched it up, drawing a line from the collarbone. Now that she knew they were costumed, she could use it against them. Instead of cracking herself on plastic and metal, she tore the cloth from the Unmaker's face. As soon as she saw the blear of pale blue eyes, she tossed the mirror dust.

The Unmaker screamed — a reedy, unamplified sound. Now that Cade knew they were human, her fear was scaled down in proportion. Two humans against a Noise-battered Cade and a soft-hearted Hatchum? She had seen enough bar fights on Andana to know what made a fair one.

She kicked low and swept the legs of the second Unmaker.

He went down with a head-crack on glass.

Fair enough.

"How many in the halls?" Cade ran out of the small room, Rennik trailing.

"Patrols of two," he said. "And a few large groups, but they were out on the perimeter. This is the heart of the ship."

Of course it was. No windows. Fewer clues about where prisoners were held. Ringed on all sides by Unmakers, so that if someone did escape, they wouldn't stay escaped for long.

"Are all of the holding cells in this cluster?" Cade asked.

"I'm not sure," Rennik said. "But I know where they took Lee."

He didn't have a chance to tell her, because a two-man patrol appeared along the far curve of the hall.

Cade didn't wait for the rush. She was the rush, streaming her voice behind her like a banner.

Before the Unmakers knew how to handle her, she had

unarmed the first guard and tested the knees of the second. By the time Rennik caught up, Cade had them fighting hand-to-hand. The little gloves of the Unmakers were slippery where they landed, and glanced off her skin. Stitches in the leather printed themselves to her cheekbone. She reached up with her right hand to check the damage, and the Unmaker snatched her fingers.

Cade lashed out with the mirror shard in her left hand, starting in on the Unmaker's robes. A thump to one side let her know that Rennik had put his guard down. With another well-aimed blow, hers went down, too.

The Unmakers blended into one black stain on the ground. This time it was Rennik who hurried off. Cade stopped to check the swelling of her cheek, to push down the wildness of her heart.

And then she ran.

She took a blind curve at top speed, arms out, and almost slammed Lee to the ground. Cade caught their combined balance and slung them both into the wall instead.

Lee pushed Cade back, holding her at arm's length.

"You *snugging spacecadet!*"

"That's one way to say thank you," Rennik said as he caught up.

Lee's laugh was so big, she could barely fit in the words. "You're right." She flew at Cade on purpose this time, arms flung over-wide, pretending to knock her down, but catching her up in a hug at the last second.

"First-class rescue."

"Come on." Cade pulled Lee's hand, tapped Rennik on the shoulder as she passed him, and they were off.

Onto a new length of hall and another batch of doors, staring at Cade white as rolled-back eyes.

If she had her up-and-functioning entanglement instead of the Noise, Cade would have been able to follow her own body to Xan, like the dreamwalk that happens when a person is pointed toward home. The turns that spin themselves before memory can catch up and garble the directions. The magnetic on-and-on, the weighted pull of it, the need.

"Hey, Cade, Renna's back the other way," Lee said.

"Where are we going?" Rennik asked. No uptick in his steps, no hitch in his voice. But Cade could see past the shallows of his calm now, to the depths of feeling. He would worry until she told him where they were headed. Unfortunately, Cade had to do more than inspect the identical doors to know that.

She needed to connect to Xan. And that meant kicking the Noise out of her head.

Cade thought back to Andana, back to Club V, and the night when her head went silent. She started with the show — labcoat in the crowd, spacesicks throbbing at the edge of the stage, lights setting their brand on Cade's skin. She had never examined that night, turned it around like a stone, looked at its underside. Now Cade blasted down the white halls, Rennik and Lee close behind, and remembered.

She followed her old self through the set, then backstage.

She met Mr. Niven again. Distrusted him again. Cade fast-forwarded through the filmstrip — she'd had enough of that white-spliced lie. When she got past it, she slowed down. Stuck on the part where the idea of entanglement took hold.

Cade had assumed that it was Xan coming out of his coma that had defeated the Noise. But Mr. Niven had never told her that. Maybe she'd put the idea together backwards. It could make all the difference. Play a line of music forwards, it was pure meaning. Play the same line backwards, it was whine and drone. Useless.

Maybe Xan hadn't turned off the Noise at all.

Maybe Cade had woken him up.

And if she had done that once, she could do it again. The music had made it happen that time. But Cade didn't have Moon-White. Besides, making sounds of the loud-enough-to-scare-off-the-static variety would bring a pack of Unmakers so fast that Cade didn't count it as an option. But there was another possibility. She had sent music — real music — to Ayumi's mind, without making a sound.

She would have to do that. But first she needed to reach out, open up, and overwhelm the Noise.

The attempt came out rusty at first, all sharp notes and stabbing rhythms. She fiddled with it while Rennik took the lead, kept her moving, eyes slanted back at her even as he rushed.

The Noise needed structure to cancel it out. Well-built, intentional, intricate music. But it demanded surprise, too, or else it would beat her to whatever punch she wanted to pull. Cade swelled over it, smothered it, ordered it to sit down and play dead.

But she couldn't quite kill it.

She tried to remember the song she'd played at Club V, remake it in miniature in her head. Verse-chorus-verse. Comfort food.

And then the bridge. Cade hit it, and for the first time, she could see where she was headed, the spot on the other bank where she wanted to land. It had been an unformed place for too long. Now it was a few steps in the right direction — a certain, small white room.

Cade was close to overcoming the Noise. She could feel it. All she had to do was insist. And that meant getting loud. So she turned the volume up, cranked it higher, until she thought her head would split down the center and pour out music in loud colors. The coma static slipped into the background. When it gave out, she stopped.

Dead in front of a door, the same as all the other doors.

But this one she tapped open.

"Cadence?"

His voice filled the space that the Noise had scraped out. It rang through her like bells.

Less than ten steps across the room to Xan, but they were the longest, strangest steps of Cade's life.

She saw him and he wasn't in her head, and she wasn't in his. He wasn't a symphony of feelings that she could slip into. He was a boy, in a too-small room, waking up. Paler than clouds. Brighter than the nearest sun.

"Hey," she said, but the word didn't matter, because it could mean whatever she needed it to, as long as she filled it up right.

"Hey," he said.

She could feel it in the corners of her eyes — a crescendo of itch. Tears came easy this time. Xan smiled with such fullness that it looked like pain. But Cade knew the difference.

"You closed the space," he said.

Cade put a hand out and touched his. Sturdy fingers, trim nails, the soft dry skin that came from never leaving a space-craft.

Just a hand. But her whole body sang bright.

Xan reached out and pulled her to him in one clean sweep. Touching someone else — Ayumi, Lee, even Rennik — was a beautiful difficulty. Being this close to Xan felt as simple and right as standing in the sun after the sandstorms passed, after days spent in deep-dwelling darkness.

As soon as Cade returned his smile, Xan's face fell into a new mold. His lips set straight, and crowded — she saw now — with scars.

"This place is filled with spacecadets," he said. "Let's drain."

CHAPTER 21

ANTI-CORRELATED A relationship defined by opposing behaviors

Xan was out of the bed in one burst. It wasn't long since he'd been beaten to empty-headed blackness, but there was no lag, no learning curve. He crossed the room in a blur, moving as fast as thought.

Or faster. Cade's mind — and her feet — slogged to catch up.

She was with Xan. They were leaving Hades together. He wasn't in league with the Unmakers. Or was he? When she reached out for Xan's thoughts, all she could feel was his need to blaze a perfect line out of that nameless ship and into the freedom of space.

With her.

The hall stood clear, with Rennik and Lee still guarding the door.

"What are they doing here?" Xan asked. Cade was struck with a sudden and absolute appreciation of the fact that Xan had been out cold when she was kissing Rennik. Her heart rate had shot to such heights that the failsafe would have snapped on, no question. The thought of it was enough to swear off kissing for the rest of time.

Cade took that back in the next breath. Now that she'd been brave enough to do it once, she couldn't imagine keeping her distance from people she wanted to kiss. She would have to develop some kind of pulse-slowing technique. She looked from Rennik's open face to Xan's impatient trace of a smile, and practiced it.

"These are my friends," Cade said, each word slow and deliberate.

"I know," Xan said. "I've seen them." *In your head,* he added, with a straight-on look at Cade.

Cade's voice picked up speed without her permission. "So what's the issue?" *You're the one we need to worry about.* She couldn't help transmitting the thought. Xan was a tractor beam for her emotions.

He stepped in, like getting close to her could somehow keep out Rennik and Lee. The space he made by putting his hands on her shoulders circled the two of them into their own little atmosphere.

"You didn't come alone," he said.

Cade thought of Ayumi, Renna, Gori, even Moon-White, all waiting. She had come anything but alone.

"I didn't know that was part of the deal."

Cade wondered at how fast she could move from the blissful overtures of first seeing Xan to the dissonance she felt now. He laughed, and it reminded her of sand grating on her ankles.

She remembered what Mr. Niven and the filmstrip had told her, once upon a time. That when two entangled people were in proximity, their moods would match. As in, oppose. It had something to do with their particles—so attuned that a change in either of them would tip the scales. They would keep this up, switching back and forth, as long as they were together. But something made it bearable. Knowing that, in some deeper place, he was the same, that they were bound in sameness. That's what it meant to match—to be perfectly one, to be diametrically different. The word held both meanings. Cade had never thought about that fact until she stared it in the beautiful, irritating face.

Xan stepped out of their little sphere and let Rennik and Lee back into the conversation with a shrug. "It's nothing personal. Just that I have a plan. And it seats two."

"Then you have a subpar plan," Lee said.

"Rennik has his own ship," Cade said, pulling Lee back a step. "They can follow us."

Nods were tipped all around and the group broke into a loose formation with Xan at the head, steering them in an unknown direction, twisting down sudden halls and sending them through doors that opened into new passages. Cade turned back to Rennik and, not caring if Xan heard, said, "Stick close."

Rennik cut a look at the back of Xan's head and mouthed the word *Very*.

But now that it was Rennik piling the suspicion on thick,

Cade wanted to defend Xan, chime out his good points, blacken the eyes of anyone who said different. She wondered if that was a part of entanglement, or just a part of her.

"Come on," Xan said, half turning as he hurtled down a new stretch of hall. "It's this way."

What is? Cade asked.

But Xan was too far to turn around and tell her now.

He slammed into a patrol at the first bend. Any residue of worry about Xan being on the side of the Unmakers was scrubbed clean in one blow. He ran at the first one and laid it flat. Then he attacked three at a time, taking out their plastic bones, cracking their shells. Xan knew just how to send them down, with strikes he must have practiced in his head for weeks. Cade sent him strength, and he sent it back in waves so wild, she had to brace herself with one hand against the wall, and regain her balance, before she dashed into the fight.

Cade's first Unmaker went down easy. With Xan awake, Cade was stronger than any human, and he was, too. It helped that she knew the Unmakers' weaknesses — Xan sent her the secrets he'd gathered, one flash at a time. The crunchable toes. The soggy bit at the back of the knees. The thin lines of flesh where robes met.

She tried it out on the second Unmaker — toes, knees, flesh — and it worked. But another Unmaker was waiting and got in too quickly, too close. An arm shot out and ground her into the nearest wall. A whiff of metal breath reminded Cade of the mechanical voice box. She faked a punch to the throat and, instead, swept her palm up at the last moment and hammered metal into the Unmaker's face. Her fingers rang and reddened. The Unmaker hit the ground.

Lee and Rennik formed a second line of defense, taking care of the few guards who rushed past Cade and Xan. But Cade didn't want her friends to have to fight at all. They had seen enough of the Unmakers for one lifetime. Lee had come with Cade, set and stubborn, all the way from Andana. Now Cade could do something to pay her back. She stationed herself right in front of Lee and took down Unmakers one by one. And because of the strength that came from her entanglement, and all those years lived from scrap to scrap at the Parentless Center and backstage at Club V, Cade was good at it.

Very good.

Fighting was a song—the beat of it breath, the harmonies bone-crack and the dull thud of skin. It wasn't pretty music. But it was electric, it was alive. Cade wouldn't smile through death to please the Unmakers. She was grim-faced, raw-knuckled, terrifying, terrified.

A fourth Unmaker went down. A fifth.

Ten in less than two minutes. And the rest of the patrol around them, sprawled on the ground.

"Not bad," Xan said. He stepped over a snapped plastic collarbone and kept running.

Now it seemed like they met a patrol every minute, but there was no stopping, no hesitation. There was just the clash, bright as moon-rise, and the horrible mess that came after it. Cade followed Xan, sure that he knew the escape route. He never doubled back or stopped to check his position. She won-dered at how well he seemed to know the entire station. But she didn't have time to ask about how he got so sure-footed.

"Almost there," Xan said.

Lee and Rennik's footsteps fell back, but Cade kept time with him even as he picked up speed. Around another bend, another patrol sprang out. Cade and Xan ran at the Unmakers, steps hitting at the same time. When the blows were struck, she felt her own and she felt Xan's. She saw two fights at the same time, and she was winning both.

"Here," Xan cried.

Cade landed a punch, looked up, and found that there was no one left to fight.

Xan jammed a button on a mundane-looking control panel. Out of a slab of plain white wall, a hatch swirled out and open. Cade turned to gather Lee and Rennik, but they had peeled off at some point. She remembered asking them not to do that. But they had a ship to get back to. Other people to keep safe.

Cade and Xan were on their own, together.

The ship looked like it was designed for one person — a single chair, tilted to face the controls, a rim of open space around it. Cade wouldn't have been comfortable in there with anyone else. The hatch sealed behind Xan.

"So," he said. "Welcome to the plan."

Xan got in the pilot's chair and warmed up the controls with a few scalelike taps.

"Have you ever flown before?" she asked, each tap louder in her ears. It seemed like a legitimate question. Xan had been in a coma for most of his life.

"Don't worry," he said. "I have the course all figured out." He unrolled a complicated schematic in crabbed handwriting, complete with strikeouts and smudges. "Simple. See?" He smiled up at her.

Cade put her own lack of smile down to the whole entanglement business.

Xan took off with a clunk that would have made Ayumi blush. Cade wrapped her arms around the back of the pilot's chair so she wouldn't crash on the nearest flat surface.

A strip of window ran around the center of the pod like a ribbon. Cade twisted back to look at the Unmaker's station, small as a batch of fingerprints, leaving its mark on Hades. The docks were quiet. No alarms, no explosion of lights, no spitting out of palm-shaped ships.

"You're not being followed," Cade said, turning back to Xan. "Why aren't you being followed?"

"Cadence," he said. "I know you're worried that they turned me somehow. But you can search my mind. You have free range in there. Do you think I could hide something that important from you?"

"I don't know," she said. "But I'll take that as an invitation to find out."

She planted herself on the wide arm of the pilot's chair and looked down at the contours of Xan's face, carved to deep gullies of concentration. It was distracting, his face. The strong bridge of his nose, the swipes of purple-gray under his eyes. She had come so far, wanting to see him like this. To be this close. Now their bodies were just another space she needed to cross. She needed to push past all of that to his thoughts.

She felt a certain amount of relief streaming through him, like a breeze—had Xan ever felt a real, planetbound breeze? Maybe the blowing of an air vent. And there was excitement, too. Cade had never found that in his head before. It was cool and crisp at the same time—like a patch of shade on a perfect day. He was excited to be with her, excited for whatever came next. But when she tried to see past the feeling to the facts of his plan, she felt—nothing.

No. Not nothing.

Blackness, and then a rush of light.

"I don't think you're hiding something from me," Cade said, "but there are parts of this I don't understand."

"We're not mind-readers, Cadence." Xan kept his eyes on the patch of space in front of them, tore the ship from the encroaching dark of a black hole. "That's not the point of entanglement."

"And what is?"

Unhappiness hit Cade—from Xan's thoughts, from his scarred face and soured posture. "Please don't expect me to echo the scientists who made us," he said. "I have ideas of my own."

Cade hated the scientists who made them, but only most of the time. They had done terrible things. To children. To mothers. But they were also the ones who'd entangled her, and she wouldn't unentangle herself, not even if she could twist time, loop it back on itself, and stop Project QE before it started. Her hate was complicated — a pit inside of her, burning but cold, an ice planet on a far-flung orbit. She could ignore it if she had to, and most of the time she did.

Xan's feelings about Firstbloom were stronger — hot at the core and on the surface.

Cade shifted the subject. "You seem to know so much about the whole process. How entanglement works. And you'd been in a coma for . . ."

She didn't want to number the years.

"The scientists took that as an opportunity to see how much they could stuff into my brain while it was in that state. I remember facts, but not learning them. They float up from a sort of . . . grayness. I'm sure I'm supposed to be grateful."

"That's how you understand so much about entanglement?"

"I woke up knowing about it, yes. Maybe that helped me figure out the connection faster." His fingers danced on the buttons. "How to control it. Turn it on, off, up, down." He smiled at her. "Not that I ever turned you down."

Cade had wondered why she'd been the slow one, lagging behind him, not understanding so much for so long. But she couldn't bring herself to be jealous, even if their difference did make him smarter and better at being entangled. Cade had a mother somewhere. That made up for a whole universe of troubles.

"Hey." Xan's focus slid off to one side of the ship. "Aren't those your friends?"

Cade turned and saw little black eyes, each one dull in the lightless reaches of space. Renna blinked at her.

Cade's smile could have lit the black between them.

Xan shrank back in the pilot's chair. The scars on his arms puckered as he reached for the controls, wrapped his hands around them. He flew a few sickly evasive maneuvers—a dip, two clunks to the left, a fumbled dodge. Renna could have outclassed him in her sleep.

"Hey!" Cade said. "Those are my friends. You said so yourself. Stop trying to shake them."

"You might want to call them off. It's dangerous out here. If you don't know where you're headed." The sweat on his forehead stood out pale on his skin like a line of shivering blisters.

Cade could do it. She could call Renna off—without tech, without trouble. She had made it to Hades and collected Xan. They were safe and away from the Unmakers. She could reach out into her friends' heads and find a way to tell them, *I don't need you anymore. Get safe. Go home.*

Instead, she turned to Xan.

"Look," Cade said, "I love a surprise as much as the next lab-altered girl, but where are we going?"

"You're going to think it's perfect." He touched his schematic like a charm, then touched her wrist. "Promise."

That one word cast a spell on Cade, sure as the opening chords of an old throat-worn song. There was no fighting it.

She had promised to cross the universe for Xan, and here she was. If he promised that they were headed to a place worth being, she would listen.

But she still didn't leave the window, didn't stop watching Renna. She imagined Rennik at the controls, smooth and calm, looking like a pane of glass but underneath molten, hot-hearted, caring too much. She missed Lee's arm around her shoulder, there when she wanted it and there when she thought she didn't. And she had more to learn from Gori. As much as she could stand. And Moon-White, she needed to get back to Moon-White, and her fingers on frets. And who would make sure Ayumi recovered and didn't go full-on spacesick? She had songs to play inside that girl's head.

That was when Cade knew — she'd lagged in her connection with Xan not because she was bad at being entangled, but because she'd been too busy making connections with people who weren't him.

"So you have a plan," Cade said, still staring at the remains of the old plan. The ship and the people who had gotten her this far. "You could have transmitted it to me at any point. Why wait?"

"I needed to know that I could trust you, Cadence," he said, looking surprised that it needed to be said.

Cade thought of the times she'd felt him hold something back and assumed he was doing it to keep her safe, to shield her from the worst of the torture.

"You were *testing me?*"

"No," he said. "That's not the word I would use. I was

taking my time. To get to know you. All the facts and ideas I had about you came from our . . . technicians," he said with a caustic rasp in his throat. "And since I couldn't trust them, how could I know to trust you?"

Cade's fingers rested on the back of the pilot's chair, inches away from Xan. Anger surged through their tips, up her arms, straight to her center. She fought it down by casting herself back to the days on Andana when she'd first learned about Xan — when she didn't trust Mr. Niven and didn't know what to make of entanglement. Before she had learned to be so fierce about Xan, to care about him as much as she cared about herself.

"I spent years being filled up on the whispers of First-bloom," he said. "How strong you were, how superior to me. It should have made me hate you, but it didn't. It fed the need to find you. To see what you were, to know for my-self. When you called me, I woke up. When I called you, you came. There's one step left, Cadence. This is the one we take together."

Cade felt the rightness of this wash over her. She moved to the side of the chair, touched his shoulder, then dropped her arm down across his chest, held him close. He smelled like sheets and sleep, like triple-washed air and ice. Clean and good and pure things. He was going to tell her, finally, the meaning of entanglement. Unfold its secrets for her, uncrum-ple the directions to the life she had been living. The purpose she'd been straining to find.

Xan looked from space to Cade and back again. "It wasn't

fully formed, when I woke up. The plan. Strange, but the people back on the station gave it to me. Of course, they didn't know that's what they were doing. Those people . . ."

"I call them Unmakers," Cade said.

Xan held her arm to his chest, clasped her there. The connection was closed. In space. In time. If someone saw them in shadow, they would look like one figure. He leaned in and pulled her toward him with the hand that wasn't working the controls. The softness of his breath was hers now. The hundred blues and the one hint of green that swirled his eyes. It was all hers.

Kissing was nothing compared to this. Not that she planned to mention that fact to Xan.

"Unmakers," he said with a laugh. "That's . . . appropriate."

"Tell me what happened." Cade could have gone swimming in his mind and come up clutching the story. But she was tired of all the grasping, the working to get to him. She wanted him to give the story to her, as a gift.

"I woke up on Firstbloom," he said. "For a minute. Less. A flicker. And then . . . I woke up again, and I was there, on that station, in that cell. You know the one." Cade saw it in one here-and-gone blink of white, courtesy of Xan's mind or her own memories — she couldn't be sure which.

"The Unmakers wanted us because they were afraid," Xan said. "Some new era of man." His voice grew large and filled the pod. "Spacesick cured! The Scattering — reversed!

Maybe even a new home planet! With the entangled leading the charge." Cade felt the optimism of those words clang in the air. But the way Xan spoke them was all brass and no substance. He shook his head. "It's the same delusion the scientists had."

"Delusion?" Cade wasn't so sure. The more she saw of what her mind could do, the more she was convinced that she could help the spacesicks. And with spacesick cleared, maybe the Scattering *could* be reversed.

A home planet? Cade thought.

That's one I haven't heard before.

"Ridiculous, right?" Xan pushed a lever forward to the sticking point. The pod sped past another string of black holes. It seemed like they were headed deeper into Hades.

"The need to stop humans from becoming more than they are now is what drives the Unmakers," Xan said. "They wouldn't stop until they had both of us. I was a captive on Firstbloom. Easy to pluck. You were harder to find and much, much harder to catch." He shot an arm around her waist. "But I knew you were coming. You were as strong as the scientists said, and more. There was no question in my mind that you would make it to the station. Even if it did take some . . . reminding."

Cade knew this part. Or at least, the version Unmother had told her. She dropped to one knee and ran a hand along Xan's arm, inspected his scars with a critical eye. Thin crosses of pure white flesh. She'd seen enough wounds to know that these could never bleed out. They were shallow, painful. Showy.

"Did you really let the Unmakers torture you?"

"Here," he said, shifting to his feet. "Take the seat for a minute."

"But I don't know how to —"

"Fly?" he said. "That's all right. It's on a sort of autopilot."

She dropped down and put her hands on the panels, at the ready, like she'd seen Rennik and Ayumi do. Her eyes slid from the view in front of her to Xan as he wrenched open the door of a small closet.

"You didn't answer me," Cade said.

Again, she could go into his head and plunder his thoughts, if it came down to that. But she wanted to hear the words.

"Xan?"

The thin closet held a spacesuit. No. Two spacesuits. He pulled out the pieces of one and started to assemble it over his clothes.

"I let the Unmakers torture me to prove that I was on their side. It was the strongest pact I could think of under the circumstances. It wasn't hard to figure out them out. All they care about, all they understand, is sacrifice. Pain. To talk to them about beauty, connection, love . . . it's a waste. So I didn't. I showed them what they wanted to see."

"And what is that?" Cade asked.

Xan strapped on the gloves and stood in front of her, suited up to his neck in thick white fabric.

"A human, ready for sacrifice."

Cade's stomach did — as Lee called it — the gravity ballet. It rose up and pressed her insides. She checked to be sure Renna was still bobbing alongside the ship. But she'd fallen back.

"Xan," she said, her voice so thin, it was almost transparent. "The Unmakers wanted me to —"

"I know what they want. I let them think I wanted the same things, the same sort of sacrifice, for the same reasons. It granted me trust, and the information I needed to help us escape. I'm sure that's why we haven't been followed. They'll send a crew after us soon enough, to be sure the job is done."

"The job?"

Something was wrong. Something in Cade's stomach. Something in her heart. And around the ship, a new smoothness in the air. Cade kept her eyes on Xan's lips.

He would explain.

"Death isn't enough for the Unmakers," he said. "Not a mundane death. Not for us. We're too dangerous. If even the least particle of us is left intact, it could be studied. Others could be entangled."

It's not enough for us to die, Cade thought. *We need to be unmade.*

"So they brought me here," Xan said. "To Hades. And they lured you . . ."

"Here. To Hades." The warning of the Matalan floated back to Cade, across time and space. From some pit of a bar on Andana to this particular nowhere, surrounded on all sides by black holes.

A place of negation.

It all rushed together in Cade's head. The place. The plot. The sacrifice that the Unmakers demanded.

It made sour, twisted sense. But it still sounded impossible when Cade said it.

"They want to feed us to a black hole."

Xan gathered her hands in his, the fabric of the suit catching on her skin.

"No, Cadence. They want us to feed *ourselves* to a black hole."

Cade untacked her eyes from Xan's face and turned. The black in front of the ship was the darkest she'd ever seen. The darkest she could imagine. So much dark that light seemed like a lie someone had told her once.

Cade focused on Xan's face, and gave him one more chance to tell her that she was wrong.

"Please," Cade said. "Tell me you didn't steer us into the blackest black hole in Hades."

Xan smiled. And didn't say a thing.

CHAPTER 22

BLACK HOLE A region of inescapable gravity

Cade looked out and saw black, black, black, stretched so wide there were no edges. She sat down at the controls, which she could push in any direction without nudging the ship's course. A seamless path straight into the black.

Cade remembered Xan's words.

"Autopilot?"

He looked up from fiddling with the second spacesuit. Blinked those innocent blues.

"You told me the ship was on a sort of *autopilot*," Cade said. "What we're *on* is a crash course with the gravity of the biggest black hole I've ever seen." She poured herself out of the pilot's chair and marched the two steps it took to get in Xan's face.

"This is the plan?"

Xan held out a helmet. "What the Unmakers don't understand is that we're not sacrificing ourselves at all."

Cade crashed the helmet to the floor. Xan winced and held his breath.

"You said you weren't on their side!" Cade cried. Her insides went hot and threatened to turn explosive. She burst out of the little atmosphere Xan liked to share with her—but all she had to look at were the black hole and the controls she couldn't work well enough to keep them out of it. So she turned back to Xan and let him have the full heat of her stare.

Cade had never felt so lied to. And lied-to was the basis of most of her life.

Xan stared back, steady in the face of her nova rage. "I'm not on their side, Cadence. And I'm not on the side of the scientists or the spacesicks or the humans who need a savior." He stepped forward. Stood so close that his pain was more than a gallery of scars. It was a thickening she could feel in the air.

"Can't you tell the difference?" he asked. "I'm on *our* side."

Cade went back to slamming at the controls. Punched in new courses, one on top of the other, only to have the control panel burst into a chorus of red lights. If Xan had reached out for her thoughts, he would have found a crackling mess. Instead he held out an armload of white.

The second spacesuit.

"You'd better put this on," he said. "I planned this. For us. I told the Unmakers that my one request was to see the inside of the black hole before I died. I wanted to see it with you, Cadence. The ship will start to collapse once we cross the event horizon, but the suits will keep us alive—"

"For how long?"

Xan shook his hanging-down head and the balance in the room shifted — fast. Xan's eyes shaded and his face went slack with disappointment. It shouldn't have been allowed. There was only room for one broken heart on this ship. Cade had come all this way to find Xan. The disappointment belonged to her. She wanted it *back*.

Tears starred Xan's cheeks. Cade fought an unwanted urge to listen.

"I thought it would make sense to you. We're entangled, Cadence. The laws of the universe are different when it comes to us. It takes a normal person a few minutes to die inside of a small black hole. But this is the largest one in the universe. And we're *not* normal.

"So light can't escape a black hole. Our thoughts move faster than the speed of light. So matter can't escape. Once we're inside, we won't want to. The Unmakers think a black hole is some kind of punishment, a netherworld, a nonverse."

"What do you think it is?"

"For us?" he said. "A paradise."

Cade tried to shake her head, but there was so much working against her. She had to wrench to twist it once, tell him *no*.

"Listen, Cadence. As soon as we cross that line, the rest of the universe will melt away. We'll be wrapped in the purest light . . . particles that have never touched a human. And all of the matter, everything that's ever fallen into it, will be our home. No more darkness, emptiness, no more nothingness to cross. No one could come and separate us. And time? Time will lose its power. You and I can fit a lifetime of thoughts into the stillness between two breaths. We can live forevers and come out the other side of them and still be together. Even when our bodies have broken down to parts, even when we're atoms marching to the center of the black hole, we'll be entangled."

A smile broke Cade's surface. Her body had become an ocean, lilting to the rhythm of those words.

"What about—"

"The rest of the universe?" Xan said. "We don't need it."

He took her hands. Patted them over the second spacesuit.

"Please," he said. "Put this on."

Cade pulled the pants over hers, struggled on the thick white jacket. But she wasn't done with her fight against the tide of oncoming black, the surge of Xan's reasons.

"You don't want a life in the universe because you haven't seen it yet," Cade said. "You've been—"

"What? Coddled? By the scientists who performed tests and experiments that put me under for fifteen years? By the Unmakers who hate our kind—their own kind—so much, they have to dress in costumes and talk to me with knives? I guess I could go to one of those terrible human-hating planets I've heard so much about. You're right that I don't know half of what's out there, Cadence."

He thought at her, strong and clear. *I know enough.*

"All of those things are as horrible as they seem," Cade said. "And worse." But . . . what was the rest? Cade had been so sure of her point, and now she couldn't even find it.

"But . . ."

"We can do better, Cadence."

He said her name like the music it was. She could listen to him say it for the rest of time.

But then there would be no other voices, and there would be no other music. There would be no loudloudloud guitars. There would be no need for new songs, because there would be no one to play them for.

Cade had songs for Ayumi. And for any spacesick who wanted to listen, for anyone who cared.

She made another dash at the controls. Searched for Renna in the window-stripe. The orbital was a dot now, far behind.

She had never thanked Renna for giving her Moon-White. She needed to get back to the ship, back to nights in the soft drumming of her bunk. She had to see Rennik again and figure out why she'd kissed him, and if she wanted to do it again. She had deliveries to make with Lee — they were days behind on Human Express.

"I have friends," Cade said.

Xan stared at her with a blankness that could have been cut from the black outside the window.

"I don't want to leave them."

Xan moved around the rim of the chair and positioned himself in front of the hatch. Settled his helmet on. Cade rushed after him and ripped it off.

"These people, Xan, all you have to do is meet them —"

"I have."

He flashed a look at her temple. Of course. Xan had seen parts of the trip to Hades as they had unfolded in her head.

His face crumpled under terrible pain and his voice turned into one long scrape, like Cade was ripping the words out of his throat, one by one. Like she was forcing him to tell her the terrible-but-true.

"The one with the pale spots on her face betrayed you. The other girl is weak. The Hatchum will never be the human you want him to be. The Darkrider tried to *kill you.* And the ship . . . is a ship."

Cade would have punched him square in the face if he were anyone else in the universe.

Xan twisted and stared out the window-stripe at the blot of Renna, almost gone.

"Those friends will leave you," he said. "They'll let you down."

Maybe, Cade thought.

But that didn't make them less worth connecting to. Rennik, Renna, Ayumi, Lee, Gori. And Cade's mother. Even if she was dead, or glassed-and-gone. Even if Cade scoured the known planets and never found her. There was a connection to be made — with her memories, with the woman her mother used to be. Cade already felt stronger for it.

If she had wanted to close herself off, shut it all down, she would have stayed on Andana.

Xan's eyes darkened in the oncoming rush of black, to a deep, cold, empty blue. He'd never had a home. Not even a makeshift home, or one that sailed through space. But Cade could change that.

"Please," she said, setting her hand to his face. "Turn the ship around. Let me show you."

He pointed to the panic-red of the control panel. Said, without a trace of regret, "It's too late."

Xan turned Cade to him, squared their shoulders, drummed up one more smile.

"I know it feels important, not to die."

Cade didn't smile. Deep inside of her, things snapped together. The words the scientists had given her. The meaning she would fill them with.

The purpose.

"We can do more than survive," Cade said.

Xan's smile flashed wide.

"Right."

Cade felt acceleration in the hole-suck. The event horizon loomed close. The sad part was that Xan would fall in thinking they understood each other perfectly.

But Cade couldn't spend her last breath on him. Before she crossed the line, she reached out to Renna and her friends onboard and anyone who might be able to listen—in ships, on planets, strangers, her mother, anyone—and sent one wild, simple thought.

Help.

Cade reached so far, so hard, that she found all of her friends in a single burst of thought, their songs all working at once, separate from each other and at the same time sliding into harmony. But it didn't stop there. Beyond them, she felt other minds, thousands, far off but bright, a waiting sea of stars.

The line between space-black and hole-black rushed to meet the ship. Cade tamped her helmet down just as Xan opened the hatch. He grabbed her hand and leapt them into the dark.

Cade flew through sheets and sheets of black, the perfect black of sleeping. Before-birth, after-death black, and just as she was starting to loosen to it she felt a new miracle and — slammed into the light.

Gold.

That's what it was inside.

Gold and warmth and closeness.

Things were falling to a perfect point in the distance. Light, ships, bits of stars. And motes of cosmic dust, billions of them, fired to brilliance by the light. Falling, slow and fast at the same time. Like Cade imagined snowflakes — plummeting from a winter-pure sky and then swirling on drafts. Never seeming to touch ground.

Cade swam at the edge of it all. Looked down and saw her outline doused in gold. It was hard for her to understand herself as the same girl who had left a seedy club on Andana.

She looked at Xan. He floated at her side, holding her hand. Soon she wouldn't have a hand to hold but he would be there, always there. He sent her the most beautiful thoughts

—thoughts like music, thoughts that moved and flowed through her, with meaning that no words could contain.

But the best thought of all belonged to Cade.

Now we'll never be alone.

So when the darkness crept in, like an ink stain, pooled and reaching, Cade almost swam away from it. Toward the center of the black hole. She almost forgot that she didn't *want* to be in this golden place.

The universe curled its dark fingers toward her.

Cade didn't understand. Now that she was in the black hole she was in it for good. Nothing could cross that line and leave. Even her thoughts could move faster than the speed of light only if they were entangled thoughts, meant for Xan.

Still, the blackness inched.

What's happening? Xan looked at her, leaking concern. Cade wanted to tell him that she had no idea, but it wasn't true. Because now she remembered.

This was what she'd asked for. Help.

Specifically, Gori.

Cade must have touched his mind. There hadn't been time to be careful—to wait for an invitation. She had breached his thoughts, but this time Gori hadn't tried to kill her. This time, he'd done the opposite. He had aligned himself with dark energy, used his influence to expand the universe in the right direction at the right rate to nudge the event horizon. He had crafted this moment, so she could live.

Cade fell farther into gold, but the darkness swelled just behind it. It came for her, and this time she answered its difficult call. She reached for it with one gravity-crushed hand and tugged on Xan's fingers with the other. He tugged back.

It's beautiful here, she thought, *but we have work to do.*

Cade sent him strength.

Come with me.

She sent him all of her sureness.

It's the right thing. Don't make me go without you.

Xan's eyes were wild, the whites tinted gold.

If Cade left him and went on her own, the Noise might stream into her head and take his place. She could be trapped with it forever, a truly broken radio. The one frequency she needed — gone.

Even if the Noise left her alone, that's what she might be for the rest of her life without him. Alone. Cade had never been able to connect before Xan. What if she couldn't do it without him there? To understand her complicated snarls of feeling? To fill her on the empty nights?

But the worst part of leaving Xan would be the one she couldn't fit into words. It tore through Cade, ruthless and complete as a final chorus.

How much she would miss him.

She looked over at Xan as he plummeted. He was falling, even though he seemed to float, and he wore a smile as he went down. Stretched his arms wide, pressed his eyes open to take in as much of this dense, black-shelled paradise as he could. In the whole time she had been entangled with him, she'd never felt something like this radiating from Xan. An emotion that wasn't tinged with fear, doubt, disappointment, or pain. He was the same person, transposed into a different key. He was all major chords here. All beaming and bright.

The darkness came again and reached for Cade.

Stay.

Xan asked with his thoughts, and with his light-drenched eyes. The word carried her from the edge of the black hole back to him. The tide of darkness washed in weaker each time. Soon it would ebb too far and Cade would be left to the gold, and an endless future with the boy she had promised to save.

Stay, Xan asked.

And she almost said *yes.*

But her mind stretched back, toward the others she had left behind. The ones on the ship. The ones scattered on planets, waiting. Xan couldn't fill all of those spaces now that Cade had opened them.

The darkness made one last, feeble push. Gori could only change the universe for her so much. Cade fought to still herself against the pull of the black hole. When the black rushed up again, she was ready.

Xan's fingers eased out of hers. His thoughts faded. He kept falling into the gold.

Cade let him go.

The rest of it was rush and blur—the blink from light to dark, like a full-body switch had been flipped. Gravity tried to screech Cade back into the black hole; it wouldn't give her up without a fight. The event horizon slid away from her body with wrenching slowness. It was minutes-that-felt-like-millennia before Renna inched close and sent Cade a lifeline.

Then she was onboard.

With the sound of familiar voices all around her. First Lee, then Rennik and Ayumi, then all of them in a round.

Is she all right?

Is she breathing?

Cadence, say something.

The whole universe pinched to sound, because her eyes couldn't focus. Someone carried her into the small hidden bedroom and it beat like Cade's heart, only slower, until she fell asleep.

Cade woke up with faces over her.

"You!" Lee attack-hugged her and Cade felt all of her organs, one at a time.

"Yeah," Cade said. "It's me."

Except that it felt like only half of her.

Lee pulled back and Cade looked up at the grouping of Rennik, Ayumi, and Gori around the bunk. She settled on Gori, who was staring.

"Thank you."

He sent Cade a blast of cosmic thought — the rush of starlight and sphere-music so sudden and brilliant that it popped her ears.

Ayumi sat at the foot of Cade's bed, crowding her toes. "You look wonderful for someone who's come out of a black hole. Not that I've seen someone come out of a black hole. I wasn't even sure a human *could,* to be honest in a painful sort of way." She pulled a notebook—the tiniest one Cade had seen yet—out of one of her pockets. "Which reminds me, do you think I could ask you—"

"—a few questions?" Cade finished. "Yeah. But maybe later."

Rennik, looking at least a foot too tall for the room, stooped down and set a plate of still steaming breakfast on her lap. She looked up at him. The words were a scrape of vocal cords.

"Egg dish?"

Rennik cut a glance at Lee. "Someone told me it was your favorite."

Lee did her best to look innocent while Cade laughed.

Rennik bent in and smoothed a wrinkle on her pillow. "I'm glad you made it back, Cadence." She listened close, and thought she heard more under the polite skin of those words, but she couldn't be sure. For now, it was enough that Rennik had said *I* instead of *we.*

Cade had more she wanted to tell Rennik, Lee, all of them. But it hurt to talk—not just because her body was recovering from exposure to an absurd amount of gravity.

Each sentence was another step away from Xan.

She could still feel him, faint, sending his thoughts as he fell. Gold and perfect. Which meant Cade could feel what she'd given up in order to come back to the harshness of space, so she could wake up in the mornings—or what she pretended were mornings—and keep fighting.

The gold thoughts were pain and perfection together on

a long, slow fade. Cade had no idea how long this doubled consciousness would last—at any point Xan could reach the center of the black hole. The light might dwindle to nothing, or she might have to live with it forever.

At least it wasn't the Noise.

The bedroom lost some of its clamor as Rennik and Lee drained out to argue with each other about the new course. Ayumi sat on the low bunk opposite Cade. Her smile was a small, lopsided offering. A real smile—not the thin-stretched emptiness of space rapture.

"Lee said I could stay on and help with the Human Express. And talk to the people she collects from, as long as I don't talk and talk and talk . . ." Ayumi looked at the place where Lee had just been standing, and smiled wider. "She thinks my ship will be useful on planets that don't have real ports."

Cade nodded. Even bobbing her chin up and down wasn't a pain-free process.

"I'd like to stay," Ayumi said. "For as long as you think I can."

Her eyes flickered to Moon-White, propped in the corner. Cade wasn't ready to play, but she would be soon. She could feel the phantom strain in her hands that came before a good session.

"Hey," Cade said. "Thanks."

Ayumi winced, her mind no doubt cutting back to what had happened in Hades. "I'm not sure I did anything thank-able."

"You did."

Lee crowded in, close behind Cade. Ayumi rushed ahead, running her fingertips all over the silent scene.

"It's a graveyard," Ayumi whispered.

"Then where are the . . . you know . . . dead people?" Lee asked.

Cade and Lee pressed farther into the low-ceilinged, open lab space. Their steps fell soft on the white, stonelike floor.

"You don't see the dead," Ayumi said. "That's not how it works."

Graveyards were an old notion, an Earth notion. Humans on Andana were cremated or given sand burials. There was so little good land there, not be wasted on humans. So Cade couldn't be sure if Ayumi was right about the lab.

She swept a look over the hush of it. No bodies. But the machines were like graves, rising white and metallic and humming Everyone Is Gone songs.

Cade and Lee fanned out to look for the tech that would restore the circle-glass. Ayumi filled her canvas sack with anything that might tell her more about the humans who had worked there, or, reaching back, about Earth. They worked out from the center of the room, overlapping each other's circles as they went, doubling each other's steps, making sure.

Cade stopped at the first bridge.

A little pane of plastic sat in the white door. A hollow tube connected the lab to another node about a quarter of a mile in the distance. The doors on both ends had been closed.

Between them, men and women were lined up in a neat row, slumped and strange. There was almost no blood. It could have been some kind of institutional naptime, but everyone's eyes were open. That made it easier for Cade to notice a certain old man, nondescript except for the wrinkles.

Mr. Niven.

Cade ripped in a breath, turned away. Her heart could have been to the expanding edges of space and back in a minute. Xan connected within seconds — she could feel his presence, but he sent nothing. Maybe he was still damp at the fact that she wouldn't fight her friends to get to him faster. Maybe he was silent at the sight of Firstbloom.

Cade decided his measured quiet was better than a brawl inside of her own body.

She stopped searching for the tech for a minute, and scoured the lab for something to offer Xan. She knew she was the one who owed him, this time. She should have been on Hades' doorstep by now. There was nothing she could send that would fill the betrayal-shaped space that had opened up between them.

Cade traced her steps back until she stood in front of a bank of cribs. She knew these from the filmstrip. She knew them from before that. Her memories steered her to a little rectangle on the far side of the grid.

She touched a thin plastic railing, tiny pillows, crisp white sheets. Cade didn't hold back the confused tumble in her chest. She sent it to Xan, along with a flash of the crib, and two words.

Welcome home.